OF ANGELS AND DEMONS

PANDEMONIUM COLLEGE KNIGHTS 3

MONA BLACK

Published by Black Wing Press.

SYNOPSIS

The factions in the College have split, some siding with the Four Houses, and some with Frankie – and let's not forget Heaven who wants her alive.
This is turning the College into a veritable war zone.

Good news is, the boys have shown their true colors and have Frankie's back, protecting her against assassins and attacks, fighting at her side.

And sleeping at her side, which is... a bonus.

How can she resist them, anyway?

When they are opening up to her.

Taking care of her.

Putting their lives on the line for her.

They still have the potential of breaking her heart, but by now that's a given. Too late to back away now. Too late to run.

Things take a turn for the worse when dear old dad's name is revealed and the angels come down to get her – but Frankie may have a plan...

*OF ANGELS AND DEMONS is book three in a next-generation series following the events in Pandemonium Academy Royals. It is a full-length paranormal reverse harem romance, meaning the main character has more than one love interest. This is book three of four, and it ends on a slight cliffhanger. There is a happily ever at the end of the series.

Warnings: This novel contains enemies-to-lovers/love-hate adult themes, foul language and humor as well as explicit content with darker elements. It contains possibly triggering themes like thoughts of death and past suicide attempts (not on page), mind-rape (not on page), loss of loved ones and depression, violence, gore, death and near-death scenes, religious themes (all made-up and never meant as the author's beliefs).

There are mm scenes and relationships. For 18+ only. Alternating points of view.*

Disclaimer: this isn't a religious book. Any mention of angels, demons, heaven and hell is made up for the purposes of this story and is by no means meant to be taken as the author's view of religious matters.

THE FOUR ROYAL HOUSES
House of Water (vampires)
House of Earth (shifters)
House of Fire (demons)
House of Air (Fae)

What to expect in this book/series:
Academy romance
Five supernatural hunks
Dynamic heroine
Friends to enemies to lovers to mates for life
Developing M/M relationships

They fall first
Characters forced into sharing a room
Heroine with evil mom
Found family
Multiple point of view

1

ASA

J lay Frankie on her bunk and step back, unsure what to do next. Holding her in my arms felt strangely pleasant. She's warm and soft when she's unconscious, not prickly and fighting.

Though I also like her prickly, fighting side...

"Frankie," Ryu says, oddly quiet, leaning against the bunk bed and reaching over to stroke her hair. "She's out again."

"I know."

"We need to wake her up and give her the pills."

But nobody else moves. It's as if we're reluctant to disturb her rest.

The medic gave us antibiotics and ibuprofen to give her. She did wake up when he examined her, declaring her wound infected, and she protested, batting at his hands. She was weak. Sick with a fever.

It's just that she's so... fucking cute. Like a kitten. Or a little bird.

Musen...

"She's saying something." Ryu frowns. "I can't make it out."

We all approach the double bunk bed as if pulled by

invisible strings, leaning close. All five of us are tall enough to tower over the bunk beds, putting us at eye-level with a curled-up, blonde girl. Her lashes are dark, as are her brows, her skin like cream, a rosy flush on her cheeks to match her lips...

"She's saying something about her aunt," Ryu says.

"What about her aunt?"

"How should I know? Something about her having kittens."

Tir frowns. "Her aunt has kittens?"

"It's an expression." Everyone turns to stare at me. "What? To have kittens. To worry and be upset."

"And that's from your study of humankind, is it, Cherub?" Rook drawls.

"I'm ignoring the silly pet names you use to bait me," I say.

"Oh, is that so?"

"Shush." Tir props his elbows on the bed. He's standing closer to her head than us. "Listen."

I can hear her now. She's asking for her aunt. And Julie.

"Who's Julie?" Rook mutters.

"Her cousin, doofus. Remember?"

"Oh, right."

"We should call her cousin over."

"Bad idea," I say.

"She's her family, Asa. I know a seraph wouldn't know anything about families but you... You must know."

"You know nothing about me," I bite out.

"Nonetheless, we should bring Juliette here. Psychological support helps."

"Antibiotics help," I say. "And she has those. She doesn't need a cousin to get better."

"You're kind of heartless, aren't you?"

"I'm not heartless," I snap. Why does it bother me? "The less her cousin knows, the better."

"Why, what is she going to do? We're all trapped here, thanks to you."

"I followed orders," I grind out. My neck burns. My hands are fisted. Yeah, this conversation is bothering me way too much. "I need to pray."

Rook's brows go up. "Say what?"

"I need to pray for guidance. This situation is confusing."

"Oh, yeah. Go pray, confused little Cherub."

"Will you stop with the cherub thing?"

Frankie sighs and rolls over on her back.

"Keep your voice down," Ryu hisses. "She needs her rest."

"She needs to wake up and take her pills," I argue, getting more annoyed by the second, "and…"

I don't know what I had been about to say, because she lifts one arm over her head, turning her pretty face to the side, and I'm left staring at her soft mouth, her neck, the soft mounds of her breasts where her tank top has rolled off one shoulder. Soft, all soft. Beckoning to be touched.

I remember her underneath me, moaning my name, her mouth reddened from kissing, her legs wrapped around me, and I can't remember why I ever wanted to go back to Heaven.

Ryu reaches for her, then retracts his hand, his eyes kind of wide.

Tir harrumphs. "Yeah, okay, she looks sweet and innocent when she sleeps. Get over it already."

Now we all turn to stare at him. "What's your problem?" I ask.

"With you?" He bares his teeth at me. "Want a list?"

I frown. "Is this about the Raziel Protocol?"

"Believe it or not," Rook says, "I don't think it's what's pissing us off."

"What would you know?" Tir snaps.

"Ooh, little Fae boy is angry."

"Fuck you."

"I'm awake, you know," she says softly. "I can hear you."

We all jump at least a foot off the ground.

"Frankie," I say.

"Don't mind Tir," Rook rushes to say. "He's upset because you haven't let him fuck you yet."

"How do you...?" Tir gapes at him. "What the *fuck, abesh?*"

"Then you should fuck," I say, "to clear your head."

Tir produces a choking sound. His cheeks color. "What?"

"Jesus, Asa." Frankie frowns at me. "Ask a girl first."

"Why, would you mind fucking Tir?"

This time a much darker blush spreads over her cheeks. Suddenly, she struggles to sit up and our attention is no longer on the sputtering Fae because she commands all of it.

"Girl, you should stay down," Rook is saying. "You have a fever."

"We got you pills," Ryu says. "You should take them."

"With water," Kass mutters. He hasn't spoken a word until now. "You should take the pills with water."

"And rest," I mutter.

While I go pray and hopefully find answers, or at least some calm. I should talk with Heaven, too. See if there's any news.

She looks at us, propped up on her elbows, all that pale hair tangled on her shoulders, her dark eyes wide. "Sorry if I freaked you out. I'm fine. Look! All good. Your precious prize is unharmed."

"Will you just... stop doing that?" I demand.

"Doing what?"

"Talkin about yourself like you're an object we're after."

"Am I not?" she asks softly.

"We're people too. We have feelings," Ryu says.

"Do you?" she asks, giving him a side glance. "What kind of feelings?"

Ryu groans. "Fuck..."

"Shut your piehole, Ryu," Kass says.

"He has a right to talk about his feelings," Frankie says.

"I wasn't... fucking talking about my feelings," Ryu says, scowling, but sounds uncertain.

"Huh." Frankie struggles to sit up and we all rush to help her. "Funny."

———

Praying isn't happening just yet.

Pills are extracted from packages and a glass is retrieved from the kitchens—Tir goes on that particular errand because apparently, he has friends in the kitchens? Fucking seriously? When did he have time to make friends?—which he brings back full, clutching it in one strong hand.

Makes me wonder if he used magic to keep the water from spilling.

And then I don't know why I am so fascinated.

I watch her shoot a wide-eyed look at Tir as she takes the glass, Kass steadying her hand so she can take the pills. Ryu is muttering something about cousins.

We're all fascinated.

But then Tir stalks away from the bed to the window. He turns his back to us, looking outside, arms folded over his chest.

"Tir." I raise my voice. "Tir, what's the matter?"

I don't expect him to whirl around and jab a finger at me. "You're wrong. She can't be an angel."

"Angel?" Frankie's dark eyes grow huge in her small face. "Me?"

"Asa might have brought up this idea that your father is an angel," Rook says.

She stares at us. "I mean... Tir is right, have you met me? I'm no angel. He should know. How was it he called me? Oh yes. A killing machine."

Rook gives me a pointed look.

I wince.

"She's a witch," Tir goes on.

"I'm sorry?"

"Her mother is one of the strongest witches in history. Her power is elemental. It feels familiar somehow. I think she might be partly Fae."

"Why are you talking about me like I'm not here?" She sounds... upset. And tired.

"This isn't all about you," Tir snaps and she flinches a little. "Besides, you hate us, remember?"

"Permission to punch him in the face?" I glare at him, and I don't even know why I'm so angry, only that he's acting like a little fucker.

"How about I punch you instead?" Tir seethes.

"Punch away," she whispers, falling back against the pillow and my anger drains away, leaving me cold. "I don't feel so good. I think I'm going to rest my eyes some more."

Rook frowns. "Are the pills not working?"

"It takes some time for medicine to work." Ryu reaches out as if to stroke her hair but pulls his hand back again. "It's not magic."

"You're all a bunch of losers," Tir says suddenly, then turns and walks out of the room, the door slamming shut behind him.

A space of silence follows his departure.

"What the Hell is the matter with him?" Rook mutters. "You don't think Jatri's death affected him, do you?"

Jatri's death. With everything going on, the death of the Fae gang's leader wasn't on my mind at all.

I walk to the window and go to my knees.

"What are you doing?" Ryu snarls. "She passed out again. Should I wake her up? Should I—?"

"She's asleep," I say, settling on the hard floor.

"How do you know?"

She mumbles something, scrunches up her cute nose, and sighs.

I lift a brow. "You were saying?"

"Fine." He scowls. "You were right this time. Don't rub my nose in it. I bet it was a coincidence."

"Dear God," I say, closing my eyes, "help me find patience."

"Hey," Rook says, "we can hear you."

"On second thought..." Getting to my feet, I head for the door. "I'll be back in a jiff."

Rook growls. "The Hell you will, Cherub. Where the fuck are you going?"

"Business meeting," I throw over my shoulder. "Keep an eye on her."

"Hey, big shot, you don't get to order us around!" Ryu calls out.

But they don't come after me.

Good, because I need a minute. Or two.

A freaking month wouldn't be enough for me to come to terms with the fuckfest that is my mind right now, and yeah, I'm well aware that an angel would never think this way.

This isn't vocabulary I learned researching Earth. These aren't thoughts and doubts from books I skimmed or TV shows I glanced at.

This is all me.

Something's wrong with me.

And hopefully, my commander can tell me what it is and how to fix it. Heaven has never seemed so far away, so out of reach. I need to get up there sooner rather than later.

———

"Asariel," the voice acknowledges me after I'm finished with my first oration.

"*Malakh Daliel.*" I bow my head. He's much lower in

hierarchy than a seraph—entire Heavens lower—but he's my new contact. I'm standing inside the men's showers because it was the only private place I could think of near our room, and the only reason I'm not on my knees is the need to be able to run at a moment's notice.

"Identity verified. Nephal rank verified. Mission Pandemonium College verified. Raziel Protocol implementation still in place. You may sp—"

"I need to speak with Raziel."

Daliel is quiet. The seconds tick by. A faucet or showerhead is dripping somewhere, the sound echoing like gunshots in my ears. Like a car crash in slow motion, each sound crisp and deafening, the pain excruciating—

"Get in here," a very human male voice says, and I'm so attuned to the angelic frequency that it takes me a moment to decipher the words.

"Are you sure nobody's in here?" another male voice asks.

"Everyone is in class."

"You sure? Haven't seen the gangs around today."

"I'm sure. Dammit, come here. Been dreaming of this all week..."

Two guys stumble into the showers, fully dressed and... kissing. One of them pushes the other against the wall and they continue kissing as if they're trying to eat each other up, hands moving under shirts, pelvises grinding...

Look away, I tell myself. *Now*.

For some reason, they make me think of the emissaries. What if it were Tir and Ryu grinding against each other like that, or Ryu... or any of them with me...

"Fuck, someone's here," one of them hisses. "Told you."

"What? No way, I checked... Oh, what the fuck? He's glowing like a glowstick."

They break apart, panting, eyes round, staring at me. I flick a hand at them and they run away like scared rabbits.

I sigh in annoyance, both at the interruption and the unexplained, sudden flare of excitement at seeing them kissing—

"Asariel!" That booming voice snaps me back to attention and the business at hand. The light blinds me, and a great wind throws me to my knees anyway as the archangel appears.

"Raziel, *Urun-en,*" I whisper.

"*Umbar umsa.* State your business."

I shift uncomfortably on my knees. I'm hard from watching those two guys kissing. Not the best state to be in while conversing with a high power that doesn't understand physical sensations.

At least, as far as I know... And why does it feel so normal and familiar to me?

"*Umbar Asariel.* Speak. Has something occurred?"

Shit. I bow my head lower, prostrating myself on the tiles. "*Urun-en.* The opposition hired new recruits, but at least we know their faces this time around. They won't get away with it, not if I have any say in it. Don't worry, I'm keeping an eye out—"

"An eye out?" Said with mild interest.

"Keeping watch. Not an actual eye out of the socket."

"...oh."

"By the way, I wanted to ask you..." I venture a glance up. He's a tall outline blazing cold light, a single eye or hole in the middle of what passes as a head. Maybe it's a mouth. Why does it matter, though? "About myself."

"Yourself?"

"Yeah, I keep having these... flashes. Images. No, not images, they're like reels of real life, human life, complete with sensations and emotions, and I know things I shouldn't about life here, and I don't fucking know why it's happening to—"

"Speak plainly," Raziel booms. "You sound more and more human. Control yourself. It's unbecoming."

"But—"

"Rising to the Seventh Heaven is no easy task. You need to try harder. Fit in. This mission could be a stepping stone."

"Stepping stone?" I frown at the archangel's still form. "But I am only returning there, I was—"

"You forget yourself," he says coldly. "Turn your face away and bow!"

The wind buffets me, and pushes me down.

You don't talk back to archangels. Right. Never question them, or their decisions. You never doubt your faith and your mission.

And you don't look them in the eye. Mouth. Whatever. I find myself lying on my stomach, shivering, shaking like a stranded fish.

An angel cast out of Heaven.

The glow diminishes. When I next glance up, Raziel is gone and I'm not any wiser than I was before.

2

FRANKIE

J'm running through the streets, glancing over my shoulder. I'm alone but the shadows chase me, and I should be with someone, but they left me to fend for myself. Men are running after me. Shadows or real, hard to tell. Menacing.

Mother, I think. *Why did you do that?*

I said I will come back, she replies, *her voice echoing all around me. Didn't I?*

I slow down. *Where are you?*

You'll never find me.

And then I scream and the shadows vanish, leaving behind piles of salt, dispersed by a cold wind.

"*Urun-en,*" a voice whispers and a light explodes over me, like a star going supernova. "*Listen...*"

"*You forget yourself,*" another voice hisses like a snake. "*Turn your face away and bow!*"

I fall to my knees, lifting an arm to protect myself from the roaring wind and the blinding light, dust and trash lashing at me, battering my face, arms, and legs, stinging like an acid hurricane.

Someone is howling and I seriously hope it's not me.

Then a hand wraps around my arm, pulling me up. "Frankie, wake up!"

"What? I'm not..." I blink, but the wind is still rushing over me and I can't see anything. It's not trash and dust that's cutting me, I realize. It's grains of salt, perfect little crystals, sharp like diamonds, slicing through my skin—

"Girl, come on, wake up," the man says. "This isn't healthy, reliving this shit every night. Wake up, Frankie."

It's the blond man. I've seen him around before... Haven't I? He feels so familiar, his name is on the tip of my tongue...

"Let's go home," he says, tugging on my arm, lifting me to my feet as if I weigh nothing, and the wind, I realize, has ceased, and the salt is gone from the air.

And I'm falling.

———

I wake up with a gasp, one arm lifted as if the man is still holding it. The man, the man, I know him from somewhere and...

"I only kill those who come after me," I breathe as my dream comes back to me, an earlier realization concretizing.

Those who come after you and those you care about, an annoying little voice in the back of my head says and I swat at the air as if, like a mosquito, it will go away.

"Frankie?" The murmur comes from beside me and I jerk away. "Easy now," the voice says, and that's when I see a dark head and a pair of muscular arms folded on the edge of my bunk. Dark-lashed, midnight-blue eyes gaze at me, looking kind of dazed—or sleepy.

"Rook." I roll on my side to face him.

"Yes, Princess? Here, in the flesh." He grins and his gaze sharpens. "How are you feeling?"

I feel like crap, but I don't say so. At least I've woken up to find myself lying on a soft surface, wrapped up in blankets like a burrito, and not lying on a street with the wind howling in my ears.

Though, wait a minute... the wind *is* howling, rattling the window.

"It's a rain storm," Ryu says, coming to stand by the bunk bed, running a hand through his red hair. He's shirtless and my gaze kind of snags on his bare chest with the silvery symbols etched in his flesh, like ritual scars. I itch to touch them. "It will pass."

Then Rook straightens from his slouch against the bunk bed, rolling his big shoulders and wouldn't you know, he's shirtless, too. I can't see what he has going on below the waist from my vantage point on the upper bunk, but my gaze follows that washboard stomach up to those impressive pecs that are littered with scars and dark marks.

When my gaze finally reaches his face, I find him smirking.

"Like what you see, Darling?" he drawls, stretching his arms over his head, making all those delicious muscles ripple. "I see you're feeling better already."

"Rook, lay off it," Ryu growls.

"Why? I live to please."

"You're a Hellhound. You're sure as Hell not here to please anybody, so cut the bullshit."

"You're no fun," Rook mutters, lowering his arms.

Pushing off the covers, I sit up and rub a hand over my eyes, mainly to keep myself from staring some more. "What are those marks? The dark ones on you, the silvery ones on Ryu. You all seem to have them, even Asa, on his cheek. Been meaning to ask you but... forgot."

More like, life got away from me. I convinced myself not to care. But curiosity won't let me rest. Simple curiosity, nothing to it.

"Our contract sigils," Rook says. "Well, and scars, but I have a feeling that's not the ones you're referring to."

"Sigils? What do you mean?"

"Our contracts are sealed into our flesh. If we fail our contracts, these sigils will kill us."

"What?" I lower my hands and clutch at the covers, staring at the both of them, standing there so... tranquil. "Are you for real? I asked before what would happen if you failed in your mission and nobody told me this."

"There are stages you go through before you admit to a complete failure," Ryu says, coming to park a hip against the bunk bed frame. He doesn't look disturbed by what he's saying. "Destroying us is the last stage. Failing once means punishment but not death. Failing twice... That depends on the contract."

Rook isn't contradicting him, so he's telling the truth, I guess. How can they both look so calm when they're playing Russian roulette here? What is it they're after that is so important to them?

Kass chooses that moment to enter the room, looking gorgeous in his black turtleneck sweater and black pants, black hair falling in his pale face.

Dammit, body, get your act together. No. Just no. Hear me?

"Whoa, man, you look like death warmed over," Ryu says, and now that he says it... I see it, too. As Kass limps over to the bed, practically dragging his leg behind him, I see how white his mouth is, his cheeks sporting a gray sheen that doesn't look healthy.

He stops by the bed, shoots me a long look I can't decipher —is he glad to see me awake or upset?—and sinks on the lower bunk.

"How is the situation out there?" Rook asks.

"Quiet. The fight is over." Kass' voice floats up to me from below and for some reason, I want to laugh.

I bend over my bunk to look at him, my hair sweeping over

my head to hang around me. His eyes go wide when he sees me. "It's weird to hear but not see you," I say. "Are you okay?"

His mouth twists. His hands are shaking, I notice. "Yeah."

But he's not. He looks so tired that my eyes feel hot. And then I'm slipping and he swears, shooting to his feet and grabbing me before I fall, head-first, to the floor.

"Fucking Hell, don't do that to me," he snarls, pulling me off the upper bunk and into his arms. "My heart's barely beating as it is. Want to stop it completely?"

I cling to him, disoriented. He takes two steps back and sits in the chair by the desk, cradling me in his lap.

"She almost fell," Ryu says, coming to lean against the desk. "Anari's fields, be careful, woman."

"She's still feverish," Kass says.

"She was hanging upside down to ogle you," Rook mutters.

"I was not," I say, indignant, even as a hot flush spreads on my face.

"I'm not half-naked like you," Kass mutters. "What's there to ogle?"

I lift a hand dreamily to his face, and draw a line down his square jaw. "You don't have to be half-naked for me to ogle."

Contradicting myself in the same breath.

"Told you she's feverish," Kass says but some of the grayness has left his skin. His eyes seem to sparkle.

"So this book..." Rook says, his deep voice drawing my attention away from my exploration of Kass' face.

"Which book?"

"This Jungle Book I have here."

I straighten and then start, reaching for the book he's holding, a reflex movement. "My book! Give it back!"

"All these notes..." He leafs through it as if it belongs to him. "Hm... Rook is so sexy, I can't keep my eyes off him. His eyes... they're so deep and alluring..."

"I didn't write that," I say automatically.

"No? Look." He brings the book closer to me and damn I'm not sure if I wrote that or not anymore, but I just glare.

I make another grab for it but I'm held back by Kass' muscular arm around my waist. "Give it back."

"Not yet. How about this bit?" Rook clears his throat theatrically. "Rook sleeps in black briefs and nothing else. His hair is loose and it's like a veil. I never thought I'd like a guy with long hair but—"

With a cry, I push off Kass and shoot to my feet. His hand closes around my wrist, pulling back as I start toward Rook, but he needn't bother. The world goes dark and I can't feel my body anymore as I go down—again.

The worst part is coming back and finding myself held in yet another pair of strong arms.

Okay, let's be honest. That's not bad. I shouldn't like it, dammit, but I can't help but enjoy the feel of a male, muscular body against mine, and the gentleness with which I'm being cradled.

"You need to stop trying to give me a heart attack," a voice rumbles against my ear, a voice I recognize as Ryu's.

"Mmf." My cheek is pressed to his pec and I try to pull back a little. My lips brush over his skin and when I lick them, they taste salty-sweet. Even his skin is delicious.

"She's back." Rook bends over me and grins. "Woo. So much live action today."

"Action? If you mean my falling all over the place..."

"Yeah, okay, so it's not like slaughtering monstrous demons from the guts of Hell." He shrugs. "But still, I admit that my stone heart may also have stopped once or twice."

"I have one question," Ryu says as he helps me sit up—in his lap. I keep landing in their laps, and is that hard length I'm feeling a part of his anatomy?

"Shoot," I mutter.

"Why didn't you comment on *my* underwear in your notes?

Wasn't it memorable enough? Maybe I should check the book myself, see what you wrote about me."

That brings me fully back to the present. I scramble to get up but Ryu won't let me.

"Gimme my book! Rook!"

"Come on, man, give her the book," Ryu says and I'm too relieved when Rook offers it to me to grumble that he listened to Ryu and not me.

"Here, Darling. Apologies."

"Don't do that again." I press the book to my chest, blowing out a breath, not resisting when Ryu pulls me back against his chest. He's sitting on his ass on the floor. It's all so ridiculous and I refuse to think about it. I'm not a fainting damsel. Never was and never will be.

My side hurts where the wound is. I wonder how soon I can be back on my feet.

"What's so special about this book?" Ryu asks.

"You wouldn't understand," I grumble.

"Try me."

I shrug. "It's just... mine. One of the few things that were mine from the start, when Aunt Mia picked me up. That and my pendant. And I've read the book a million times and it's... It's me."

"*You*?" Rook eyes the book skeptically. "Isn't it a book about a little boy?"

"Yeah. Just... don't ask."

"But I *am* asking," Rook says. "I want to understand you."

"Why?"

He snorts softly. "You wouldn't believe me if I told you."

"That's a weird thing to say. And reading my personal diary doesn't help me believe you."

"That's your diary? I think you're mainly using it to write soft porn about us."

I frown and open my mouth to tell him where to shove it, when the door flies open, and Asa appears.

"What's going on?" His eyes zero in on me—on the floor, in Ryu's lap, clutching my book to my chest, probably looking like a hot mess—and then take in the room. "Where's Tir?"

"Off sulking somewhere?" Rook suggests.

"Sulking? Why?" I ask.

"Because you won't sleep with him."

"Are you serious?"

"No, he's not," Asa says.

"Yes, he is," Ryu counters.

Asa comes to stand in front of us, reaching down to give me a hand. "You should be in bed, resting. That infection is serious to knock you down like that."

"Is it?" I clasp his hand, let him pull me to my feet, and then his arms come around me and I'm pressed to his chest, my book caught between us. "Asa..."

And then it's too much. I shove away from him, and when he doesn't instantly let me go, I beat at his chest with one fist, letting out a cry of frustration.

This time he does let go and I stumble back a step.

"Frankie," he starts, frowning.

"No. What is wrong with you?" I breathe, "all of you? And with me? This isn't right. I shouldn't like you. I *hate* you. Don't you get it?"

"I wasn't..." Asa huffs. His hands curl into fists at his sides. "I don't know what you want from me."

"Nothing! I want nothing! Stop acting like you care, that's all. It's so frigging confusing!" I bat at him with my book, then rethink that and gather it back to my chest. "I don't want to like you. You sold me out! I'm trying to figure out what I am and you're the nets sent to fish me out and put me in a glass bowl to be studied or tortured. Why would I like you?"

"Come on, Frankie," Ryu whispers.

"*Come on?* Really? That's all you have to say?"

Rook steps up to me. To his credit, he doesn't try to touch me. "Hush, Darling. Just rest. Fever is like being drunk. You may blurt out things you don't want anyone knowing."

"You know *everything* about me," I retort, my breath catching. "Everything."

"That's not true." This time, he reaches for my hand. "Let's get you back in bed."

"No." I twist away. "I want to talk to my aunt." My throat feels clogged with tears and there's no way I'm going to let them fall. I cling to this demand, this idea that if I talk to Aunt Mia, everything will be okay. "I need to."

"Well..." Rook looks from me to the others. "We're still in angelic lockdown and you're in no state to leave this room, but you can still talk to her, I guess. Let me show you how."

3

FRANKIE

"Sit down before you fall," Kass says and I obey without thinking, sitting on Tir's bunk. Then I glare at him for good measure.

"Now," Rook says, sitting down beside me, "close your eyes."

"You're not going to put a spider on me or something? For laughs?"

His dark brows hit his hairline. "What did I say about not oversharing when you have a fever? You will probably regret telling us this later on."

Ryu snickers, then turns it into a cough. "Yeah," he mutters nonsensically.

"I knew about the spiders," Kass says.

"You did?" Rook glances at him, his brows still somewhere near his hairline. "And didn't share?"

"Yeah, that's right. Are you going to go sulk with Tir, keep him company?"

"Guys." My head is pounding, my stomach is churning. "Please."

"Sorry, Princess." Rook manages to shake the shock off his

face, and it's kind of funny, but my head hurts and I want someone who really cares for me to talk to.

Someone who isn't using me.

"You say you don't believe we care for you," Rook whispers.

Oops, did I say that out loud?

"It's okay," he says. "Probably better for everyone if you don't believe it. Here, close your eyes and feel your spark of magic. You're so elemental, I won't even bother with teaching you a demonblood spell. You're practically a creature of air, aren't you? Witch with some Fae or angel in you, if these guys are right, and they must be. I opened my big mouth to talk about demons but your demonblood is not really..."

"What is it?" I breathe.

He has dropped his hand to my waist. He strokes upward a little, over the bandage—and jerks.

"Rook?" Asa is suddenly crouching in front of us. "You felt something."

"Yeah, sorry to break it to you, Cherub, but I was right. She does have some demonblood in her, after all."

"Let me see." Asa's hand joins Rook's on my side and I'm so shaken by what's happening I don't even think about pushing them away. Asa's fingers ghost over the bandage. Then he snatches them away. "*Abad nili hedug, Musen.*"

"No idea what you just said, but you look unhappy."

He said, "Keep us safe, little bird," I think, but how the Hell would I know a language I've never learned? This time I bat their hands away. "So I'm not an angel. Told you so already."

"But..."

"Show me the spell."

Wordlessly, Rook lifts his fingers and draws some symbols on the air. "Try this," he says, "and try to draw on your power. You may have to pull some energy from around you. You can use me as your source, I won't mind, though it might be easier to try Ryu who is more elemental, being a shifter."

"Gee, thanks for volunteering me," Ryu mutters but comes to sit on my other side, nodding at me. "Go on. Make your magical phone call, so you can get some rest."

"You really don't mind if I draw on you?"

"I wouldn't relinquish this honor to anyone else," he says softly.

Still confusing me, still acting as if they give a damn. Is this how professional bodyguarding looks? I have no experience with such, but it feels a lot more friendly and personal to me.

Then again, I'm still confusing lust with feelings. *Go me*. I just never learn.

It's the fever, like Rook said. I need to talk to Aunt Mia, then sleep this infection off, if that's a thing.

Closing my eyes, laying a hand on Ryu's arm—ooh, nice biceps, wait, let me stroke my hand down to his forearm, I mean, let me place my hand lower—I take a deep breath and concentrate on the spark inside me.

It's faint as I've never fanned it, always trying to ignore it. It's a word, I think, but I can't make it out. It's a word but it's also a flame and a drop of water and a sparkling crystal. It's a word of power, or a sound of power—or a *scream*—

"Feeling Ryu's power?" Rook asks.

"I'm... not sure," I whisper.

"Or his muscles?"

I grin. But sorting through the elements I feel is tricky. Is he the crystal? Is that the earth? I do feel a burst of energy inside me, though, so that must be it.

"Now think of your aunt," Rook says, "picture her, picture how her magic feels, and call out to her. Ping her, Frankie."

"But how?"

"Give your magic a little nudge, or a little pull. It depends on the magic user."

"It's advanced magic," Ryu says, "you can't expect her to master it without—"

I nudge. And then I pull.

Something sparks in me.

My heart is pounding and I feel a little dizzy. It's like a sense of impending doom. It's because it's magic, I realize. I'm using my magic and nobody is dying.

I almost cry with relief.

And I feel her, I feel my aunt—I feel her warm, multifaceted magic that's filled with my four uncles' energies and love, I feel her surprise when she senses me.

"*Frankie?*" she whispers and her face appears before me.

Oh. Why didn't anyone teach me to do this? Ah right, the fear I might just level the city made phone calls a better bet. But this is wonderful.

"Auntie?" I breathe and I'm horrified when my voice breaks. She's my aunt, but in reality, she's the only mom I've ever known. Her house is my home, her family is mine, too. If I know how to love, it's thanks to her, my uncles, and my cousins.

"Oh, Honey," she cries, "I've missed you so much. We all have. Boys, gather around! It's Frankie!"

"Are you having a magical Facetime with your family?" Kass asks, poking his head over my shoulder.

"Who are they?" Aunt Mia asks as the Wonderboys gather around me.

"Just... some guys." I turn to them. "Please, I want to speak to her alone."

After a few thunderous beats of silence, Ryu clears his throat. "You heard her. Get out."

"You too," I tell him.

His jaw tightens. "Fuck. Really? Don't you need my power?"

"I think I'll be fine."

The look of disappointment on his face is so funny.

"We'll be right outside the door," Asa says as he starts dragging everyone out. "Call us if you need anything, all right?"

I watch them file out, faces set in unhappy frowns. The door closes.

And then it's just me and my family, and I finally sink down and weep, because with your family, the people who love you, you can break down and not suffer for it. You can be weak and yet loved.

You can just *be*.

I'll never get anything like this again and it feels like I've already lost it forever.

————

"Honeybug," Aunt Mia says, leaning forward, her face filling my vision. "You're using magic to call us. Are you sure this is safe? With the incidents—"

"It's okay. I'm... I think I figured something out."

"And what's that?" Asked carefully. Gently.

"My scream, the killing scream, I only seem to use it when somebody tries to kill me or kill... others near me." I glance at the closed door, and swallow hard. I wonder if they can hear me.

"It protects you," she whispers. "Wait... Who tried to kill you? Dad never told me that! What happened? What—?"

Uncle Emrys steps in front of her. "Frankie, were you attacked?"

I wince. "Yeah. Look, Uncle Rys—"

"I'm going to kill some people," he grunts. "Fuck that angelic dome, fuck that, I'm coming over."

"Settle down," Aunt Mia pushes him aside. "Whatever happened, you are okay, right?"

"I'm fine," I mumble.

"Julie said she's been looking for you. We were going crazy with worry."

"I'll talk to her," I promise.

"We talked with Ms. Deveroux, the dean. She said there were some riots at the school? Is that when it happened?"

"Yes, but like I said, I'm fine. Look..." I can be weak with them, I can cry, but how much of the truth can I tell them? "Auntie... and Uncles. Has Granddad told you about the last incident, before I came to the College?"

"Bits and pieces. I swear it was like pulling teeth."

I swallow past the knot in my throat. "Well, it happened again. Here."

"Honey. Please. Tell us what happened. Your uncles are about to start kicking down the walls to get to you if you don't reassure them that you're okay."

I hate making them worried, I hate it, but the truth will come out sooner or later. So I tell them what happened.

They are cursing by the time I finish, the men tangled around my aunt, holding her as if she's about to come apart.

But she doesn't. My aunt has a core of steel. "Are you okay? You're sure you didn't get hurt?"

"No, no, don't worry."

"Why are you so flushed?" Uncle Sindri demands. "Are you sick?"

"I'm okay," I insist.

I can afford these small lies, I decide. I will be fine tomorrow. I've worried them enough.

"You'd tell us?" Uncle Ashton asks. "If something was really wrong, if you needed help?"

"And what can you do?" I shake my head. "We're closed off from the world."

"We know people there. Promise me you'll tell us if you need something," Uncle Jason says.

"I promise," I whisper. "I just wanted to see you. Talk to you. I'd love..."

"What, Honeybug?" My aunt is giving me a sweet smile, but her face is strained.

"A hug? Like we used to do when I was little. All of you hugging me."

She nods. "The group hug."

"Yeah, that."

"You can feel it, though, can't you? That, in our thoughts, we are hugging you."

And that's the last thing I see before the magic fizzles, as I lie back against the pillow and close my eyes. Their beloved faces.

I'll never find love like that ever again, will I? I think as fevered sleep draws me back under.

4

RYU

*H*er family.

Though I'm standing outside the room's closed door, I can hear what she says, no matter how softly. My shifter senses make sure of that.

But I don't know if my mind can take it. She has a family she loves, this target of ours. She may play it tough, but her voice is choked with tears as she talks to them. She misses them. She needs them. She wants to hug them.

I feel that in my fucking black soul. This need, this yearning, this ache for the people we care for and who are too far away, out of reach.

I lost everyone I loved. She shouldn't have to go through that. She shouldn't be kept away from them. Shouldn't be used and traded.

She's a weapon.

But she's also a girl, a living, breathing girl with feelings that echo mine and it shouldn't matter, but right now she's got ahold of my stupid heart and I can't breathe. My chest feels too fucking tight.

"I think she's done with her call," Rook says. He's parked his hip against the wall, muscular arms folded over his chest, his long black hair pulled back in a haphazard knot at the back of his corded neck. Only he can make long hair look sexy on a man.

Fuck, why am I thinking such thoughts? I've always been straight. Attracted to women. I was married to one and never desired anyone else. Not even in the long cold nights of war where men often took solace in one another's arms, or found sexual relief.

Even as a fox, I preferred females.

Why now, of all times, on this accursed mission did my mind and body decide they fancy dicks and the men attached to them, too?

And why is my heart beating a weird double beat when it comes to the girl inside the room?

Kuso.

I've always been cursed, haunted by my ghosts, desperate to end it all. I've never been confused about what I want. What lies ahead. Nothing can make the wound inside me better. Nothing can heal me.

So why am I softly smiling?

After a while, quiet falls inside the room. Asa opens the door and we troop back inside, oddly quiet. Subdued. It's this whole business of her being unwell. I think it affected all of us, even Asa who doesn't seem to have an actual fucking heart.

He now kneels by Tir's bunk bed where she's lying with her eyes closed like Sleeping Beauty, one hand hovering over her face.

Except Tir. Who isn't here. Where the fuck is he?

The faint unease in my gut can't be worry about that *baka*... can it? I shouldn't give a flying fuck about any of these assholes, sexy as they may be. Or about this girl, pretty and sweet and hot as she appears.

Dammit.

"She fell asleep," Asa whispers way too loudly and I'm struck by an insane urge to laugh at his serious face. He still seems undecided about whether to touch her or not.

Approaching, I take her hand in mine. "I will sit with her," I say. "And tell her a story. To call her back."

Asa gives me an undecipherable look as I sit on the bed with her. "A story."

"My story." I look down at her small face. "Once upon a time, I thought I'd become a printer."

"A printer?" Kass frowns. "Like the machine?"

"When I was young, there weren't any digital printing machines, *baka*."

"In Japan?"

"No, like I told you before, I was born and raised right here. My grandmother on my father's side was Japanese. I dreamed I'd purchase a press machine, not a linotype, mind you. I loved the idea of typesetting every page. It was part of the fun. Choosing each tiny letter, setting it perfectly in the frame, adding the pictures..."

"You're weird," Rook mutters.

"I disagree," Asa says softly. "It sounds like something I'd love to do."

"Go, Cherub." Rook snickers softly. "I bet you'd be perfect at it, jamming the letters in, glaring at the machine until it worked the way you wanted."

Asa shrugs.

Truth is, of all the guys, I least expected him to say that, to sound interested.

"How about you?" I ask him.

Asa's gaze is still unreadable. "I didn't grow up on earth. I wasn't expected to choose a path, a career. I'm a seraph."

There's something in his voice that has me gazing at him across the room, though. He's lying down on his top bunk, arms

folded behind his head, gazing up at the ceiling. Something...
uncertain.

"I was a barista for a while," Kass says. He's standing by the
window, his favorite spot in the room.

"Wait, really?"

"Doesn't sound like much? I was happy. It was a quiet life."

"And then you were turned?"

"Amazing deduction powers you have there, buddy," he says
drily. "Yeah, then I got turned and was recruited into the
military ranks of the House of Water."

"Why would they recruit a barista-turned-vampire into
their army?"

Kass shrugs. "I volunteered."

"You what?"

"I had my reasons."

"I'll bet. Well, I'm like the angel," Rook mutters from his
sprawl on the mattress on the floor. He's throwing and catching
a pen he probably filched from my stuff. "I've thought about it
though."

"About what?"

"What I'd rather be. I want to travel the world, go to parties,
swim in the ocean, trudge through the jungles. I want to work
all sorts of jobs and meet people. I want to get drunk and have
loads of sex. *Ha.* I mean, nothing stops us from doing what we
want in the future, right?"

"Nothing stops us... is relative. Wishful thinking. Failing
this contract will stop us," Kass mutters. He suddenly walks
over to me. "What is it? You look like you realized something
terrible."

"No, nothing terrible," I say. "Just a realization."

The realization that in my case, succeeding is what will stop
me, but I stopped dreaming of a future long ago, so it doesn't
matter, does it?

"You can still follow your dreams," Rook says, still lying on the mattress, though he's stopped playing with the pen and has twisted around to look at us.

"Yeah, I will follow my dreams," I whisper and unwittingly look down where the scars show on the inside of my wrists.

Kass' gaze follows mine and he grabs my arm. "Ryu..."

"Don't. Fucking don't." I jerk my arm away and in the same motion disentangle myself from the sleeping girl by my side. "Where the Hell is Tir? I should go find him."

"Leave the fucker to sulk his fill," Kass says.

"Suck?" Rook mutters.

"Sulk, *idiota*."

"Sorry." Rook shrugs and smirks. "Your Italian accent is too strong."

"Fuck you."

"Hey, I understood that. Was it in Italian? Do you—?"

"Have you ever had a dog?" Asa asks and we all go still as if someone hit the pause button.

"What the fuck?" I whisper after a moment.

"A dog," Asa says. "You know, the animal."

"We know what dogs are."

He rolls his head to the side to look at us. He has a faraway expression on his face. "A white dog. Big... fluffy. They are so charming, aren't they?"

"Charming. Not the word I'd use for the slobbering beasts, but yeah. Why, thinking of getting one once we're done here? Oh wait, no, you're going back to Heaven to dance around as a fucking singing flame because that's your dream, isn't it?"

He frowns, and sits up, almost hitting his head on the ceiling. "Going back to Heaven is my reward."

"That's not what I asked."

He jumps off the top bunk, feet landing solidly on the floor with a thump, and heads to the door, a determined look on his face.

"And where are you off to now?" I snap, confusion turning to anger in me.

"To pray."

"Again? Prayers won't answer your questions, *baka*, not if they haven't done so by now. Go look for Tir instead, tell him to get his ass back in here."

He gives no answer, and then he's gone, closing the door softly behind him.

Well, damn.

Praying.

I think of my Inari shrine. I still have it. That wasn't taken from me. But I haven't sat to meditate or pray since it all went to Hell. Or even practice with my *shuriken* or my *katana*. You could say I didn't have time with all the shit that went down.

But that's bullshit. You always find time for something when it's important to you. And you should always find time to be alone with yourself to make sure you still like one another.

I could grab my shrine and go elsewhere to pray, like Asa does, or my weapons, for some privacy and quiet, only I... I glance back at Frankie.

I don't want to leave her alone when she's unwell.

She's not alone. Rook and Kass will be with her.

All the same, I can't walk out right now. Is it a sense of duty keeping me here?

Would Inari reply to me? Or would I be the one replying to myself? When has she ever said anything to my prayers? When has she helped me?

She didn't bring those I lost back.

It's up to me to take care of those I have in my life right now, so I return to the bunk and sit down beside Frankie. Maybe it *is* duty, what I feel. Who knows? Intense feelings are hard to tell apart, at least for me. Sorting through them is nigh impossible. Anger lies close to sorrow, relief lies close to pleasure, and contentment lies close to love.

Losing the photos of my family felt like someone cut off a limb. Like they took away my memories of my family. I'm unsure I can remember their faces without the pictures. I feel like I can't hold onto them, like they're slipping through my fingers.

But she's real. She's warm and solid when I pull the covers over her body. I remember the first days of meeting her, her smile, her questions, her interest in my notebooks and pens, the relaxed air about her.

Feels like ages ago when it hasn't been any time at all.

What wouldn't I give to go back to that. To pretending I was a normal student, just a guy, free to live my life, study and learn. Be with her.

But how? She doesn't trust me. I'm supposed to give her up. She hates me. I'm supposed to feel nothing toward her.

This is messed up.

I glance at Rook who has sat on the desk, Kass in the chair, and I wonder what is on their minds. What they feel. What they have to lose.

I had told myself that it pays naught to care, that I should cut all ties, yet here we are, all together in this room, in this venture, guarding Frankie and not knowing how to win.

Is there a way? Looks like a lose-lose situation to me, and that's coming from someone whose goal is to let go of the rope.

Do I want to?

I startle myself so badly with this question that I bang my head on the headboard as I scramble to get back up.

"Ryu?" Rook gets up. "What is it?"

"Nothing." My hands are shaking. My breath comes in shallow gasps. What the fuck is wrong with me? I've been begging for release from this life for too fucking long to have doubts now. I took on this fucking mission for that.

"Don't *nothing* me. Is Frankie okay?"

"She's fine. Look for yourself."

With a frown cast my way, he sits down on the bed beside her. He doesn't touch her, just watches her, his head bowed.

"I'll go get us some food from the kitchens," I say, itching to get out of here, walk the tension and the crazy thoughts off. "We haven't eaten since yesterday."

"Not fucking hungry," Kass mutters.

"You need to eat, man. And feed on someone. You look like shit."

"So you've all made a point of telling me."

His gray eyes have dark circles framing them. His face looks too thin for someone who hasn't only eaten in a day. The way he's holding himself in the chair speaks of self-control and pain.

He still looks beautiful.

Fuck.

Yeah, getting out of here right the fuck now would be wise, before I say anything I'll definitely regret later. After I've eaten and had a decent night's sleep, my rational mind will return to its senses.

But a knock comes on the door.

"Could be Tir," Rook says absently.

"Tir wouldn't knock."

"Be careful," Kass says, starting to rise from the chair as I throw the door open.

It's a short, dark-haired girl, quite pretty. Her brows wing up when she sees me.

I know her.

"Hi," she says. "Is Franks here? I mean, Francesca. Can I see her? I'm her cousin."

5

FRANKIE

I hear voices. Familiar, warm, male voices that keep the dreams at bay as I drown in the covers and a familiar sexy scent.

Tir, I think. *Smells like Tir.*

But he's not here. Am I in his bed?

A touch on my arm. Covers wrapping me up in more warmth. A weight dipping the mattress. A soft argument that later fades away.

And then a different presence sits down beside me.

"Franks?" a girl's soft voice says, dragging me up through layers of sleep.

With some effort, I lift my heavy lids. "Jules!" I reach for her hand and she grabs both of mine in hers. "What are you doing here?"

"Mom pinged me. Said you seemed sick. Asked me to check on you. Your hands are so warm. What happened?"

"Infection, apparently."

"What? Why?"

"She was wounded during the attack," Rook says and her head whips around so fast I'm scared for her. Is she turning

Exorcist on me? "We hadn't realized she got an infection. Us supernaturals rarely get those. Which makes it... weird that it has brought her down like that, to be honest."

"Oh my God. You're all here," she blurts out.

Rook shrugs. "Right now? Only three of us, as you can see."

Kass gives a small wave from his seat.

"I didn't notice you," Juliette goes on.

"That's impossible." Rook looks affronted. "I'm sure you did, don't be shy."

"My fault, Darling," Ryu drawls in a fair imitation of Rook, "I tend to blind the girls with my looks."

And I snicker, unable to help myself.

"But otherwise... you're all here?" Juliette's eyes are wide, her cheeks flushed.

"Yeah, all five of us. Welcome to the den of monsters."

I roll my eyes. "Don't mind Rook. He's a little theatrical."

He grins, and tips an imaginary hat. "Finally, some recognition. I want to add Thespian to my curriculum vitae. Rook Greysill, Hellhound and budding actor at your service, my ladies."

"Obviously," I mutter but he still looks ridiculously pleased, for whatever reason.

Julie is ogling the three of them—because of course, they're half-naked, fabulously bare-chested, a fact I had sort of lost track of as I'd talked to Auntie and Uncles and then fallen asleep. Yeah, they are a sight for sore eyes, definitely. They're all lounging about, all muscular chests, bulging biceps, and chiseled jaws as if it's just another Tuesday.

I can't believe Julie is here. I bet she can't believe any of this, either, but tugging on her hands, I'm reminded of something urgent I need to ask her, and not in front of the boys.

Ugh.

"Rook. I need to talk to my cousin..."

"So talk," he says. "We'll be quiet, I promise. I was just about to brush my hair and paint my toenails."

I blink. "You were?"

"Fine, no, I wasn't, but I'll still be quiet while doing manly things like push-ups. I'll keep my caveman grunting to a minimum."

Julie giggles and blushes. "Is he for real?"

"Couldn't tell you. Sometimes I'm not so sure myself." I lift my head off the pillow to glare a little at a still-grinning Rook. "Please? Just for five minutes."

"But—"

"Girly matters." My cousin gives him one of her patented sharky smiles. "Not meant for male ears."

"What the fuck," Rook mutters. "Now I'm definitely curious."

I glance at Kass, making puppy eyes, and he sighs. "Out, guys. Let's give them some privacy."

"For real? Pussy-whipped," Rook mutters at him as he stalks out of the room. "Behave girls. Don't do anything I wouldn't do."

"Who's the pussy-whipped?" Kass snarks as he heaves himself out of the chair and limps after him. "You're the one who couldn't keep his hands and dick away and slept with her."

Julie's brows arch.

Oops.

Ryu gives us a last, lingering look and closes the door behind them.

"So... about what Rook said." I let go of her hands to sit up and prop the pillow behind me so I can lean on it. "I may have screwed up..."

———

"You slept with three of them," Julie says.

"Yeah."

"Since yesterday."

"Uh-huh."

"Without using any protection."

I wince. "Right, about that—"

"And that's just the cherry on the cake because they are on various missions to deliver you to their respective Houses— and/or Heaven—for their own means. Auntie told me about that, too. She was so pissed at the world. My dads were swearing up and down they'd tear Heaven apart to force the dome off so they can come pick you up, take you into hiding."

"Been there, tried that," I mutter. Sudden panic grips me. "Julie, you can't let them try any of that. This is bigger than us. Just the thought of any of you in danger makes me want to hurl. Promise me. Promise you'll convince them not to do anything rash."

"They are concerned."

"I know. But there's nothing they can do."

"And what do you suggest, we leave you to be taken God knows where and experimented on? These people could hurt you badly, Franks. They could kill you or make you disappear."

"Well, I'm a dangerous weapon, apparently, and maybe it's better if I'm taken out of circulation."

"Never say that again. You're my cousin!" Her eyes fill with tears. "You're like a sister to me! Stop referring to yourself like... like an object, something they can take and put away!"

"Sorry." My eyes burn. And then something dawns on me, something that has lurked for a while at the back of my mind. "You're not afraid of me."

"Of course not!"

"Maybe I wasn't clear. I have killed people, Jules. I'm dangerous."

"I *know* you," she says fiercely. "I grew up with you. You'd never hurt anyone who didn't mean you harm. If you're a weapon, then you were used in self-defense, and that's not a crime."

I wish I could believe that was all there was to it. I wish I could just wash the guilt I feel off me and trust that I'm not a bad guy. Not having much success with it so far. Because no matter the reasons for killing someone, you did something that can't be undone.

...right?

I sigh. "Okay, let's stick to first things first."

"Which are?"

"I had sex with three guys. Without protection. Julie, what do I do?"

"Oh, dear."

"Because one thing worse than taking me away and experimenting on me is doing it while I'm pregnant... right?"

She pales. "Oh my God. Hadn't thought of it that way. Franks..."

"Focus, Jules. I'm trying not to fall apart here." My voice cracks and I have to take a breath, push the fear back down because hate-fucking the boys was one thing. Being afraid of bringing a child into this world is quite another. "Help me. Tell me what to do."

"You're right. When was your ovulation?"

"My *ov*... are you for real? You think I keep track of my cycle when all this shit is going down? I normally don't anyway, even under normal circumstances."

"Why not?"

"You think it's something Granddad would have taught me?" I scoff. "Buying panty liners, tampons and sanitary towels is always such a joy. He keeps forgetting what they are for and I have to explain the female reproduction system all over again."

"Oh boy." She tucks a strand of hair out of her face, smiles sadly. "I've really missed you, you know. Growing up with my brothers only wasn't as much fun as having you around. I've been so sad that we didn't get a chance to go through puberty together, exchange period and ovulation secrets and boy crushes..."

And now it won't happen either, but I don't say it.

"I'm sorry," I blurt out. "Sorry I'm the way I am, that my mom is a world-class bitch and my dad an asshole with a big—"

"Franks."

"A big power." I stick my tongue out at her. "That's what I was going to say. Now tell me what to do. About the sexing issue. I'd go to the medic, but I'm still too sick. There's a pill I should take, right?"

"Morning-after pill? I'll go bring you one, just in case. I mean... have you had sex before? Did they... you know. Come inside of you?"

"I know how sex works," I mutter. "And yes."

Now she puts on her teacher face, the one she always used growing up when we played house. She always played as a teacher and enjoyed telling me how to do just about everything. "I'll find you a pill and then we'll use magic for any future encounters."

"Contraceptive magic?"

She suddenly grins. "Assuming you want to keep having sex with these guys, that is."

Now my skin must be blistering, it's so hot. "Not sure."

"Just in case, then." She wiggles her fingers. "It's a spell."

"Is everything about magic in this College?"

"Of course it is, didn't you know? It's a magic university."

"I've spent years with Granddad avoiding magic," I whisper. "I don't even know what I can do... except damage and death. And magical phone calls."

Then I think of Tir and have to swallow hard because I still don't know if I can do more. If I can undo some of the damage and what that means.

"You pinged Mom without killing anyone. You're doing great."

Yeah, there's that.

"I'll go find the medic," she says, "ask for the pill. I bet I can convince her to give it to me without too much fuss."

"And the spell?"

"Lift your tank top." When I'm too slow to comply, she pulls down the blanket and pushes my tank top up herself. She lays her hands on my stomach and whispers something under her breath. Heat spreads through me, making me gasp, then cold. So cold I bat at her hands, a whole-body shiver gripping me.

"What are you doing?"

"Freezing your ovaries." She giggles, and lifts her hands off me. "I was being serious. All done."

"So easy? Is this... a permanent spell?"

Nope." She smiles. "It's good for a while. It depends on the person, how long it will last, but a month for sure."

"Okay. That's something." I pull down my tank top and pull up the blanket, feeling a little shaky. Shakier. "Thank you."

"I should get going. Get you that pill." She rises from the bed. "By the way, did I mention that your guys are hot?"

"They aren't my guys," I say flatly.

"You just have casual sex with them."

"Hate sex," I correct her. "And now it's over."

"If you say so." She waves at me, turns to go but pauses before she opens the door and glances back at me. "If not Granddad, then Mom and the Dads will find a way to get you out of here. I'm sure they will. Don't worry."

"I'm not worried," I lie and smile at her. "I'm sure everything will be all right."

6

FRANKIE

*E*verything is not all right. Julie brings me the frigging pill and it makes me sick like a dog.

I throw up.

And then throw up some more, the fever and the spell and the pill making for a shitty cocktail.

Did I mention earlier that I felt like crap? Well, now I feel worse.

All the joy.

"She's still sick," Kass all but yells at Rook. "Do something!"

"Like what, sucky boy? Whatever her cousin gave her didn't sit well with her. Frankie, what did Juliette give you?"

"None of your business," I grind out and heave some more.

Great.

Gross.

So sexy.

Not that I want to feel sexy for these guys. Nope. Not even for hate sex. I need some distance. Yep. That's what I need.

No distancing is happening now, though, with Asa holding my hair back and Rook returning with a washed-out trashcan only for me to upchuck some more.

Julie didn't warn me it would be this bad.

Then again, if I spewed the entire pill out when I first heaved, as I did, did it work at all? Doubtful.

All this puking my guts out for nothing.

"Easy, girl." Kass wipes my face with a wet towel as I lean back against Asa. "You should drink some water."

"Here." Ryu presses a glass to my lips. "Take small sips. See if you can keep it down."

I'm too exhausted to mind that they're all hovering like mother hens and manhandling me—gently, mind you—on the bed and over its edge where I can empty my stomach contents over and over. Then Asa is braiding my hair to keep it out of my face, Ryu is muttering something about getting me some ginger ale, Kass cleans up my face again, lingering over my cheeks, and Rook returns with a freshly washed—for the hundredth time—trash can to place in front of me.

I feel like a pampered princess.

A sick, puking princess, but pampered nonetheless. It's a feeling I haven't had since I left home with Granddad years ago, and it shouldn't touch me. This isn't my family. The motives of these guys aren't pure and self-sacrificing. I know this and yet...

Don't ever forget it, Franks. You keep choosing to forget it, dammit.

What a pity.

I'm not happy feeling so weak, depending on them.

But at the same time, I admit I like the gentleness they show me. I've seen them fight and they're all sharp edges and power, but right now, with me, they seem afraid to break me, and I am breakable. At this moment, I am.

And I like their strength as they lift me and lay me against a mound of pillows, which, in hindsight, must be all of their pillows stacked together behind me.

I like everything about them today, and my God is that dangerous. It's a glimpse into the kind of men and partners they could be, how it could have been if they really liked and wanted me.

My heart is at risk. It's just as breakable as my body, as if the two are connected, as if the physical weakness is eroding the walls around my emotions and undoing all my good work in putting them back up.

This is a siege on my heart.

I'm not prepared. I didn't have time to build up my defenses. In the whirlwind of the past twenty-four hours, I was mainly concerned with not dying and not killing everyone by accident, so I didn't have a moment to sit and meditate, gather up my wits like bricks in the wall and fortify my resolve not to let anyone in.

Especially these five.

The five guys I can't stop thinking about, can't stop wanting. *So fucking unfair.*

———

I wake up curled up against a warm, hard, male body. It's like a furnace, exuding heat, and the muscles locked around me are taut as steel, his chest—has to be his chest, as his heartbeat pounds under my ear—a perfect pillow.

Scent of wood smoke and pepper...

"Ward the door." The chest on which my cheek is resting rumbles. "Don't let anyone in."

"I already warded it," Kass says.

"Ward it some more. Damn these people."

It's Rook, I think. The scent and the voice... Definitely Rook. He's the guy whose muscular chest I'm using as a pillow.

"What's going on?" I breathe.

His arms tighten around me. "Don't worry. We got your back."

"Is there an attack?" I try to unfold from the cage of his arms but don't manage to budge an inch. "Rook?"

"We're dealing with it," he says, his voice grave.

Something else is at the back of my mind and it takes me a moment to retrieve it. "And Tir? Did he come back?"

"He'll be fine," Rook rumbles.

"So he didn't." I manage to push back enough that his hold relaxes and I can look up at his handsome face. "Go find him."

"He's a Hunter, Sweetheart. He can take care of himself."

"No, you don't understand. He tends to self-destruct."

His dark brows bunch together. "Self-destruct?"

"He tends to go looking for trouble to blow off steam," I explain. "Didn't you notice?"

"Then he's an idiot."

"He's a *person*." I stare at where my hand is pressed to his pec. Why is Rook shirtless? Just to torture me? "I think Jatri's death affected him in some way I don't understand."

He's quiet for a moment. He nods at someone, and I realize I've almost forgotten the other boys inside the room. "Rest, girl. Don't get your panties in a wad over him."

"You don't get it." I want to get up and go after him myself, but even this short stretch of conversation is tiring me out. My head is pounding and my lids feel heavy. "I think he's in trouble. He may get hurt. He barely came back from the dead."

"What?"

"I can't stand the thought of losing him again, of him dying again—"

"Again? But he didn't die."

"Yeah. Shit, you're right." I close my eyes. Force them open again. "But for a moment there, I was sure he did. I swear his heart stopped and he wasn't breathing."

"When was that?"

"When he opened the portal and hauled me away from you."

He's still frowning. "You're no doctor, Sweets."

"No, but when you stop breathing you die, don't you?"

"You do. After a while." He sounds troubled. "But I'm sure he never really died."

Sounds of crashing and smashing come from the other end of the room, and I jerk. "What's that?"

"Just the fucking angels. Go back to sleep. Everything is okay. We will be okay."

Everything is okay. We will be okay. His words echo inside my mind, blotting out the noise until it all fades away.

———

I find myself on a familiar dark street with a sadly familiar sense of dread winding through me. Ash is blowing on the cold wind, making me shiver. Echoes of voices wind around me but nobody is there.

Everyone is dead.

Because I killed them.

I rub my hands up and down my arms. Strangely, I'm only dressed in my underwear, which makes me frown. I'm supposed to be wearing sturdy, full-coverage clothing—and boots. I look down at my bare feet.

This isn't right.

Why am I not cold?

The cold is a ball of ice in my gut, burning me, hollowing me out, but I'm otherwise all right standing in the middle of the city in winter in my underthings.

Yet I feel exposed—not to the elements but to gazes. Nobody is there and yet I could swear I feel eyes on my bared skin, leaving ghostly trails in their wake.

Then steps crunch on the asphalt and I turn around with a gasp.

Favrash... The word echoes against the insides of my skull. *Favrash...*

The blond man is approaching me, carrying his staff in one hand. He looks a little worse for wear, his T-shirt bloodied, his jeans torn in places. His feet are bare, too, I notice.

His eyes are blazing dark and I take a step back.

"Oh, it's you," I mutter. "Again. What do you want?"

"Checking on you." His voice is a low rumble, calm and reassuring, not matching the fury in his eyes.

"And why are you so mad?"

That seems to startle him. His pale brows wing up. "I don't... know what I'm doing," he admits. "I'm so out of my depth." He clutches his staff. It has a long string hanging from it, fluttering in the wind whistling through the streets and alleys. "I came here thinking I knew exactly what to do, that I was ready to do anything to achieve my goal, but now... Now I wonder if I was mistaken. About many things."

That's quite the speech, and yet... I squint at his handsome face and as I stare, it starts to shift—small changes, his dark eyes turning a pale green, his cheekbones becoming more defined, and that string on his staff keeps fluttering, distracting me.

"What's that?" I demand, pointing at the staff. "That string hanging off it?"

"This? It's the string of my bow. When it's unstrung, I use it as a staff."

"Your bow." I gape at him because finally it all clicks into place and his face shifts some more, turning into the familiar face of a certain annoying, sexy Fae. "Tir. It's you. Of course it's you. Jesus, how didn't I recognize you from the start?"

"Pardon me, *elenyi?*"

Even his speech patterns have changed now that I know who he is. It's as if recognizing what I'm seeing changes it to fit better what I *know* it is. Pointed ears now poke out of that pale hair and when he speaks, I catch glimpses of sharp teeth.

"In my dreams. It's you. You're a dreamwalker."

He dips his head in acknowledgment. "It is one of my powers. I didn't expect you to know me in the dreamworld."

"Is it glamour?"

"Of sorts. It takes special skill to alter your appearance in the dreamscape. Then again, you weren't supposed to see me at all. Your powers are... unexpected."

"Gee, thanks. You're asleep now, too?"

"Not quite. I'm in a trance."

"And why the Hell are you stalking my dreams?"

"It's my power, the one I was chosen for when I was given this mission. I started doing it when I first met you, trying to find answers, make sure you were the one I was told to find, that you were really dangerous."

"And now?"

"Now... I can't seem to stop myself." He sounds troubled.

"Wow. Um, awesome." I mean, *brows, meet my hairline.* "You do know that's creepy stalker behavior, right?"

He shrugs. "I am a monster. What did you expect? I'm Wild Hunt. Not used to boundaries. And I want... to be around you. Though I shouldn't."

He doesn't look like a monster. It would help if he did, but even when he transforms into a horned half-beast... he's still beautiful.

"Do you want me to stop visiting your dreams?" he asks.

As if anyone should even ask the question.

I open my mouth to say yes, but strangely, I hesitate. My dreams are mainly nightmares and having him there is... comforting. What do I do?

Just like him, I have no clue what I'm doing.

He takes my hand and I let him. I squeeze his fingers and

the icy ball of dread inside me thaws a little, and all I can think of is, this is not good.

Not good that I like his hand around mine so much, that I relax when he's here, that I feel safe and protected.

Not good at all...

7

TIR

I stay out late.

That sounds like fun, at least for most young guys my age at this college. Or the age I'm supposed to be. Not fucking confusing at all, is it?

Most guys here aren't old like us. They really are twenty-something men—and the occasional girl—who were sent here by their influential supernatural families to learn the rudiments of their magic and develop their powers.

It's been a long while since I've felt young.

Since I've felt anything but fear and anger.

Being inside her dreams only served to drive this fact home. She feels so young in them and I feel... too many things. I want to grab and hustle her away, hide her, and keep her safe. I keep returning to them, hoping to see the nightmare turn into a peaceful dream, go from bad memories to pleasant ones.

But the only time I've seen her relax was when I took her hand in mine and she gripped my fingers back. It felt so right, like she trusted me to help, like she wanted me there.

A load of bull.

Visiting her dreams at this point is a mistake, a lapse in judgment, a loss of self-control and it's time I stopped.

My dreams have been heavy, too, to be honest, in the few moments of sleep I've managed to catch over the past weeks. So much has happened.

My hunt for Frankie.

The unlikely friendship we struck.

The unexpected lust for her.

Then my failure to deliver Frankie to the Unseelie king.

My punishment for it.

The assassins and Jatri's demise.

And now being captured once again by the Fae gang as I was on my way back to the room.

"Fuck off," I hiss and throw my elbow back into the stomach of the guy holding me. "You don't know what you're doing. My patience is at an all-time low. Get your mitts off me! If you touch me again, I'll turn you into a frog and step on you, got it?"

"Let him go," a familiar, hated voice says and it's Cirdan, Jatri's second in command.

The guy releases me and I shove him away and straighten my T-shirt. "What, are you the new king of the College Fae? How impressive for your CV, Cirdan."

He is just frowning at me, as if what he sees isn't making any sense. "So you're Wild Hunt."

"I doubt that was news for you, but if it was, then I have to wonder why Jatri had you as his second."

"I'm from a powerful family, obviously," he says with an annoyed huff and I snort at his lack of embarrassment. I'd like his frankness and realistic view of the world if I didn't suspect he believes he's a great catch in each and every way that counts because of his family.

"Good for you," I scoff, brush my hands on my pants and turn to go. "If that was all, then I have places to be."

"Wait, Tirius. I'm not... I won't take Jatri's place."

I halt. "And why the Hell not?"

"Because we need a strong Fae to lead us," a girl from the Unseelie Court says, marked by her scaly skin. "And you're the strongest Fae at the College. A member of the Wild Hunt."

Slowly I turn back around. "Wait, let me get this straight. You want me to *replace Jatri?*"

The faces around me are solemn. Cirdan lifts his hands, palms up, in a shrug as if to say, *what can you do?*

"His body has barely cooled," I go on, the unreality of the situation setting in. "And you're already looking for a replacement?"

"A gang without a leader is a dangerous monster," Cirdan says.

"And a gang with a monster for a leader isn't much better," I mutter.

"You're not a monster. Not to us," Cirdan says, opening his hands like a peace offering. "We're Fae. Our Unseelie side is beastly and monstrous, we're used to that. To your friends, you may seem that way, I don't know. Especially when you take your true form. Have you asked them?"

I take a step back as if he's punched me in the gut. "None of your goddamn business," I breathe.

The guys are as much monsters as I am. They wouldn't judge me for being a Hunter, for having horns and black claws. Would they?

And how will your family feel about that, T?

Fuck.

I turn and walk away, ignoring their calls to go back and talk. Talk about what? What do I care about leading the Fae gang of bullies and assholes? Why should I care?

And as for my friends... What friends? We're not friends. This is fucking shit.

Even if I'm worried about Frankie, worried about them.

This isn't right.

I don't need this burden.

As if being told that my family has now been informed that I'm a criminal not deserving of their concern and losing hope wasn't punishment enough.

As if being told that next time I fail, their memory of me will be erased wasn't cruel enough.

How long will they cling to the memory of me? As if the child they once knew still exists, as if the long years I spent with the Wild Hunt never happened. What am I clinging to?

Kraish... I locked up all those questions together with my feelings for my family. Had to, or I'd have crashed and burned when the Wild Hunt took me away. Now the box keeps leaking fear and uncertainty and more questions than ever and...

More feelings.

Warm feelings I shouldn't be able to feel with this damn heart of mine that was turned to stone long ago, all pleasure and niceness burned out of it by Arawn himself.

So what the fuck am I doing?

Kraish bedash.

I should focus on the mission and nothing else, erase all doubt from my mind, and just keep going. It's the only thing that's worked before and now is not the time to consider other choices.

———

There's a girl in my bed.

Talk about Goldilocks vibes.

Rewind. I stealthily enter the room and seek my bunk, roll into my bed in the dark—only to find another person there who shifts and whispers something I can't make out.

A girl.

And it's the one girl I've been trying to avoid.

With a sigh, she turns and rolls against me, throwing her

arms around me. Automatically, I do the same, pulling her against me, and my mind blanks out while my traitorous *kerel* body crows *yes, yes, fucking finally!*

Which is absurd. I'm just holding her against me, nothing more than that, and she's all soft curves and sweet fragrance, though I can smell something slightly sickly about her that has me tightening my hold on her as if that way I can keep her safe and well. She's shivering and I pull the blankets on top of both of us, nuzzle her hair.

This is the girl whose dreams I walk, whose fear I've felt in my bones. I've seen the desolate dreamscapes in which she wanders every night and though I feel like a voyeur, I feel so close to her right now. Closer with every dream I invade.

She must hate me.

When she wakes up in the morning, she will realize who's holding her and hate me even more. She'll be spitting mad.

It feels like a stolen moment, like flying with her in the clouds inside the pages of a fairytale—which is ironic, seeing as fairytales are the chronicles of my people and they went from being terrifying tales of warning to humans to prettified and sanitized bedtime stories for kids.

She makes me feel that way right now. Innocent, somehow. Free. Ready to take on the world and hope for a happy ending.

I should know better.

I *do* know fucking better. This is idiocy. Lunacy. Self-destruction at its best.

But I don't let go.

———

Sleep has dragged me under for good, for the first time since my arrival at the College, and the only reason I know it is because I'm caught by surprise.

I'm always on my fucking guard, so the last thing I expect is to find myself being hauled out of bed and thrown to the floor. It's hard and cold and the encounter with my hips and ribs startles a yelp out of me.

Ow, bruises meet floor. A pleasure.

"The fuck is wrong with you?" I grouse at the guys standing over me. "Has the bullying now moved into our bedroom?"

Rook and Kass.

Their expressions shift to startled for a second. Is it because I haven't gone beastly and killed them yet?

Or... because I said *bedroom* and not just room? *Our* bedroom?

Then their eyes harden again.

"You just walk away," Rook accuses, "and she's so sick she can't keep anything down, and where the *fuck* were you?"

I scowl. "I don't answer to you."

"We're a team, fucker." His dark blue eyes flash. "Are you denying it? Want out? Want to sleep in another room? We don't mind."

Sudden panic hits and I scramble to my feet, noticing that the bed is empty. "Where's Frankie? Wait... You said she's sick? I thought I smelled sickness on her."

"You thought right."

"Where is she?" I turn in a circle. "What the fuck..."

"Calm the fuck down," Kass says, running a hand through his wild dark hair. "She went to take a shower."

I reel. "Alone?"

"Are you fucking with me right now? Testing my fucking patience?" Kass growls. "Of course she's not alone, now less than ever. Think we'd let her walk around alone when she's still dizzy and running a fever?"

"A fever... right." I grab onto the bunk bed until I'm sure my legs can hold me. My nerves are frayed, to say the least. "Her wound. It didn't seem she was hurt so bad."

"You talk about it as if it wasn't last night we brought her here, together, motherfucker, and then you walked out and didn't come back!"

I lift my fist, shake it at him. "Calm your tits, Kass. I went out to walk around and blow off some steam, get my head on straight. I hadn't planned on staying out all night."

They exchange glances. "What happened?"

"The Fae gang happened. Again. I swear, those assholes always choose the time to grab me."

"The Hell?" Rook comes forward, stopping when I raise my other fist, too. "Are you okay? Did they beat you up again?"

"Stop right there."

"Tir..." He lays a hand on my shoulder, startling me. "Tell us."

I blink, lowering my fists, surprised at the concern. "No. This time they didn't."

"Good, or I'd go right now and smash their heads in."

I realize my mouth is hanging open. "You would?"

Warmth unspools in my chest, warm threads like sticky toffee, tangling everything up, catching small emotions here and there like moths and toying with them.

He hauls me closer and squeezes my shoulder. "I swear I'd make them eat their balls."

A disturbing image perhaps, at least for normal people, but we're not normal. It makes me grin. I fight it, turn my face away, because another emotion wells inside of me, another crack in the wall.

Dammit.

I think of my strange encounter. What if I said yes to Cirdan? What if I led the gang? Could I then protect Frankie better? Would I have more clout with the Seelie and the Unseelie Courts?

"Tell me about Frankie," I deflect before they ask anything more about the gang and the night I spent outside our room. "Did you say she was throwing up?"

"Like a dog, man." Kass shakes his head, his anger seeming to evaporate. "I thought she was doing better, and then her cousin came to visit and brought her a pill that made her so fucking sick."

"And what was that pill?"

"Hell if I know."

Pushing off Rook, I stumble to the window and brace my hands on the desk set before it. The chair has been pulled to the side, against one of the bunk beds. Outside, the light is gray, the sky overcast. You can see one side of the other dorm, the one with the private, luxury rooms for the scions of the big Houses and everyone whose family has some clout, and on the other the campus park.

"Something else is bothering you," Rook says.

"Yeah, genius, spot on. A lot of things are bothering me, wouldn't you know it."

"Spit it out. Don't be shy."

"Fuck you."

"Come on, trickster. What else happened?"

"Nothing... much." The almost-lie twists my tongue. How often have I wished I could lie freely? That I wouldn't feel a stab in my guts every time I do? The curse of the Fae won't let me, not that it's ever stopped me.

"It's about Frankie, isn't it?"

Not that hard to guess, I suppose. "How did she get up without me realizing? I'm a Hunter of the Wild Hunt."

"You should have seen yourself." Rook chuckles. "You were all wrapped around her like an octopus, snoring away."

"Shut up. I don't snore."

"Sure, sure. Mouth open and drooling and all."

"That doesn't explain how I let her go without waking up."

Kass approaches us. "No idea, man, but you fought us in your sleep. Threatened to kill us and cursed our ancestors when we tried to pry her from your arms."

I wince. "Still not explaining how—"

"We replaced her with a pillow," Kass says.

"The fuck? A pillow?" I sputter. "And I was fine with that replacement? Are you messing with me?"

"It was *her* pillow. It was still warm and smelled like her," he concedes. "Probably why."

I expect them to laugh at me some more, tell me what an idiot I am to accept a pillow as a replacement for our girl, to tell me how stupid I am for a Fae, how stupid a race the Fae are, and all the usual ribbing between races I've endured and been a part of all of my life.

A Wild Hunt Fae, after all, is shunned by every side, including the Fae side. We're the black sheep of the Fae world, the amoral bloodthirsty bogeymen, the embodiment of all that goes bump in the night.

But they're quiet.

All three of us are standing there at the window, around the desk, arms folded over our chests as if we were arranged to mirror each other, and there's a certain sense of... calm and camaraderie that sets my heart thumping in a different rhythm. I feel my shoulders relaxing, my spine allowing a bit of a slouch, my head bowing forward. My jaw unclenching enough to allow a smile.

What's going on here? It's as if we're becoming friends. Brothers in arms, bonding over Frankie and our concern for her—our missions, okay. Whatever.

Then Rook shoots me a heated look, his eyes traveling up and down my body, and yeah, okay, brothers with benefits? I never thought he might want to get his rocks off with me again, but the look says he definitely does, which is cool with me. I feel my dick stiffening under his gaze.

And my mind whispers, *Why not?*

When he slings an arm over Kass' shoulders, making him jerk in surprise, I snicker.

When he nuzzles his neck, the look on Kass' face is so priceless I have to lean against the desk, choking on laughter.

"You do know you smell amazing, don't you?" Rook sniffs at Kass' neck, then his hand slides up to cradle Kass' head, fingers digging into the wild black hair at the back. "You're a sexy fucker, Kassander. I want to fuck you."

And Kass... blushes.

Like a virginal schoolgirl.

I'm fascinated.

Especially when Kass, badass foul-mouthed vampire, doesn't tell him to stop, instead turning his head into the touch, lips parting.

Fuck... He does look hot.

"You're half-incubus," I say. "You need sex. You both do. You should do it. I'd watch."

"No," Kass says as Rook leans in to run his mouth over the side of his neck, "you fucking peeping tom, get your own peepshow... oh yeah..."

Arawn, this is so damn funny. This time I bow over, laughing out loud. And yet the warmth in my chest remains, as does my hard-on.

"Stop... laughing," Kass manages, red seeping into his eyes. "I can't... do this..."

This time Rook draws back, brow furrowing. "What is it you can't do?"

"Sex!" Kass pulls back this time, eyes dark and wild, flushed all over.

"Why the fuck not? No pun intended."

"Well, intend your puns, goddammit," I mutter on autopilot, dying of curiosity. "Kass, why the no fucking rule? I'd do you myself, I confess, if you don't want Rook."

"It's not that!" he snaps. "It's not Rook. I want him. I want you. Wanting you isn't the issue here."

"I knew you were hard for us," Rook says, smirking.

"Then what is it?" I ask.

"I will lose control!" Kass all but yells at us, fists balling at his sides. "I'll lose all fucking control and fucking... rape you, bite you, suck you dry in all and every way."

Silence spreads between us.

Then I laugh. "My man, you think we're human? Think you can overpower and kill us? You've found your match here."

He shakes his head, dark hair flying, face red, and Mab's tits, he's so damn fuckable it's all I can do not to grab him and kiss him.

Talk about loss of self-control... If he's afraid of that, he should look inside my head. It's as if a bomb went off in there. A goddamn clusterfuck.

Rook runs his hands through his long hair, distracting me again. He pulls it back in a bun and parks his ass on the desk. "Going to shower?" he changes the topic.

I sniff my armpits. "I think I'm good."

"Frankie won't like it," Kass mutters, sitting down on his bunk, acting as if the last few minutes of conversation never happened.

"I bet you she likes our smelly armpits just fine," Rook says. "Trust me on this. Who wants a guy who smells of roses instead of male musk?"

"You talk as if she'll want to sleep with us," I mutter.

"She does. If you can't tell, then trust the expert."

Kass' cheekbones turn redder. I see hope flash in his eyes. He wants her. Just like he wants me and Rook. His stony façade is cracking right through and I can read him like a book.

I want it, too. I shouldn't be hoping for that, any of that, with any of them. None of us should.

But life is like a train wreck. You may tell yourself you can jump off at the last minute, but the crash always comes too soon.

8

FRANKIE

*W*aking up was a bit of a blur. I had a sense of strong arms holding me against a muscular, warm chest, a feeling of safety and well-being like one of those dreams I had as a child, before the first incident and the nightmares that took over my sleep.

A scent of lightning and attractive male winds through my senses.

His heart is beating under my ear, a steady, reassuring thump-thump that eases mine. In the last year, I've always woken up in a panic from a nightmare, so this... is new.

Pleasurable.

No, that's too lightly said. It's calm and relaxing and glorious, this chance to luxuriate in the warmth and the feel of that male body against mine, and not in a lusty way. It just feels...nice.

And then I'm gently but firmly disentangled from his arms, pulled to the other side of the bed by more sets of capable hands, and held against another firm chest, my head pillowed on a muscled shoulder.

"Asa," I whisper.

"How are you feeling today?" He folds a muscular arm behind his head, pale hair mussed. His bright blue eyes are warm, gazing down at me.

Gah, so gorgeous.

"Better," I say after taking stock, shifting a little in his arms. "I stink."

"Shower, then." He sits up, hauling me up to sit with him. I don't expect him to surge to his feet with me in his arms, cradled to his powerful chest, and yet that's exactly what he does.

"I'm coming with you," Ryu says, grabbing my towel.

"You can put me down, Asa," I whisper. "I can walk."

But when he shakes his head stubbornly, I don't insist. I'm still in this hazy place right after waking up, after coming out of sickness when your limbs feel wobbly and your head heavy. It's nice to be held in Asa's arms.

Everything... is so nice.

It's as if I'm on drugs, and I giggle against his shoulder at the thought.

"What's so funny?" Ryu meets my gaze over Asa's shoulder, following behind us as we exit the room. He closes the door behind us, then his green gaze is back on me, questioning. He's a sight to behold, in his loose, red pajama bottoms and a black tank top thrown on top, his red hair clinging to his temples and neck, his muscular arms bare.

"I was just thinking that I like this," I whisper, and then I don't know why I spoke my thoughts out loud. It was the last thing I was about to say, and heat climbs up my neck.

The smile that flashes over his handsome face is sudden and breathtaking. "You do?"

I curse myself inwardly. This hazy, beautiful place I am at won't last. "I feel like I'm on drugs," I confess.

Ryu's smile falls.

"It's the weakness from the fever and throwing up," Asa rumbles, reaching the girls' showers. "It will pass."

Now I feel downright wretched and Ryu's face mirrors it. He looks like he's swallowed something bitter.

"Right," he says. "It will."

I expect Asa to put me down but he strides into the girls' showers with supreme confidence.

"No," I say, patting his chest, "no, Asa. You'll scare the girls. Wait outside."

"I won't," he says, and that's it, apparently.

Ryu follows us inside, too, and the dark look on his face gives no indication of the bright smile he wore moments before, brooking no more arguments from me.

One girl brushes by us, fleeing the showers, a towel wrapped around herself, her eyes wide. She pushes the door open, pours herself out, and the door thwacks closed again.

It's just me and two of the boys in the showers.

Two of the boys I've had sex with before.

The boys I hate.

The boys I like.

The boys I'm so damn confused about.

There's nothing sexual about the way they undress me. Ryu turns on the water and checks the temperature. He brought my shower gel and my shampoo, not my conditioner but I'm already impressed by the forethought when my mind is all foggy.

And that's when he starts undressing, too. A little too late, as he's already soaked. Or maybe that's why. He peels the wet tank top off himself, muscles rippling frigging everywhere, making the silvery marks on his skin dance. His small nipples are tight, his stomach is a perfect six-pack.

My God, who thought fox men could be so ripped?

And so hot?

Okay, yeah, I may have checked out his half-hard cock,

which is deliciously thick and long, and sue me, but having sex with someone and having the luxury of looking your fill of their body are two very distinct things.

But while I'm in the midst of ogling my fox shifter, Asa passes me to a very naked Ryu and he pushes down his sweats, starting to undress, too.

Whoa, it's as if every time I see their bodies, I'm caught off guard, left panting like a bitch in heat, though right now I'm sort of dizzy and not sure it's from seeing Asa naked.

My gaze lazily wanders down his perfect body, from his massive shoulders and bulging biceps, to his hard pecs and chiseled stomach and lower... yes, I'm now staring at the angel's cock, that's half-hard, like Ryu's, and hardening under my gaze, rising from between his thick thighs.

I swallow hard. *Hot.*

But my gaze wanders lower, down his muscular legs to his feet.

His feet are bare.

Both of them came here barefoot, I realize. The spray is already plastering their hair to their heads, running over their powerful bodies, and I'm mesmerized. I can't stop staring at them.

But I'm too tired to feel the usual bolt of lust, while the sense of warmth and safety lingers as Asa mutters something and pulls me back to his chest.

"I'll hold her," he says.

I almost blurt out I don't need him to hold me, but leaning back against him feels good. I close my eyes as Ryu shampoos my hair, then rinses it off, making sure to keep the suds out of my eyes, using one hand as a barrier. They bathe me as you'd bathe a babe—and I actually remember my uncles and aunt bathing my youngest cousin like that.

I want to ask Ryu if he was there when his children were little, if he bathed them like this.

I want to ask him if he has descendants who are still around, if his children had children and they in their turn had more...

Ryu twists my hair into a rope and rings out the water. Then he grabs the shower gel and starts lathering my body.

And the lust finally ignites, the easy, friendly washing turning sensual as his hands move over me like a caress.

Asa's cock thickens at my back as Ryu's hands move over my shoulders, down my arms, and then over my breasts, his thumbs circling my nipples, slipping in the suds, making me moan.

"Dammit," Asa breathes in my neck, his cock twitching in the small of my back, "touch her, Ryu, do it..."

"Kiss her," Ryu counter-commands, and my gaze dips to his long, hard cock before Asa grips my chin and turns my head up to kiss me.

My knees go weak when Ryu puts his mouth on my breasts. Asa is keeping me up easily, with an arm wrapped around my waist as he kisses the living Hell out of me. Gone is any awkwardness and inexperience. This is a man who has kissed a lot, I think, moaning against his lips, right before his tongue invades and tangles with mine.

Ryu sucks on my nipples, toys with them, rubbing and lightly pinching them. We never had foreplay before and that's a damn pity, is my only thought, before his mouth trails lower, down my belly, and between my legs.

He lifts one of my legs over his shoulder, opening me up, and just goes to town on me.

He's also very experienced, I think, shuddering as he eats me out, his tongue and lips working together to bring me to the brink, and then take me higher and higher, until I'm shaking and rocking against his mouth.

I can't catch my breath. I have to close my eyes because I'm afraid of passing out, black edging my sight. The pleasure is mounting, and Asa's mouth ruthlessly torments mine, coaxing more and more sensation, sending streaks of heat right between my legs where Ryu is stroking me with his tongue and lips, until I find myself on the precipice.

And I fall.

I cry out against Asa's lips and fall back against him, shuddering, while Ryu continues licking and sucking, prolonging my orgasm.

They don't speak a word. Don't ask if I'm okay, if I liked it. Ryu finally pulls away, and Asa slowly sinks down to his knees, his back to the tiled wall, lowering me with him. Ryu is now facing me, his eyes gone feral—really feral, the pupils vertical.

Just like a fox, I think, and am not shocked to see the fox ears poking out of his wet hair. Without thought, I throw an arm around him, the other around Asa, and we all huddle together on the floor, the spray falling on us like warm rainfall.

It's like a rain of stars, and I don't want to think—about reality checks, about tomorrow, about what in the world I'm doing. I want to stay here, in this moment.

All that's missing, I think, *are my other Wonderboys.*

And isn't that a crazy thought to have?

9

FRANKIE

"I smell sex," Tir says the moment we walk through the door into our shared bedroom. I have Ryu's arm around me and Asa is holding my hand.

"No, you don't," Ryu says, pulling me inside the room and leading me to the bunk beds. "You don't have a shifter's or a vampire's nose."

"Well, *I* can smell sex," Kass says. "The scent is so strong I bet even mere humans would smell it."

"Well, fuck." Ryu grins. "Can't hide anything from you, can we?"

I feel hot all over. I swear, the skin of my face must be blistering, and I can't blame the fever for it anymore. Annoyed at myself, I lift my chin and sit down on Tir's bunk. Can my legs carry me up the ladder to my bunk? I'm not sure so I just sit there and pretend I don't care if Tir, Kass, and Rook are upset with me.

Sex isn't a sin. Consensual sex among adults is most certainly fine. And I don't have to report to anyone or feel ashamed of it.

"Was it good?" Kass asks, and I tilt my chin a little higher, ready for a comeback, but I'm surprised to see only heat in his eyes.

"It was," I admit.

"I bet it was," Rook smirks. "Though I can bet you a thousand dollars—if I had them naturally—that these two guys have the bluest balls in the history of blue balls. Cobalt, probably. Prussian. Or ultramarine."

Kass snickers softly.

"You said you smelled sex," Tir accuses.

"So I did," Kass cheerfully says. He seems more relaxed than before. "I wonder what happened."

But then I jerk back in surprise when Tir drops to his knees in front of me and takes my hands.

"Frankie," he whispers. "I didn't know you were so sick yesterday or I'd have freed myself sooner to come back."

"Freed yourself?" I frown at him, then glance at Kass and Rook. "What did I miss?"

"The Fae gang caught him," Rook says.

"Serves you right for wandering around by yourself after we started a war," Ryu mutters, "my friend."

"We didn't start the war," Asa states. "Somebody else did."

"What did they want with you?" I ask Tir, afraid of what I'll hear, the sense of safety, security, and warmth slowly getting replaced by cold fear. "Did they hurt you?"

His eyes widen. He bows his head over my hands. "I'm fine. They wanted to talk to me about Jatri's death."

"What about his death?"

"They asked you to take Jatri's place, didn't they, Tir?" Rook says.

"How would you know that?" Tir glares.

"There's a void of power," Rook says as if it's self-evident. "Like when the Black Queen Witch refused to kill the White Queen Witch and left an imbalance in the world. Out of kindness and compassion, out of hope, sure, but kindness and compassion have no place in war."

I shiver. "That's not true."

"It means," he goes on, "that the White Queen Witch is still alive and trying to return."

"You do remember that the White Queen Witch is my mother, right? Imprisoned and guarded at all times?"

"Oh, I do. And her return will be through you."

Jeez. Talk about breaking a sweet moment. I pull my hands away from Tir's. "Why are we talking about this now? I'm not my mother. I don't want to take over the world, neither for myself nor to serve it to her on a platter."

"No," Asa says, "you're not your mother."

And leaves it at that. Nobody else offers any comment, and I don't know what to make of it. Their faces look solemn, eyes pensive, brows wrinkled.

If it's taking them so much brain power to work out what I said, or to decide if they believe me or not, then nothing has changed.

Of course it hasn't.

My mind is finally clearing up—from the fever, the pill, the spell, the mindblowing release in the showers—and I pull myself away in every possible sense. I'm ready to try the ladder now and nobody stops me when I get up and grab the rails.

"I'll be on my bunk if anyone needs me," I mutter. "Thanks for your help."

Not that I think they'll need me. I've been the needy one. *Jesus.* I'm worn out but I hope by tomorrow I'll be ready to get back into the swing of things.

Classes. Research. A call to Granddad. Maybe through magic even if he shits bricks when he realizes. Accepting my power and my fate.

No big deal, right? Right back to the daily grind. No rest for the wicked, as they say.

Though the short break has sure been nice...

———

For a long while, I drift in and out of sleep.

The boys come and go, but there's always one of them inside the room. One time there is Rook, lying on Asa's bunk across from me, throwing and catching an apple. Another there's Asa, standing still as a statue by the window and I imagine I see the shadow of wings behind him. Then there's a hushed argument between Tir and Kass during which Tir flicks his fingers at Kass' jaw and actually makes Kass grin. Then, when I finally fully wake and my eyes remain open, I find Ryu watching me from his perch on the desk below me, holding an open notebook in his lap, a pen thrown inside.

Which reminds me of something...

I fish my book from under my pillow, letting out a relieved breath.

"Always with that book," he says when he catches my eye. He's smiling but his eyes still have that distant look from earlier.

"What? Some girls sleep with their teddy bears until they're grannies. I sleep with my book."

"You're the furthest from a granny I have ever seen."

"...thanks?"

"You're welcome." He shrugs.

Smiling in spite of myself, I rummage inside my bag that's still wedged between me and the wall and find the pen he gave me.

Then I throw it at his head.

He ducks, eyes going comically wide, but I'm gratified to see that I caught him completely by surprise. Not even his supernatural shifter speed saves him from a hit to the head.

"What was that for?" he grumbles and bends to retrieve the pen. His brows knit. "This is the pen I gave you."

"I'm returning it to you."

"It was a gift," he says softly just as the other guys file inside. Jesus, it's as if they heard me waking up or something.

"I don't want your gifts."

"Why are you upset again?"

"Because nothing changed?" My smile is now long gone. "I mean, is this it? We're going to go on pretending we like each other, that we're friends with benefits brought together by circumstances? Like nothing ever happened?"

"Pretending we mean nothing to each other you mean? We'll have to live with it, like you are."

I frown back at him. What he said makes no sense. It almost sounds like... they are pretending we mean nothing to each other? So... we do mean something to each other?

My head hurts...

"And let me state for the record," Tir growls, "I never saw those benefits you speak of."

"Hear, hear," Kass mutters.

"Girl, you look much better." Rook stands in front of the bunk bed and rests his arms on my mattress. "Now give it to me straight, how do you feel? No lies, no hiding. Think you can walk around on your own?"

"She'd have to get up and try walking first," Tir says, elbowing him and taking his place. "Right, *elenyi*? Don't be stupidly brave, Frankie, don't try and act as if you're well before you feel it, okay?"

There they go again, confusing me. Why can't they be obnoxious, loathsome villains all the time? Also, why can't they be ugly and you know... not sexy? Their hotness is really making my life hard. How can I pretend to ignore it? Pretend not to want them?

"Pretending we mean nothing to each other."

That word—*pretend*—keeps coming up.

"Come down, Frankie," Ryu says, half-climbing up the ladder and reaching for me. "Let's see if you got your sea legs back."

"Back?" I mutter, letting him pull me to the ladder, then starting down facing outward, looking down at the five of them. "We're not at sea."

"The world has always been a stormy sea," he says and it makes sense.

He climbs down looking up at me and then stands and waits for me to reach the ground. His hands hover at my elbows as he waits for me to take a few steps.

"Seaworthy," he whispers and for some reason it makes my throat go tight.

His approving tone shouldn't make me feel like this.

The expectation and hope in their eyes shouldn't make me teary-eyed.

This is insane.

My feet hit the floor and I stand there, taking them in, all five of them—shirtless and tall, muscular and sexy. Beautiful.

The image will live rent-free in my memory for years to come. When I'm old and gray, I will remember this and sigh lustfully.

Why can't this be real? Why can't I be with them? Stay with them?

I have often thought I must be paying for having been a bitch in a past life. That, or for my mother's sins.

Either way, karma is Hell.

———

"Whoa, steady, girl." Rook grabs me when I sway on my feet as I look around for my shoes. I woke up dressed in a long T-shirt that doesn't belong to me and no panties, which reminded me that I fell asleep in a towel, and then slept in Tir's arms... in this T-shirt.

Which now smells of him and of everyone at once, making my body clench with desire.

And okay, fine, I'm still a little dizzy.

Getting out of this exhaustion is taking way too long. How can a wound that looks mostly healed and barely even stings make me so sick? As for the pill's chemicals, they have to be out of my system by now.

Asa and Tir left for the kitchens to get us all some much-needed breakfast, while Kass is dozing on his bunk bed and I'm trying real hard not to worry about his pallor and dark circles under his eyes. I need to push him to get another donor, but every time I open my mouth to tell him, something stops me.

"Sit down," Rook says, pushing me into the chair by the desk. "What's taking those guys so long, huh? I could demolish a sandwich or two right now. Or a lunch buffet. I could eat all the meals of the week in one go, I'm fucking starving. I'd eat the plates, too, I swear."

I stifle a laugh. Then right on cue, my stomach rumbles and I set my jaw, refusing to be embarrassed by this, too. But my skin is sadly too prone to blushing and betrays me.

For some reason, it makes Rook grin. His long black hair hangs around him like a cloak, over his muscular chest with its dark symbols, his midnight-blue eyes sparkling, and though he can sometimes pass for a human man, right now he looks every bit the supernatural creature that he is. "You can't go to classes yet."

"That makes you happy?"

"Yes. You stay here so we can keep an eye on you."

"Fine." I feel too wobbly to argue about that. Not many options. I wouldn't like to fall and break a bone. In fact, that would limit my options even more.

"You have a desk right here. You can study in the room. We'll bring you the homework."

"But I also need to at least do research. I still don't know what my father was, if there's any chance..." I swallow thickly. "Any chance of stopping my curse."

"Of course." He says it so easily, as if his mission doesn't matter, as if solving my problem won't result in his failure and punishment.

But what should I do, let Heaven or the Houses grab me? Juliette was right. We don't know what they might do to me.

"Yeah?"

"Yes." He looks away, brow furrowing. "Tell us what you need and we'll bring you the titles. Or we can accompany you to the library, I suppose. When you're feeling a little better."

Then I need to know. "Was it you who brought the desk and chair from your room along with the mattresses?"

He shrugs. "I thought you might want to sit and study by the window sometimes."

Aw. I grit my teeth even as warmth fills my chest at his thoughtfulness. "Thank you."

He goes still in the course of pulling back his long hair. "Don't mention it, Darling."

I itch to touch his mane, pet it, comb my fingers through it, see how soft it is. Is it weird? Isn't that a thing girlfriends are supposed to do with one another? He's definitely not a girl. Despite the long hair and the pretty face, he's most definitely male, all angles and muscular planes, jagged edges and prickly confidence.

Also, he's a badass.

And hot.

Getting repetitive there, brain. Yeah, they're hot, we've noticed. Move on, will you?

My mind only sends back a smug silence.

Is it weird that I have these conversations with myself? Am I certifiable?

Wait, better not answer that. I'm not prepared for the answer.

The door flies open revealing the guys with our food—and with the unexpected side effect of Kass leaping upright with a snarl, whipping out his lash and cracking it on the floor, his eyes as wild as his black hair.

"*Ma che cazzo,*" he whispers, stumbling forward a few steps, his grip on the lash going white-knuckled. Then he frowns, shakes his head, and rubs at his eyes with one hand. "What the *fuck* is going on here?"

Rook sighs. "Rise and shine, baby boy. Chow time."

"*What*?"

Rook grabs Kass by the shoulder and guides him to sit back on his bunk. "Soon you'll need a transfusion, you know that? You need a fucking donor, Kass. You'll be a liability if you don't. Face the music."

Tough but true, and my heart clenches because I'm so close to offering to be his donor again when I know it's a frigging bad idea.

He glances at me as if hearing my thoughts. "I don't need a donor," he grumbles. "I don't *want* a donor."

"So you'd rather die?"

"Got you some meat rolls and protein shakes." Tir nods at Kass, his arms full of stuff. "That should help."

Kass looks startled again, dark brows winging up. "Thanks."

"We got a bit of everything," Asa says, and his dimpled smile lights up the room like sunshine. He's carrying a huge tray piled high with food which he sets up on the desk. "Dig in."

Rook snatches a sandwich, bites into it, and groans. "I swear this is almost as good as an orgasm."

By this point the aromas of warm bread, butter, and fried bacon have my stomach trying to consume itself. I reach for a bread roll but Asa beats me to it. He grabs a bread roll already stuffed with bacon and egg and passes it to me along with a bottle of water.

"Coffee?" he asks.

"Why, yes, I'll have one, thank you," Rook says around a huge bite of sandwich. In fact, I think he has stuffed the entire bun inside his mouth. He looks like a squirrel with an entire cache of walnuts inside his cheeks.

I almost choke on my bite of sandwich from laughing so hard.

We're all stuffing our faces and for a long time, the only sound is the scrunching of plastic wraps, munching, and the occasional moan of pleasure.

Which I do my best to ignore.

Hard to do, when they're all sitting and standing around me, producing those sounds. It's as if they're doing it on purpose to see my reaction...

Then I catch a glimpse of Rook watching me as he moans and yeah, they *are* doing it on purpose.

"Dickheads," I mutter, finishing my sandwich and reaching for a sausage roll. More can play this game.

So I give my full attention to my sausage roll, nibbling at it, and closing my eyes as I groan with pleasure at the taste.

Instantly, all other sounds cease and I open my eyes to find five pairs of eyes boring into me, dark and heated.

Looks like it worked... Maybe a little too well, judging by the growing tents in their pants, most of which are at eye level with me.

I swallow hard.

I need another shower, stat, and make it a cold one this time.

"We need..." I clear my throat, trying to think of a

distracting subject. "Well, *I* need to talk to the demon and the vampire gang leaders."

"Kalissa Aimee and Sebastian La Fontaine?"

"The very same. They sounded like they wanted to negotiate a truce with us."

"Broker a deal, you mean," Rook says.

"I thought you said this is war."

"I think it's more of a trading situation."

"Isn't war the same thing?" I ask.

"Yeah, but with more violence."

"Right... So I need to talk to them, and I need my pendant." I take a sip of my coffee and wince. It's too sweet. Rook must have added, like, four sugar cubes to it.

"Why is that pendant important? Where did you get it?"

"It comes from my mother. Maybe there's a clue there as to who I am, something I failed to notice but..." I gather myself. "Maybe you guys can take a look, tell me if I missed something."

The silence in the room shifts.

The light in their eyes seems to brighten.

"Then we'll get that pendant for you," Rook says, "and Tir's earrings, and a deal that will protect you at least until we solve the mystery of your birth."

He says *"we"* with such ease, as if it's self-evident that they will help me, and they are all nodding as if it is.

And as for what comes after that, not a word.

Which is just as well. I'd rather not have fake promises of a happy-ever-after when we all know it's probably never going to happen.

10

ROOK

*S*he's sitting there, her small face serious, her food forgotten, as she talks about parlaying with the demons and vampires like it's no big deal, about finding out what sort of monster her father is and about her curse.

This girl is brave.

I've seen people break down and give up when fate throws a wrench in their lives. They go down and stay down, but not her. I knew nothing about her when I arrived at the College except that she might be dangerous.

But seeing her with her family, I know she has a lot to lose if things continue on their set trajectory, the trajectory I helped arrange.

Unlike me. I don't have anything except... except for hope, but that's neither here nor there. I come from nothing, and if I end up with nothing, then...

She's the opposite of me. And having a lot to lose, having tasted happiness, makes the fight all the more tragic. I don't want her to lose all that.

If I lose, then... then I've never even tasted that forbidden fruit. Here, at this stupid College, I've had more pleasure and more moments of joy than I've ever had in my life.

They could be enough, if I chose. If I decided they are. That I'm satisfied and don't need to really live a life in the world, a good life, a time without fear and pain, without killing and maiming. A happy retirement.

Why should I deserve that anyway?

I glance at Kass who's still pale as a ghost even after eating and chugging down the protein shakes Tir brought him.

At Asa who's hovering protectively near Frankie, his back propped against the bunk bed.

At Tir who's frowning at something we said, his food half-forgotten in his hand.

At Ryu who's demolishing a burger—where did he get that? —with his ass parked against the edge of the desk to be as close as possible to the food.

Or to Frankie.

I like these fuckers, I like them way too much. It's goddamn annoying. They're so sexy they get my dick hard all the time, just like she does. And they're... good. Better than I ever suspected they'd be, at least. They have their moments of insanity and violence, their own agendas, their murky pasts, their demons—*har har* funny, since now I'm one of the said demons—but they've been working together, fighting together, back-to-back, both in the chaos of battle and in the bedroom, with and around Frankie.

I've never had this sort of... relationship with anyone before. I've always been a lone wolf. The Hellhound they always sent on suicide missions.

That hasn't really changed, it seems. This mission is starting to feel suicidal.

I mean... What am I even considering? Fail my mission to give Frankie a chance? A chance to do what? Dammit, doubts will be the death of me.

Have I gone mad?

Because even if I do step back, if I fail my mission on purpose, there are four other guys in this room with me waiting to jump on the opportunity to get her for themselves.

And even if they fail, the rest of the fucking world is lurking out there, waiting for their chance to grab her for themselves. I mean, look at her. A pretty, sassy girl whose scream can turn armies into piles of ash. Or salt, whatever. Makes no difference, does it? Death is death, though I'm more partial to pepper myself.

And she's only just discovering her powers.

Who knows what the next level will be like.

I should be fucking terrified of her.

Not want into her panties again.

I'm an insatiable monster at the best of times, and somehow with her, it's even worse.

Or better. Everything feels better with her. She's like all the fizzy cocktails and wines, all the decadent cakes and ice creams, all the trips and excitement I've always wanted and may never have.

"Speaking of which," Ryu says. "You're a veteran of the Battle of Adesh. Tell us about it."

"Hm?" I look up from the coffee mug in my hand. The coffee has long since gone cold but I swig it down anyway. "What was that?"

I hate spacing out and missing parts of action or conversation. You never know what vital information you missed out on.

"I was saying, you're a veteran of the Battle of Adesh," Ryu says.

"And so what?"

"You might have met a friend of Kass'."

I frown. "What friend?"

"Nobody," Kass says, his voice like gravel. "Ryu, will you just fucking drop it?"

"His name is Brody," Ryu says.

"Ryu," Frankie mutters, frowning.

"How would you know about Brody?" Kass looks murderous.

"You talk in your sleep. You kept apologizing to him."

"Fuck you," Kass seethes.

Ryu sighs. "Was he your boyfriend?"

"You asshole," Kass breathes and goes after him, only for Tir to grab him and hold him back.

"Leave it, Kass," he says. "Whether he was your boyfriend or not shouldn't be an issue."

"It's not. It's not that, dammit." More struggling. "He has no right—"

"Kass, stop it," Tir says, turning to Ryu. "And you, drop it."

"It's important," Ryu says.

I narrow my eyes at the kitsune. Kitsune are as much tricksters as the Fae. They have a weird kinship. And Ryu likes to push and prod.

It feels like an innate need to find out the truth, pushing him past other people's boundaries. He's a nuisance in a pretty package. But he's not grinning or smirking. Doesn't look like he's having fun at Kass' expense. He looks serious, though there's also something manic about him that's making less and less sense. As if he's trying to... fix this. Fix us. While we're flying toward total destruction.

"Ryu," Frankie says, "that's private, you can't just—"

"I knew a Brody once," I say and quiet drops like a stone, crushing us.

Kass, it's Kass I'm watching. He goes still, eyes wide, face pale, jerking backward against Tir, and I'm not even sure he knows what he's doing or where he is right now.

"You knew him?" he whispers. "Back then?"

"I had my mission. He had his. Do you...?" I don't know what is going on here, why he's looking at me with both dread and excitement, who this Brody was to him, except... A boyfriend? Is Ryu right? "I didn't see him during that battle. It was... messy. Bloody. Went on forever. I happened to meet him in the aftermath, in the war hospital."

Frankie's eyes are now as big as Kass' and I don't know what the fuck to do. Should I go on or stop right here?

"Did he say anything?" Kass asks, leaving me no option but to dive deeper into my nightmares.

"About?"

"Anything that stuck with you." Tir has released him and he's standing there, brows knitted, cheeks way too pale, dark hair in his face.

"You really have to be more specific."

"I never saw him after that battle," he blurts out. "Never saw him again alive."

Fuck... What is Ryu trying to do? The damn fox is acting like a puppeteer, setting events into motion. Does he even know what he's doing?

"Brody was a vampire like you, wasn't he?" I say. "And he was important to you."

His jaw is tight. "Tell me."

"Not unless you reply to my question. How important was he to you?"

"This entire fucking mission is about him, goddammit." Kass is suddenly in my space, in my face, pressing me back against the bunk bed. "Was he my lover? Yeah, he was. Did I love him? No. But I was supposed to bring him back!"

"Back where?"

"Back to life!"

I stare at him. I stare and he stares back, eyes wild, until Tir slings an arm around Kass again.

"Why don't you sit down?" he suggests mildly.

Kass shakes him off. "I just want to know what he said. If he said anything. About me."

Shit. I remember the conversation I had with the man perfectly. He was talkative. I thought he was hilarious back then. My self-destructive streak liked his views and lifestyle.

"No," I say. "He didn't."

"Are you sure?"

Fuck, as the memory clears, I realize I need to change the topic and quick, before Kass corners me.

"Tell me about him," Kass is saying. "Did he tell you what was his undercover mission for the House of Water?"

"If it was undercover, why would he tell him, genius?" Ryu mutters.

I cut him an icy look and he shuts up. "Were the two of you together long? How did you meet?"

Kass finally sits down, suddenly, as if his strings have been cut. "He helped me when I needed help the most. When my family was at its worst."

"He saved your family?"

Kass shakes his head. "He saved me *from* my goddamn family."

"Why?" Frankie whispers. "What did they do to you?"

A mirthless laugh leaves Kass' lips. "I... I like guys as well as girls. They believed I would burn in Hell for it. As if being half-demon and half-vampire wouldn't ensure that. What would the people say, they kept telling me. A mafia king's son has a reputation to uphold. An image to project. It didn't matter that I wasn't the oldest, the heir. Because you never know, right? You never know who lives or dies."

"Kass," Tir says, but Kass doesn't seem to hear him.

"I'd been in love with a lovely man. They said if I wanted him to live, I had to let him go and get married to a bride of their choosing."

"Jesus," Frankie whispers.

"She was a nice girl. None of this was her fault. We had two girls. Such sweet children. I told myself it was fine. I didn't love her, but I loved the girls and I would be fine."

My gut is starting to cramp with stress at this story. I can't take it when children are starring in tragic stories. It's my turn to say, "Kass..."

"Then I met him. Brody. I didn't look for it. Tried to be a good son, you know? A good husband and father. *Porca miseria...* I should have known I'd fail. I always fucking fail people around me."

"What happened to the girls and your wife?" Frankie whispers, her eyes huge in her face. She's expecting the worst, just like me.

"She took the kids and left. Said she didn't deserve such disrespect. She was right. It doesn't matter that we hadn't slept together after we made the youngest. And though I missed them, I really did, I was happy for a while with Brody." He turns his gaze to the window, his eyes miserable. "I turned him."

"He was a fucking *human*?" I breathe.

Oh no. This is even worse. Bad idea, Rook. You should have said you'd never met the guy. Caught by surprise, I hadn't thought of the implications.

"He begged me to. Said he wanted to be with me forever. And then he told me he was leaving on a secret mission. I knew he was involved with the House of Water higher-ups, he let it slip once... And I thought for a while that... that he'd wanted to be turned so he could become this super spy, super soldier. But his feelings were real. They had to be."

At least the kids and the wife are alive. I sag a little with relief. "Yeah," I say, unthinkingly.

Brody. That massive giant asshole.

Something in me wants to protect Kass for some reason, but at the same time, I need to set this straight. Nobody deserves to live a lie, do they?

"I had no idea he died," Kass says. "Nobody contacted me. When he stopped answering his phone, I waited and waited and then started checking hospitals. And then death lists. He never listed me as a close contact. But of course he wouldn't. His job—"

"That's bullshit," Ryu says.

Fuck.

"What's wrong with me?" Kass mutters. "All this doesn't matter. He didn't tell you anything about me, he'd always been discreet. In the midst of war, why would he even think about me?" He runs his hands through his wild hair. "He was declared dead, but he's a vampire. Hard to kill, aren't we?" Another mirthless laugh that's like a stab to my chest. "He's in stasis. It's not easy to bring him back but I promised him I will. Joined the ranks of the vampire army. Took this mission for him. If I succeed, he will be brought back by the Council of the House of Water."

Frankie's eyes are shimmering like she's about to cry. The guys' faces are furious.

Brody. That sad fucker.

"I always wondered what happened," Kass is muttering, "if he talked with anyone, if he ever mentioned me, but now I know he said nothing—"

I rub a hand over my face. "Okay, fine, he spoke to me."

Kass blinks at me. "What?"

"I said that Brody fellow, he spoke to me. But not about you, Kass. Listen, we were high on painkillers and sedating spells at the time. We were high as kites and he was gravely wounded, though I admit I hadn't thought he was so bad off. Like I said, the drugs and spells."

"Stop rambling, Rook," Kass whispers. "Tell me what he said. What did he say?"

I wince.

"The truth," Kass says, *begs*, and Ryu is nailing me with that unnervingly flat stare of an animal who won't offer judgment but wants what is real.

"He told me he had a plaything back home," I say, the words like rusty nails on my tongue and trust me, I'm not into the usual BDSM shit demons are. "A boytoy. His little Giocca."

Kass surges to his feet, then sways, barely catching himself. "What did you say?"

Tir makes a small sound that's almost like a protest. He's standing beside the bed where Kass is seated, concern on his face. But this rockslide is already underway. There's no stopping it.

"It wasn't about you, Kass, like I said."

"Fuck you. That was his nickname for me. *Giocattolino.* Little toy."

"I'm quite sure it wasn't you."

"He didn't have other lovers. Only me. What else did he say? Did he say if he tried to contact me, if his phone had a problem then, if—"

"He made crude jokes," I say. "About how he'd turn his little Giocca and promise him they'd be together forever, but then he'd leave him and visit a different bed every night."

"Turn him?" Kass lets out a dry laugh. "That makes no sense. I'm the one who turned him, that must have been a joke... right?"

"That boy, that man he was seeing, it wasn't you."

"It can't be. You're mistaken."

"Kass... this boy toy was a blond human. His name was Evan. And Brody had a list of men he'd planned on visiting when he returned from the war. He showed me that list."

A wounded groan leaves Kass' lips. The rest of the blood is draining from his face. He looks as if he's seen a ghost—or as if the ghost he was seeing turned out to be a prank. A betrayal. That's what he's seeing.

And I lifted the veil for him but I don't feel proud of myself. Not one fucking bit. He's staring at me but he's not seeing me.

Brody, you motherfucker.

What do I do? I'm not used to offering comfort, to finding the right words to ease someone's pain. What words would do such a moment justice anyway? What good are false reassurances that everything will be okay?

And yet I want to give that to him—not false claims but a solid embrace, a steadying hand, and a listening ear if he wants to rant and rage.

He's silent, though.

I see Frankie make an abortive movement toward him, but it's too late.

Nobody is prepared to stop Kass when he walks to the door, yanks it open, and strides out, the door banging shut behind him.

Well, shit.

11

FRANKIE

I hate that broken look on Kass' face as he storms out of the room. Hate it with the power of a thousand burning suns.

I'm balling my hands into fists as if I can fight something and make this right, but I'm helpless with a fury that has nowhere to go.

"You shouldn't have told him what you did," I whisper.

"You mean the truth?" Rook says acidly.

"You did the right thing," Ryu says.

"And you." Tir turns on him, pointing an accusing finger. "Why did you have to dig that up, huh?"

"We need to be honest with one another," Ryu says. "You said that. No? One of you said that."

"And so what? You'll go around ripping everyone's heart out and stomping on it to get your truth?"

Ryu gazes back at him. "It was fine when it was me whose heart was being ripped out, was it?"

Tir snarls. "You're *punishing* us for that? For asking about you?"

"It was a good thing. A relief. I now gave it to Kass."

"But—"

"He was suffering. When you find an animal suffering, you put them out of their misery."

"We're not animals!"

"Are you sure about that?" Ryu asks quietly.

A shifter who remained in animal form for... how many years? A lifetime. Enough to have a family and lose them, too. Are we asking too much of Ryu? He's straightforward like an arrow to the heart.

I'm shivering and can't seem to stop. It's not a fever this time, or physical weakness. Saving Brody was Kass' goal, his reward for going on this insane mission, and now he just found out that Brody was a shithead who didn't care about him.

Broken dreams.

A broken heart.

And there I go again. Caring when I shouldn't.

"I'll go after him," Ryu says out of the blue, and without waiting for a reply, he follows Kass out.

"Ryu! What the fuck!" Rook starts after him but the door bangs shut a second time. "Motherfucker..."

He's already gone.

"Well," Rook says, deflating. He reaches for the tray on the desk. "Not sure he can make things any worse than they already are."

"Are you seriously still hungry?" Tir demands. "After all this?"

"I'm always hungry. I'm a growing demon."

"Your waistline will be the one growing if you keep that up."

"Oh, I see." He wags his brows. "You're concerned about my figure."

"Rook—"

"First off, I haven't eaten in two days. Pardon me if I need more than a sandwich to be sated. And second, *Faeling*, I have amazing metabolism. Watch this donut vanish." He eats it in two bites and licks his fingers, watching Tir from under his lashes. "See?"

I laugh quietly, not feeling it much, and his gaze snaps to me.

"I like it when you laugh," he says.

I shake my head, my laughter fading. "Another donut?" I dangle one right in front of him and he sighs.

"Fuck me, it has frigging sprinkles. You sure, Darling?"

"Yes, you can have it."

"A woman after my own heart. Hell, you only live once, right? Give it here."

I grin. "The way to your heart is paved with donuts?"

"Don't be crass. The pavement is made of waffles with syrup. The donuts are just decorative."

"You do have a sweet tooth."

"All my teeth are sweet." He licks his fingers. "Look, I've had a shitty life, all told, and I'm not saying this to garner sympathy. Truth is, my only purpose with this mission is to live a little. Have fun. Eat sweets and good burgers. Maybe a sausage roll or two." He winks at me. "Lick some cream."

"Be serious."

"Why? I've been serious all my life. Dead earnest. Devoted to the cause, my life sacrificed on the altar of duty, like Ryu's. I've fought and fought and almost died again and again in other people's stupid wars. I've seen my friends die one by one, and yet I am still alive. Against all odds, I've made it here. And all I've asked was for a chance to *live*."

"That's what you asked for?" I whisper. "That's your prize?"

"It may not seem that big a deal to you, Sweetheart, but where I'm coming from? It's the greatest gift imaginable. This human world is a paradise few of us ever dream to tread."

"You're on a sugar high."

"Shit, is that why I'm spilling my heart out? Or maybe it's

contagious, since Ryu and Kass started it." He shrugs his strong shoulders. "Doesn't matter. It wasn't that big a secret."

Only he hasn't really said much, has he? He dances around the topic of his past, waxing poetic about a possible future here on earth. That would be his consolation prize, his recompense.

Which he will only get once he delivers me to his masters in Hell.

Crap, I'm so tired. It's mental as well as physical, and to top it all, I've stuffed myself silly with food and now all I want is to curl up on the bed once more and go back to sleep.

Preferably with one of the hunks curled around me.

Stop it. Bad Frankie.

But what does it matter in the end? It won't change anything, my traitorous mind insists. Hate-sex, hate-cuddling. Same difference.

Not even as you start finding out about their stories, one by one, about why they went on these missions? About how broken they are? How justified they may be?

No. Nobody is ever justified in delivering another person to the crazy kings and queens of the Houses—and the out-of-touch cruel Heavenly supervisors.

Delivering you to justice, you mean? Saving the world from you?

But I'm not trying to destroy the world.

I'm not.

Even if nobody seems inclined to believe it, including my own subconscious.

———

"Are you sure you wouldn't rather stay here and rest some more?" Tir demands, brows drawn together.

"Yes, I'm sure." A wave of dizziness hits me and I lean against the desk. At least I've stopped throwing up and my fever is all but gone.

"Girl…" Ryu slides an arm around me, steadying me. "You really should rest some more. Take it from us. We've had infected wounds before and they take their sweet time to heal."

"As if any of you would have stayed in bed for a second," I scoff. "I bet you just kept going, fever and all, refusing to allow anyone to care for you."

Rook snickers. "She's got us all sussed."

"You're guys. I know guys. I grew up with two male cousins and four uncles, and they'd rather die than be seen as in any need of help."

"That's you." Rook points at Kass who shakes his head. "And Asa. Not me. You can pamper me any time, Princess."

"You're a headcase, demon." Tir folds his arms over his chest and tilts his head back a little. "I'd rather walk around with a knife in my leg than lie down. Kass?"

"Definitely."

"There you go," I mutter. "Called it."

Ryu sighs.

They came back last night looking oddly subdued, but calm. They didn't seem inclined to talk about the why, and the silence that reigned in the room during the night had a sharp edge to it. Kass hasn't spoken a word since then and he looks sick, dark circles under his pretty eyes and deep hollows in his cheeks.

This boy is suffering. I have this terrible urge to hug him but his expression is tight and I'm not sure he'd appreciate it.

Macho males, like I said.

"Yeah, I'm weak, what can I do," Rook says cheerfully. "I'd stab my own leg to have Frankie take care of me."

"Be serious," I whisper, but I end up snickering when he waggles his brows at me and leers.

Jesus, these boys.

"So what's it gonna be?" Tir is still frowning and lounging

in a very manly way against the desk, those muscular arms drawing my attention every time I turn his way.

"The library," I decide. "My time is running out. What's the use of doing homework when I should be trying to break this curse?"

"Let's see if they fixed the shelves," Rook mutters.

"Not sure what you're hoping for, Frankie," Tir says softly. "This isn't a curse. It's how you are. Finding out what it is won't change it."

"But what if there is a way to get rid of it?"

"That would be unusual. Magical gifts don't usually come with a return policy."

"I want to try."

"Say no more," Rook says. "Right, guys? We said we'd help in any way we can. Besides, I doubt any of you is dying to go to class, right? Anyone here excited about Herbs and Dongs? Yeah, didn't think so."

"Herbs and *Dongs*? Is that even a class?" Tir frowns.

"No idea, I just made it up. Seemed legit."

I should stop laughing at his antics.

I should stop laughing, period.

This isn't funny at all...

———

The library is mostly empty. We hurried through breakfast—Tir went to visit his kitchen friends again and I promise I did my best not to feel jealous of the girl there but it's a losing battle, which annoys me—and brought back a tray loaded with a mountain of food which was consumed within minutes. I swear men eat their weight in food on a daily basis.

Anyway, we were done quickly and so we've been in the library for more than an hour now and my five bodyguards are starting to show signs of boredom.

I mean, they have been searching together with me, I have no complaints on that front, going through shelves, looking for any title that could contain the answers to my question of origin, but right now they seem to be on a break.

I realized that one by one they'd moved away from the shelves to a table on the side where people sit to study, and now I can hear the low timbre of their voices.

I lean back and catch a glimpse of them arrayed around one end of the long table. Kass and Asa are seated in chairs, Tir is perched on the edge of the table, while Ryu and Rook are standing by the side.

They're discussing something.

Without me.

I refuse to feel hurt about the exclusion, but it burns like acid in my stomach regardless. Of course we're not a real team. I should be glad of all and every reminder of this fact. Getting back to my research should be the only thing that matters, only just as I'm about to move to the next row of shelves, I hear Rook laugh softly and it's real laughter, quiet and heartfelt, nothing like his usual snickering and guffawing and all his theatrical posturing. It sounds like the crackling of a fire, the gusts of smoke puffing up a chimney.

Like a song.

Transfixed, I linger a second too long.

"So..." Rook's laughter tapers off. "Ryu went to get Kass last night and...? Gimme all the juicy details. Did you two kiss? Did you fuck and make up?"

I prick my ears, my hand gripping a shelf with huge, ancient tomes. They seem to shift, seen out of the corner of my eye. Just how magical are the books here?

"Get your head out of the gutter, demon," Ryu says. "We did none of that."

"Is that so?" Rook, though, is undeterred. Maybe he feels

bad for telling Kass the truth? "Is that a hickey on your neck, bat boy?"

"You know damn well it isn't," Kass says. "It's a bruise from the fight in the auditorium."

He sounds calm, normal. Nothing like the broken-hearted man of last night. How well is he hiding his sadness?

"Looks like teeth marks to me."

"That's because they *are* teeth marks. Someone tried to rip my throat out. Happy?"

"Let me see." Rook moves closer to Kass and I expect Kass to punch him when Rook puts his hands on his neck.

He doesn't, though.

"It does look like someone tried to rip your throat out. Damn, man. Though you could be into kinky sex, what do I know?"

"And you think I'm into kinky sex, too?" Ryu asks drily, winning a snort out of Kass. "What, Kass?"

"You can never tell who's into kink," Kass says.

"Like you?"

"Wouldn't you like to know," Kass says, deadpan.

"Now you sound like Rook."

"Oh please. I don't sound like that." Rook still has his hands on Kass, though now they've moved to his shoulders. He seems to be giving him a massage. "I'm very refined."

"The refined circles of Hell," Tir mutters.

"Even in the deepest gutter," Rook says, "you can see the stars. Even there you'll find intellectuals and prophets."

"You make them sound like assholes."

"Usually they are."

Move, I tell myself. *This isn't interesting anymore, is it? I mean, it's not about sex, you nympho. You shouldn't care about their conversations.*

But God, I like their easy banter. It makes my chest feel warm. Makes me want to smile.

Have I mentioned that these guys are a hazard? A danger to my resolve to keep my distance?

Yeah, only a million times by now.

Move your ass, Franks. Get back to work. Your problems won't resolve themselves. If only eye candy was the right medicine.

"Did you say that her scream turns people into piles of salt?" Tir asks. "Cause it's been on my mind."

I freeze. How am I supposed to even pretend to focus on research when they're discussing stuff like that within earshot? Discussing *me*.

I should move further away, not to hear them.

But my feet are rooted to the spot and I'm annoyed. Shouldn't I be present when they talk about me?

"Now is not the time for this discussion," Rook says, moving away from Kass. "Frankie should be here for it."

Now I want to kiss him.

"Since when do angels turn people to salt?" Tir insists.

"Since ever. You do know the story of Lot's wife," Rook says. "No? You need to work on your education, boy. Off to class you go."

"But it's just... How come I didn't realize it was salt?" Tir is muttering, practically to himself. "The heat of the battle, probably. I mean, salt is my element. I should have felt it. Are you sure it was salt?"

"Whoa, back up." Rook frowns at Tir. "Your element? What gives?"

Tir shrugs. "I need it. Since I joined the Wild Hunt."

"It's not your average salt," Asa says with that grave voice of his that makes me want to kiss his mouth and lick his dimples.

Gah.

"Define non-average salt," Tir says.

Asa sighs. "Not table salt?"

"Aha. Keep going. You almost made sense for a second there."

"Big crystals of salt," Asa grunts.

"Salt *is* composed of crystals," Ryu mutters. "Just FYI."

"Is it?" Tir blinks.

"Sorry, is this too much for your itty-bitty brain?"

"What? Who even talks like that?"

"The crystals aren't polygonal," Asa says. "They're fractal."

"Fractal doesn't exclude polygonal," Rook says. "Wait, is it like *Fleur de sel*? Those pyramidal structures?"

"Perhaps," Asa concedes.

"What the Hell are you two talking about?" Tir grumbles. "I don't get it."

"They look more like snowflakes," Asa says, "rather than diamonds."

"Which is why we mistook it for ash," Rook mutters. "I insist, though, that Frankie should be here for this discussion."

"Frankie can hear us just fine," Asa says. "Right, Frankie?"

Dammit.

Kass is looking right at me. He can probably hear my heartbeat from across the room. How did I ever think I could hide from these guys?

"Frankie, come over!" Ryu beckons.

"Shh..." the librarian glares at us. She's abandoned her nest of books on the left of the library doors to come scold the boys. "Quiet. This is a library!"

Oops.

I step out from behind the wall of shelves and find them looking sheepish. Well, most of them are. Asa is looking kind of blank and Rook is smirking.

The librarian glances at me. "You. I've seen you around before."

She's a kindly older lady with pink-streaked hair, dressed in a long floral dress under which pointy black boots peak out. She's never spoken to me before—then again, I tend to go quietly about my business, though last time I was here...

I blush, remember how Rook took me against the bookshelves. Thank God this is another librarian, because the things he told that one...

"You don't see many girls around this College," Rook says, grinning at her. "You must remember every single one of them that crosses your path, especially the ones that I fu—"

"Actually, not here," she says, frowning at me. "It wasn't here."

Now everyone is staring at her.

"Then where?" I ask. "Where else have you seen me?"

"A school on the other side of the country where I used to work, maybe twenty years ago. A Pandemonium Academy offshoot, called Mephisto Academy."

"Oh... Yeah, no. That wasn't me," I whisper.

"Your hair is different," she says. "It's so pale now. Used to be so dark."

"Like I said, that wasn't me." I swallow hard. "You met my mother."

12

FRANKIE

"*S*he was a quiet girl," the librarian says, sitting down with us, tucking her pinkish hair behind her ears. She's wearing dangling silver earrings that look like they're from India. *That's how I want to be when I grow old,* I think randomly before I remember I may not live to see old age, the way things are evolving. "Can't believe I mistook you for her. From closer up, you do look quite different. That girl was troubled."

That's putting it mildly. "And I'm not?"

She laughs lightly, as if I'm making a joke. Little does she know. "I don't know you, really. You said your name is Franka?"

"Frankie. From Francesca."

"Right. I must have known her before she had you. Feels like yesterday. Nothing makes you feel as old as meeting the grown-up children of the children you used to know."

"But when you met my mother, she wasn't a child, was she?"

"No, she was a troubled young woman. I knew the story, of course. Everyone did at the school. I mean, the news we got was curated and we all knew that, too, but she was the White Queen

Witch who tried to take over the world and was defeated. That was enough. She barely talked to anyone. She had a hard time."

"She deserved to have a hard time," I mutter. I don't want to feel empathy, not for the mother who had me by mistake and gave me up, then refused to cough up the name of the father.

"Your mother liked books. You must have gotten that from her."

"Got it from my aunt," I grumble. "Hundred percent sure about it."

When Tir steps behind me, placing his hands on my shoulders, I welcome the distraction and warmth of him.

"Okay?" he asks. Just that.

I nod, even though it really is not. "Did she ever say anything to you? Did she ever mention anyone?"

"I'm trying to remember. It was some time ago, you see." Her thin fingers tap a rhythm on the tabletop. "I mean, yes, she said things. Not to me, obviously. But occasionally she would just... lose it. She'd throw her food tray at her bodyguards, yell obscenities. *"I will come back,"* she kept saying. *"I will come back and take the crown that is owed me and rule the world."* She had no problem saying it. Didn't care if you heard her. All the cops and bodyguards following her. But that was anger talking. She was upset, which is understandable."

"Understandable? She's a criminal! She tortured and planned to kill people! She planned to take over the world!"

"I know." The librarian taps her fingers some more. "She didn't seem so evil. A pretty, young woman. Some people thought it seemed unjust. I mean... killing someone, or stealing something are tangible things. Things you can imagine happening. Taking over the world... not so much. It's too huge a thing. It didn't feel... attached to her, if you get my meaning."

I glance at Rook. He shrugs. *Told you so,* he mouths.

That she wanted to come back to the world? Yeah, for sure. But I didn't actually think she was ready to fight to take the throne back, fight my aunt after the clemency shown to her. After the horrible things that she did, I thought she'd feel a modicum of guilt and the need for penance.

I suppose, deep inside, I wanted her to repent and become a good person. Maybe one day look for me. We could have a coffee and a chat, and she'd give me a good reason why she gave me up and never looked for me. Maybe she was told she had to give me away and to never contact me. Not what Aunt Mia told me, but you never know, right?

Jesus. I thought I had come to terms with my reality, that I had accepted that my mother was a narcissist and a psychopath who was never interested in her child or anything and anyone but herself.

Funny how you discover how deluded you have been from time to time. A nice little shock to shake you up, wake you from your foolish daydreams, and remind you that you're an adult and need to stop hiding your head in the sand.

Face the truth.

"If she was always with her guards," I whisper, "how did I come into being? She was watched at all times. She never had any time alone with anyone but then how did she have me? Through a vision? The unholy ghost? Maybe my father was a ghost."

"I've heard of weirder things," Rook mutters.

"Ha," the librarian says.

"Ha, what?"

"She used to haunt my library, much like you are doing. And she used to meet a man there."

"Oh my God." I gape at her. "Why haven't you ever said that to anyone?"

"Nobody came to ask me."

"She left the school before anyone knew your mother was pregnant," Asa says. "Nobody thought to ask her."

Jesus Christ on a stick.

"So... wait, back up, back up." I lift a finger. "Used to meet a man, you say. You saw him? You've seen my father?"

"Holy fuck," Rook says.

"Who was he?" I demand.

"Oh, no idea," the old librarian says. "Remember, I saw him fleetingly, and only a couple of times. At first, I thought he was one of her bodyguards, but then I realized that he was someone I'd have noticed before, someone... powerful."

Excitement courses through me. I lean forward, folding my arms on the table. "What did he look like?"

"He was a handsome devil, tall and nicely dressed but in old-fashioned clothes." The librarian smiles, eyes gone distant. "Know what I mean? Like someone from a fairytale or an old book, in a dark frock and pants and a ruffled shirt, a black cloak with a hood thrown over it all. Very brooding. Your tall, dark and handsome type. Only his hair was so blond it was almost white. I remember thinking it was very striking. Like yours."

I let out a controlled breath. A clue. I have his hair. We have a description for the first time ever. Never underestimate librarians and generally ladies who read. "Anything else?"

"Oh, I thought once that he wore a kind of crown."

"A crown?"

"More like... a tiara? Do men wear tiaras? It was a golden filigree diadem wrapped around his head. I mean, these are modern times, men can wear whatever they like. Still, I don't know who would wear such a thing."

The guys are glancing questioningly at one another but nobody seems to have any ideas about this man in the tiara who got so friendly with my mother.

"I only know," she goes on, "that one morning before I was reassigned here, she sat in the library, playing with a pendant hanging around her neck and said to me—or to herself, who's to know?—these words that stuck with me. *"A child shall be born,* a child shall be born, they say, and she will be given a choice between Heaven and Hell, between this life and the next." Such odd words."

"What does that even mean?" I breathe. "Could it be any more cryptic? Seriously. We all have these choices. Be good or bad, live or die."

She stares at me, frowns, then claps a hand over her mouth. "A child. Oh, dear me. I hadn't thought that she meant a child would be born to her. What if she was already pregnant with you at the time?"

"Possibly. That pendant she was wearing that morning... do you remember it?"

"Vaguely. It looked like the symbol of a flower inside a circle."

All air leaves my lungs. I grab Kass' hand—he's sitting next to me—and squeeze it. "That's my pendant. The one she left with me. Like a clue, to figure out who my father is. It's an *ouroboros*, a snake biting its tail and a flower inside. It's my pendant!"

"You're jumping to conclusions there. You don't know if there's a clue in that pendant or if she happened to have it and passed it on to you," the librarian says.

"It is the only clue I have."

"She has a point," Kass says.

"Yeah, the point being that we need to get that pendant back. Thank you, my lady." Rook, ever the handsome, reckless rake, takes her hand and kisses it. "You have helped us enormously."

Her cheeks color. "My pleasure, young man."

"Thank you," I echo, giving her a wan smile. "You really helped us more than you can ever know."

"My pleasure. You seem nice. For what it's worth, I don't believe that children have to turn out the same as their parents. You can be your own person."

"I'm working on that," I whisper, choking down any number of other responses.

If I'm taken away, how will I be able to work on anything?

I can hear her saying as she walks away, "Whew, those boys sure are pretty. Lucky girl."

I am and I'm not. But at least I know what I need to do next:

Talk to the demons.

And by that, I mean Kalissa.

———

"Let's go." Grabbing my backpack, I head out of the library, any lingering dizziness be damned. This conversation has lit a fire under my butt and I need to get to the bottom of this, at long last. Hope is burning hotter than ever, burning inside my head, inside my gut, and I refuse to acknowledge it.

"Wait up, girl... just wait." Rook reaches my side first, the other Wonderboys squabbling over something behind us, something about... sleeping arrangements? "So, research is over, just like that?"

"We finally have a clue, a clue that all the books I went through refused to cough up. I need that pendant, see if it has any other secrets to offer."

"You had that pendant on you all your life, correct? Why would it offer up anything new now?"

"Why are you so negative? We now know my *father*," I almost choke on the word, "has pale hair and a crown and... and..."

"And that's all you have to go on, Sweetheart."

We both stop. "Crap. You're right. That's not much of a progress, is it?"

He tucks a strand of hair behind my ear, looking earnest and concerned, a striking young man in the halls of a college, not a demon boy whose real face is almost half gone and his heart probably full of evil.

I'm shivering—with cold, with reaction, with confusion. The other boys are catching up with us by now, casting us weird looks.

"What's up?" Tir asks, reaching us first.

"What do you think, fucker? We have new clues." Rook's gaze doesn't leave mine. "Bound to leave our girl unsettled."

"Our girl."

As if that takes away any of the confusion.

"You said I had no real clues, and the truth is, I don't know what I'm doing," I confess. "I don't know what my mother expects from me. Take her place? Put her back in power? How? I wouldn't even if I knew how. And I'm clearly not a witch. I can't draw energy from the elements and do magic."

"You haven't seriously tried yet."

"Like this, you mean?" I snap my fingers, channeling my anger and fear into the act—and sparks fly over them.

"Ow." Rook swats at them like flies. "Give a man a warning."

"Sure. Next time."

"It's elemental but... what did you draw on?"

"My anger," I whisper.

"Not an element? Wait, is that an angelic thing, drawing on an emotion?" Kass turns to Asa. "Is it possible?"

Asa shrugs. "Could be."

"So we have more possible clues," I say, "than just my father's hair. Angelic magic. Turning people to salt."

"Fleur de sel," Rook says.

"Whatever. Together with the symbol on my pendant, maybe we can piece something together."

I'm frowning at Rook, as if challenging him to provide more arguments against the probabilities of success of my undertaking, but he's silent. He nods slightly.

"You're right," he finally says. "Let's go."

More hissing convos are happening behind me as we head toward the school building. Assuming Kalissa is in class and not out here, plotting my demise—or hopefully my initiation as an ally of her gang, which should be less bloody.

You never know with demons, of course.

"What's the matter, Rook?" Kass is saying. "You act as if you don't want her to find out who her father is. Is it so bad if he's an angel?"

"If he is, he's no common angel."

My ears prick again but I'm distracted by Tir's growling stomach.

"Sounds like you swallowed a wolf for dinner," Ryu mutters. "Whole. And alive."

"That was the burger I had," Tir says, straight-faced.

"And... now we finally know what burgers sound like."

I'm generally distracted, I guess, what with the five hunks accompanying me and the latest news about my mother doing it in the library and getting caught by the librarian.

Is kinky sex hereditary?

Is sex in a library considered kinky?

Also, *ew,* I really should stop thinking about how I was conceived. It's icky somehow. Especially with a mother I don't even want to get to know, like, ever.

Tir grabs my arm and tugs me toward him. "All good?" he asks and I open my mouth to reply God knows what, maybe, *sure.*

And then a crash all but throws me on my face. Heat explodes on my side just as one of the boys moves to flank me.

An attack! Oh no, we're back to this? That's the only thought I have time for before Asa grabs me, lifting me off my feet, and turns, offering his back to whatever is happening like a shield. He grunts, his face paling, and I clutch at him, terrified.

"Asa?"

He nods as if to say he's okay—but is he?

A scream is building up in my chest, rising like a wave. It's as if my lungs are full of dark water, full of mud, and I need to spit it out, vomit that scream into the world.

"You're okay," Asa whispers. "We're okay."

Gritting my teeth, I swallow convulsively, doing my best to keep it down. His words and his arms around me help to control the urge.

Over his shoulder, I catch glimpses of Tir whipping out his bow and arrows, firing arrows so fast his hands are a blur, and Ryu throwing *shuriken* after *shuriken*. How many does he have on him and where the Hell is he hiding them?

Kass and Rook are using their whips while running toward our attackers and I wince, thinking of Kass' bad hip, but he's as fast as Rook, if not faster.

"Put me down," I say and am startled when he obeys.

"No heroics," he snaps. "Stay here."

I glare at him, not sure why he thinks I'd follow his orders, but at least this time I came prepared. Not that I really expected this attack, as evidenced by my total shock when that thing crashed past me...

"What was that explosion anyway?" I ask.

I take out my knives, consider whether throwing them is a good idea—then I'll be left with only my small switchblade. But I see a guy creeping up behind Ryu and I throw one without another thought, hitting him in the back.

He topples over.

"It was an exploding dart," Asa is saying. "The tip is set to explode when it hits, but they missed you. How the Hell could I have been so careless? If Tir hadn't pulled you to him right in that moment—"

"Not your fault." I throw my other knife at a girl about to

plunge a dagger into Rook's back while he's shoving a man off Kass.

"I'm your guardian." His sword glints as he stabs at a vampire rushing us with his long fangs bared. "This is my duty."

"I don't have a guardian angel," I say, flicking my switchblade open and cutting at a Fae who's so stupid he thought to get close to me. Though the burst of magic from my fingers seems to have zapped him before my blade even touched him. *Oops.* It's as if I'm leaking magic without realizing it. "And if I do, he must be off getting drunk by now."

"You do have a guardian angel now," he says quietly. "You have me."

"Don't say things like that," I whisper. "Don't say things you don't mean."

Things that can't be true.

And then it's as if a switch is flipped—*switchblade magic, haha*—and magic erupts around us. Rook is pulsing darkness. Tir is a whirlwind of steel and night, maiming and killing. Kass lifts his hands and people go down, bleeding. Where Ryu walks, his tail swishing behind him, the earth shakes and plants burst out.

Wow... These guys have power. It shouldn't be so sexy, this show of death and pain, but it is. Damn my girly parts, but it is.

"I thought you weren't supposed to use magic to kill," I say.

Asa grins. "Looks like we decided to break some rules again."

And his own Glory blazes forth, turning him incandescent. His sword becomes a white flame, searing everyone it touches. A werewolf runs at us, howling, and the sword twitches as if sentient, finding him and turning him into a puff of smoke.

Holy shit...

The scream is still pulsing inside me, making my lungs feel thick and turning my breathing shallow. Power. It wants out. It's a crawling feeling under my skin, deep in my chest, low in my fingers. It's a thousand fire ants that I struggle to contain—and yet when a demon crawls behind us, I point my blade at him and he yells, turning tail and running away.

Okay, maybe it wasn't magic, that bit. Maybe he just changed his mind about losing his life in this stupid fight.

The battle is turning now like a great tide, pushing the attackers away. The boys slash and cut and shove with their magic. The pavement under our feet is cracked and uneven, the walls scratched and splashed with blood. The boys seem to move in bursts, faster than the eye can register, finishing off the attackers.

Those still left standing start to run.

I'm breathing hard, even though I haven't done much fighting. The place is suddenly empty—although I slowly become aware of students watching us from windows and doorways. There's even a couple on a bench behind a tree, no more than thirty feet away, staring at us with round eyes full of shock.

"You're welcome for the show," I mutter under my breath.

Someone is carefully approaching us, one slow step after another, his face pale, hands held up as if he's afraid we'll shoot.

What is he doing?

Okay, so the picture we present might be a little intimidating.

Tir's black-on-black eyes gaze at us impassively. Ryu is more fox than man. Rook is half man and half shadow, his maimed side not quite there. As for Kass, his long fangs are out and his eyes are red.

We're a sight.

And Asa... Asa is glowing, and I swear I see the brilliance of huge wings rise behind him, big enough to reach the sky.

Oh yes, and we are surrounded by heaps of wounded

people. Possibly a few dead? I know that later, probably in my sleep, I'll feel guilty about that and spend the rest of my life expiating my sins in my nightmares.

But I didn't scream.

I didn't.

Small or not-so-small victories. I'll take it. We won today and avoided getting hurt ourselves. I didn't turn people into table salt, or whatever that salt is, and we're all still standing.

The guy is finally close enough for me to see how terrified he looks. He looks very human, though I know no humans are allowed in this college.

"What do you want?" Asa grinds out.

The guy swallows hard. "The dean... the dean wants to see you."

Right. It's a miracle it didn't happen before now. I mean, we seem to be at the heart of every fight. She will understand when I explain. After all, she's a family friend.

Right then Asa's glow diminishes and he goes down to one knee.

And then he faceplants.

13

KASS

*A*fter the initial shock of the attack, we fight and it's like moving through mire, exhaustion dragging me down. But I find my rhythm and push past it, the way I've been taught, pushing past weariness to the other side where you go berserk and just keep moving as if your body doesn't belong to you.

Men keep going down. Lines of fire appear at random places on my body where blades, fangs and claws rip into me. I'm fighting back-to-back with Rook and it's heady, to have people I trust again when danger closes in from every side.

My magic is simmering under my skin and I ruthlessly suppress it. Orders, engraved in my flesh. The contract. Not supposed to break the rules.

I may have lost my reason to go on, my reason to see this mission through, but that doesn't mean I'll stop fighting. After all, if I fail, the punishment will be dire.

Funny how you don't think about the consequences of failure when you enter a risky competition. You always think you'll win.

I'm not so sure anymore, but I'll keep fighting.

For her.

And for these men who have been kinder to me than anyone else ever has. Kinder and more honest, and the memory of Brody's lies makes me grind my teeth and find more energy reserves to keep going.

We're right at the heart of this uneven battle—my bread and butter, honestly, if only I wasn't starving for blood and sex and feeling like roadkill—when something shifts.

It's like a spark igniting inside of me and I catch a glimpse of Frankie suddenly... flickering.

Like a flame.

A magic throb goes through me, through everyone and everything, and Asa staggers, turning to look at her. He says something to her.

And it's as if the bindings of my contract fade, the restraints they put on me fall away. Using magic with the marks on my body was possible but painful, but now magic bursts out of me.

I'm a vampire and an incubus, a demonblood creature, but I'm suddenly tapping into a deeper part of myself. Elemental magic, I think, water and fire, and it erupts out of me.

Holy shit. It pulls me into myself and snaps the reins on my frail control. I'm a starving vampire and I'm full of unused magic.

I unleash it, and people fall around me, blood pouring out of them as they collapse. It feels good to release the pent-up tension and energy, lash at them with the essence of what I am instead of my Bitch.

I keep my lash by my side, though, as the remaining attackers turn and run, and it takes me a good fucking while to accept that the fight is over.

Or at least it seems that way to me, as time has stretched and everything moves slow, every moment elastic and ponderous.

Tir turns to me, panting harshly, his horns and hair black, his face streaked with blood. Rook grabs my arm and says something to me but though I can see his lips moving, I can't hear a thing. Ryu is grinning, and I stare at him, at his dark nose and whiskers, the fox ears, the sharp teeth.

I feel like laughing. I feel a little crazy.

Then everyone is turning to look at something.

Someone.

A guy is standing there, knees knocking together. Narrow-shouldered, pimply, he looks too young for this place. He smells partly like a shifter but mostly like sour fear.

I see him through a red haze. My gaze zeroes in at the pulse beating at his neck, my fangs aching, but his scent is off-putting. That's not the blood I need. Meanwhile, the heartbeats of the men and the girl around me grow louder and louder, the rush of blood in their veins deafening. Their scents hit me through the million other smells—hot and spicy and sweet—and I want them all. I want to bite them and fuck them all.

Merda.

Battle-lust and blood-lust.

And something else, something that digs deeper into me, deeper than any other feeling has ever burrowed, not with Brody, not with anyone.

Before I have any time to analyze it, though, and while the guy is telling us something I can't hear... Asa goes down.

Which is... sort of funny. And unfair, when I made myself keep going, when my head is spinning and my bad leg is barely holding me up.

I think I'm high. High on pain and exhaustion, high on power and hope.

Frankie is on her knees, shaking Asa who seems to be out cold, and the others slowly gather around them. Did I mention that everything is moving too slowly?

That hasn't changed, and as the adrenaline and the pure shot of euphoria from my magic starts to fade, my body lets me know in no fucking uncertain terms that it's currently not so happy with me.

I approach, each step heavy, my bad leg dragging behind me, my mind finally slowing down to match the speed of the world. "What's wrong with him?"

"His back is bleeding. It's pretty torn up." Rook has peeled Asa's T-shirt off, and yeah, it's kind of mangled.

Flashes me right back to the battles I took part in, the fields strewn with corpses and mangled flesh, and my gorge rises, bitter and sour in my mouth.

"He grabbed me and turned me away from the blast, taking the brunt of it," Frankie is saying, her voice a little choked.

"He's an angel. He'll be fine."

That could have been her, I think, *and she's no angel, is she?*

Is she?

"That arrow was spelled to kill," I say. "We need to put wards on ourselves for such attacks. We've been remiss in our duty."

Rook glances up at me, his gaze questioning. "After learning of Brody's assholery, you still believe in your mission?"

"It's not about Brody. It's about protecting her. And all of you. I don't need a mission or a contract to believe in that."

He nods, something like approval crossing his deep blue eyes, and then he's helping Ryu lift Asa up.

"Frankie, what if you can help him?" Tir says.

She frowns, those slender brows knitting over bright eyes. "How?"

"You can heal people."

"Who says?" She glances at us, as if looking for answers. "I don't think so."

"You brought me back," Tir says. "From death."

"No," she shakes her head. "I only pulled out the arrow poisoning your blood."

"You healed me. Called me back," Tir says, a stubborn light in his eyes.

"Tir, I tried to pull energy from nature to heal you, but nothing happened. I don't know what I did, Tir. Maybe the others are right. Maybe you were just unconscious."

"Or maybe you didn't realize what you did."

"Green grass," Rook mutters.

She turns her cute frown on him. "What?"

"When I took her from you, Tir, the grass was green. The trees swaying, full of leaves. She didn't draw power from around her. Ergo, it wasn't elemental magic that brought you back."

"So are we talking about an angel? Or a necromancer?"

Dammit. Maybe it's just attrition, but I'm actually starting to consider an angelic lineage as a real possibility. I mean, apart from her granddad, obviously. Someone powerful.

If the expressions the others are wearing are anything to go by, they are considering the same.

"Don't talk about this too loud," I caution. "Can't let anyone hear you. We have to discuss it in private."

"Why?" she whispers and I see my worry mirrored in the others' eyes.

"Because," I tell her, "killing people is easy and acceptable, piles of salt notwithstanding. Bringing people back from the dead? Big no-no. First of all, Heaven doesn't like it. It loves having the monopoly on resurrection. And second, it makes your value to everyone's eyes go up to astronomical highs. Very unusual ability, that. Very sought after, understandably."

"But—"

"*Ragazza,*" I tell her, "if you think the powers-that-be wanted you badly before, wait until they realize what you may be able to do now. There's no length to which they won't go to get you. Do you understand? To get you or to end you."

———

The slight man acting as a messenger for the dean is sent back to report the delay in complying with her request, and I follow behind with Frankie as Rook and Ryu carry Asa to our room, Tir going ahead to open doors and get the bed ready.

Asa is half-awake already, occasionally trying to shove everyone off him, but not succeeding.

Meanwhile, I feel half-dead.

Maybe I *am* half-dead.

I snort softly at myself, my thoughts twisting around themselves. *Are you half-alive if you're half-vampire?*

Frankie bumps a little into me as we go up the stairs and a jolt of fire goes through me, my demonic and vampiric sides colliding, needing.

So damn dizzy right now. I brace a hand on the wall not to fall while I draw a long breath of her natural perfume, my senses filling with flowers and honey. My gums ache with the need to bite. My hands ache with the need to touch her.

My dick aches with the need to fuck her, hard despite being long overdue for a feed, all the blood I possess pooling south.

"He's going to be a terrible patient, isn't he?" Ryu is muttering. "Fuck me."

"He won't stay in bed for long," Rook says, "mark my words."

Just as I thought.

"Bring him in here!" Tir calls out from the top of the stairs. "Let's put him on my bunk. Kass needs his."

I stop. Can't do this. All of this. They're trying to help me, making sure I have a lower bunk, not an upper one, and not a mattress on the floor because of my leg. And not mentioning again what an idiot I've been with Brody. Their concern is bound to turn to pity any moment now, if it hasn't already, and I've let down my defenses, let them see me at my weakest.

My weakest then and now, as my body has finally betrayed me.

"Kass?" She reaches for me and if she touches me again, I won't be able to control myself.

"Don't," I warn her.

"What is it?"

"Bloodlust. I'll attack you if you touch me again."

"Kass..." Her eyes are wide and worried, and it's the last thing I need.

"Go. Go to the room. You want to be with Asa," I say, trying to keep my voice steadier than I feel. "He took the brunt of the blast for you. Go thank him."

"I'm not leaving you here."

"I may be weak but my need right now is greater than me. I will feed on you if you don't go. I need sustenance, and you're like a drug. After tasting you, nobody else will fucking do."

She lifts her chin. "I'm not going anywhere."

"Don't you get it? You're in danger."

"And don't *you* get it?" she whispers. "I want to be with all of you. I don't like it, but I can't seem to be able to help myself. I want you to feed on me. I want you inside of me. I want *you*, Kass, and it's killing me."

A grunt leaves my lips. My thoughts don't make much sense, except, *want her, want her, want her.* "Go," I make myself say again. "I'll find someone else to feed on. Just go."

Instead, she steps closer and lifts a hand to my face. "Come here."

"Frankie—"

Her hand cups my jaw, fingers light on my neck, and my whole body jerks toward her. I grab her hips and haul her against me, a groan leaving my throat.

This is... everything.

She looks into my eyes as I taste her lips. Before I can deepen the kiss, she draws back.

"I hate you," she whispers, though her eyes are wide and dark and full of something hot that doesn't look like anger. "I hate you all so much."

"I hate myself, too," I agree and then we're kissing like we're each other's air, fighting with our tongues and lips and teeth to take over. My fangs cut her lip a little and a drop of her blood touches my tongue.

Her sweetness explodes through my senses, hitting me like a sledgehammer, and I slide down the wall, my ass thumping on the steps. I blink dazedly at her as she lowers herself over me, straddling me, and that's another hit of sensation burning down my synapses.

Fuck.

Whoa.

I feel like I'm on drugs, like that time I took the pills Sebastian gave me when I had first arrived, the pills he'd forced us to take. High. Loopy. Grinning for no reason other than the world is here and I exist in it.

And she's in my lap.

Her mouth returns to mine, kissing my slack lips until the fragments of my mind get back together, and I kiss her back. Her hands fumble at my belt and, fueled by that one tiny drop—because fuck her blood is like cocaine—I grab the fly of her pants and tear it apart. She squeals, jerking back, as I tear her pants and panties off her, letting shreds hang around her hips.

I slip a hand between her pale thighs and fuck me, she's so slick and hot. She moans, placing her hands on my shoulders, riding my fingers, and they slip inside her. Tight. So damn tight and slippery and my dick swells more, throbbing painfully.

I let my head thunk back against the wall, cursing under my breath. The last of my control—what control?—is slipping away fast. This is the last of my energy, and my mind is streamlining, honing its need like a blade, discarding any thought other than biting and fucking. If I don't do it now, I may slip into a coma.

She doesn't know how close I am to going under.

Nobody here does.

It's complicated being half-demon and half-vampire, and both halves need her now.

Then her hands are back on my crotch and *fuuuuuuuuuuuuck* I'm about to bust. Her fingers—unlike mine —retain their fine motor skills, undoing my fly and freeing my burning dick. It swings up and I almost shout out with relief as it hovers between us.

"I want you," she whispers, and puts a dainty hand around my diamond-hard cock, nearly driving me mad. My fingers inside her twitch and she moans, riding them some more.

She's dripping wet, her cream coating my hand, and when I pull my fingers out, I bring them to her mouth. "Lick them," I say hoarsely, barely recognizing the sound of my own voice.

Her pink tongue darts out and she obeys, licking each of the two fingers clean, every sweep of her tongue almost driving me over the edge.

"Enough," I bark.

I don't care if we are on the stairs of the dormitories where anyone can pass by and see us. Who knows, maybe someone already has. I couldn't give a fuck.

I lift her up and lower her on top of my cock. I hiss as her heat envelops me, her pussy tightening around my hard-on.

"Kass," she moans my name and it's the best sound in the fucking world. I want to hear it again, so I rock into her, and she says it again.

God. Fuck. Yes. Every rocking of my hips slides my cock in and out of her pussy, mere inches, but it feels like I've fucking died and gone to Heaven. Her tits are almost in my face, and I want to lick them, but she's still dressed from the waist up and I can't relinquish my grip on her hips. It's impossible. I'm locked into the act of fucking her, no other space left in my head for anything else.

And then she says, "Bite me."

I want to argue, to warn her that the pleasure might be too much. It has on occasion stopped humans' hearts.

But she's not human.

And I'm way past caution and even the ability to speak. My brain has shut down, my fangs have slipped out, and everything is crimson and blood and need. I tilt my head and put my mouth on her silky neck, then bite down, my fangs piercing her flesh.

Her blood is cinnamon honey and caramel cream.

I've died.

I've returned to life.

I'm hovering in the in-between.

And then her blood hits my bloodstream, my veins, my arteries, my heart. This girl punches me right in the heart, and the world erupts with light.

14

FRANKIE

"*K*ass!" I moan his name over and over as waves of ecstasy hit me, drowning me. I'm riding his thick cock, and his fangs are in my flesh. He's sucking on my neck as his cock pistons in and out of me, and I'm dying of pleasure.

We're on the staircase of the dormitories. At some point, I lost all sense of decency and propriety, all sense of reason and resolution, and find myself in Kass' lap, grinding against his very hard erection and eating out his mouth.

And now, somehow, I've ended up impaled on him, not caring if anyone sees and hears my moans and pleas for more. His mouth on my neck has gone from painful to wonderful, and I feel like I'm dying of pleasure. It buffets me like a great storm, making my body clench and shudder. My nipples are hard, my pussy fisted around his cock, my belly tight, and I'm bent over him, my head tilted to the side as he sucks on my blood, his hips rolling upward again and again.

Making me come again and again and again.

A pressure in my chest lets loose along with my core, a flame flares. A crack sounds from behind me. I ignore it.

Another crack I distantly feel. Can't focus on that. I can only ride the pleasure that threatens to pull me under. It's orgasm after orgasm, my core tightening to the point of pain only to spasm and contract and release once more.

So this is what it's like to be sucked and fucked by a vampire incubus, I think dizzily and I almost laugh because it somehow rhymes.

Like a song, I think next, and it's like an echo inside my head.

After a while, minutes, hours, days, who knows, the pleasure ebbs. I'm draped over him and I loll in his arms when his fangs retract, my head resting on his shoulder.

"Mm..." I feel drunk. Happy. Sated. He kisses my neck softly, and I make a small encouraging sound because it's like a caress through the rosy haze.

"We broke the staircase," he says. "Look."

"What, I have to move my head?" I shift a little and try to look sideways at what he's nodding at.

The rail of the staircase has broken in several places.

The steps have cracked around us, forming a pattern. It's a star, with us in its middle, the points spreading up on the steps and on the walls.

"Whoa. We did this?"

"Magic," he says. "Hi, guys."

"What?" Suddenly I become aware of two tall shadows looming over us and I scramble to sit up. Kass pulls me into his arms.

"So this is what good sex does," Tir mutters, crossing his arms over his chest. "*Wallbanging* I think they call it, only you had no headboard to bang and instead decided to destroy the stairs of the dormitory."

"It wasn't quite premeditated. You've noticed her magic tends to escape her," Rook says, coming to stand beside Tir, leaning against him nonchalantly. "Hm... I see our vampire has gotten some, at last. About time."

Kass gives them the finger, but only for a second, his hand returning to my waist, then my back, stroking.

Feels nice.

I could fall asleep right here, in his arms. His cock is still half-hard inside me and every tiny shift of my body sparks more pleasure.

"You should take her," Kass says, his voice vibrating in his chest, against me, soothing. "The double feeding has put her into a languor."

"Into a what?" I whisper.

"A sedated state a human normally enters after a vampire has fed on them," Rook explains. "You're not human but double-feeding, as he said, takes a lot out of you."

"Live and learn." I giggle a little. Hiccup. "I don't want to move."

Kass chuckles low. I love the sound. It's pure male satisfaction and delight. "Did I wear you out, my pretty?"

"You could say that." I hiccup again. Snuggle against him. "I wanna stay here."

"How is Asa?" Kass asks quietly over my head and that wakes me up a little more.

"Yes, how is he?"

"He'll live," Tir replies. "He's all up in our asses asking why you're not in the room with him and to make sure you're okay. Controlling *abesh.*"

"Said you shouldn't play with your food," Rook adds with a wink.

Kass laughs, shaking me.

I smile against his neck.

"Come on." Rook slides his arms around me, pulling me up. "I think I'll put you in bed with Asa. That will shut him up."

I like the sound of snuggling with Asa, too, so I let him manhandle me like a doll. I wince when Kass' cock slips out of me. Wetness spills between my thighs.

Thank God for Juliette's spell, I think as I lean against Rook. *The lack of condoms in my life seems to be very disproportionate to the insane amount of sex I'm getting.*

By a lot.

As in, zero condoms versus daily sex.

"There is no insane amount of sex," Rook says, guiding me toward the rooms, a grin in his voice. "Sex is good for us."

"Shit, did I say that out loud?"

"I like a girl who enjoys sex," Rook goes on, "and no lie. I like you."

God, I like him, too.

Kass comes after us and slips an arm around me. He barely limps, I realize, and glancing sideways, I see that he's slightly flushed, his eyes bright.

My God, he's so pretty. Gone is the grayness from his skin, the sunken cheeks. I bet any boy or girl crossing our path will swoon at the sight of him.

"In fact..." As Tir joins us, he turns and walks backward, giving Kass an obvious once-over, his eyes darkening. He licks his lips. "I wouldn't mind some double-feeding, if you're looking for volunteers."

I almost laugh out loud when Kass does a double take.

"You could have a buffet," I tell Kass, nudging him with my hip. "Or tapas."

He stares at me. "You really wouldn't mind if—"

"You share me. Why would I mind if we shared you, too? If you'd like that, of course."

Kass chokes a little. Then he chuckles again.

Did I mention I love that sound?

Rook leans in and kisses the top of my head. "God, I *really* like you."

"Thanks," I stammer, now hot all over—but in a cozy, *nice* way. Okay, also a turned-on but not urgent way.

Is this what Stockholm syndrome is? Falling for your

captors? I never understood how that could happen to anyone, but now...

Now I think I do...

———

Ryu is waiting for us at the open door of the room. He glances right and left as we approach. "Got an eyeful?" he snarls at the world in general. "Close your doors before I shift and tear your throats out."

Sure enough, quite a few doors click shut quickly down the corridor as we reach the room. An exaggerated hush follows.

"Wow," Rook says. "This fox has claws."

"And teeth," Ryu replies, lips pulling back, his canines glinting white.

"Ah-huh."

Ryu's normally moss-green eyes flash yellow as he steps inside and we follow, Tir staying back to close the door. He turns the lock, too.

It occurs to me that had he done that a week ago, I'd have kicked him in the nuts and unlocked the door. Kept the key, too. Now I'm happy he did, so we can have some privacy.

As if I feel safe with these guys.

As if I trust them not to hurt me.

Asa is lying on Tir's bunk on his side. When we enter, he lifts himself up on one elbow and nails me with that sky-blue gaze. "Frankie."

"I'm right here," I say, a small lump in my throat. "How are you doing?"

He reaches for me and I hurry over, not even pretending nonchalance. He catches my hand, tugging, and I sit down beside him.

His blond hair is longer than ever. I thread my fingers through the golden locks, tugging a little, and he groans.

"Why is your hair longer with every passing day?"

"Isn't everyone's?"

"Not like yours. It grows insanely fast. Must be an angel thing."

His blue eyes move over me, checking me over. "Are you okay? You stayed back. It's been at least half an hour. I thought the worst."

"She was with Kass," Tir says.

"Doing the horizontal tango," Rook adds. "Or whatever they call it nowadays."

A hot blush seeps into my face and neck. "I didn't realize we were gone that long."

"It was clearly enough time to be fu—"

"Come here." Asa gestures with his hand, his pale brows drawn over those blue, blue eyes. With his golden hair now reaching his chin, he looks absurdly young and pretty, as if he's aging backward.

"Where?"

He pulls me down until I end up curled on the bed beside him. "Right here."

His large hand closes over my neck, tugging until our foreheads almost touch. He's radiating heat and smells of musk and blood. Such human scents. He *looks* human.

Inhumanly beautiful, true, but the lines of pain bracketing his mouth and the dark smudges under his eyes soften that brutal perfection.

I stroke his jaw, his cheek, and his eyes close, a long breath leaving him. Our foreheads touch, his breath feathering over my mouth. He needed to touch me, he needed to be touched. I hadn't realized how tense his strong body was, but now I feel him relaxing in stages.

When I pull my hand away, he grabs it, presses it back to his face.

"Stay," he slurs, already half-asleep—or passed out, not

sure, though the other guys don't look concerned, so the bleeding must have stopped.

"I'll stay," I promise. "Sleep now. You need to get well. You shouldn't have stepped in the way of an explosive for me."

"Anytime," he grunts, his lashes fluttering closed. "I told you, I'm your guardian angel."

I don't want to cry but I swear my eyes sting with tears as his breathing evens out and he's off to dreamland, his hand still on the back of my head, fingers tangled in my hair.

Why? Why am I so touched? Why do I trust them now? Why do I feel things for them?

Why am I so stupid to fall for them all over again?

Not fair at all.

15

FRANKIE

I come awake in degrees, surfacing from slightly disturbing images of people turning into statues and then crumbling and getting blown away by the wind. I can't remember their faces but I'm pretty sure that, at least in my dream, I knew them.

I'm toasty warm and I have a weighted blanket on top of me.

Wait, no. Wrong. That's a heavy, male arm wrapped around me, and a muscular leg thrown over mine. The hand pressed to my middle is strong and long-fingered, a small white scar bisecting the roughened knuckles. My back is pressed to a hard chest and we're lying on a bunk bed...

Asa, I think, the memory returning.

I study his hand and bask in a sort of weird joy, discovering about this little scar on his right hand, and how he feels spooning me. Such intimate details and...

Wait. We're spooning. Asa and I.

And then I notice the other four guys in the room and remember how this is a bad idea.

Gah.

How can something that feels so right be wrong?

He blows out a small breath when I shift and I go still, not to wake him up, turning my attention to the other guys instead.

"… will blow a fuse if I say no," Tir is saying.

"So what?" Rook says. "They're a bunch of assholes. Who cares? Let them blow a gasket."

"We don't need more of said assholes breathing down our neck," Tir says.

A knock comes on the door, and they all turn to stare at it. Nobody moves to open it.

"Must be the dean sending us another guy to request our presence in her office. Poor thing must be shitting his pants, waiting to see if we open."

"Cast your eye on the orchard where I grow my fucks and you shall see that it is barren," Kass intones.

I swallow a hysterical giggle.

Asa's arm around me tightens. His hips roll a little, and *uh-oh*. That's some morning wood there. It feels more like a battering ram.

"Sooner or later, we'll have to talk to the dean," Ryu argues.

Kass shrugs. "Then later rather than sooner. We need breakfast." He's standing with his arms folded over his chest. It's uncanny how a feeding has healed him so much. He no longer looks tired and wounded. He looks powerful.

"We keep having breakfasts and skipping the rest of the meals. No wonder I'm always hungry," Rook complains.

"You're a bottomless hole, my friend," Ryu says, sounding impressed. "I bet three meals a day wouldn't be enough for you."

"Yeah, keep poking fun. I bet you had enough to eat in the forest. Hell consists mostly of barren wastelands. I've had my fill of worms and insects, thank you."

There's a lull in the conversation during which they all stare at him as if trying to decide whether he's serious.

The worst thing is that he isn't cracking up. He looks solemn, and maybe a little sad.

That tight feeling in my chest is by now familiar.

But this time I attempt to sit up, at the same time attempting to lift Asa's hand—and arm and leg—off me.

...bad idea.

He's suddenly on top of me, pressing down his impressive anatomy—miles of hard muscles, weighing me down, plus other hard parts of him.

Specifically, one very thick, very long, and very, *very* hard part.

I gasp, the entire assault combo frying my brain.

"Children," Rook says, "can you not fuck right at this moment? We're having a serious conversation."

"Fuck your conversation," Asa growls.

Then he kisses the Hell out of me.

There's slow clapping.

"Nice," Tir says. "Now can you avoid putting your dick inside her so we can have some breakfast?"

Asa sighs, sits back. "You really need to get laid, Tir."

"And you're really not a Seraph," Tir mutters, "no matter what you say. The evidence is here for all of us to see."

Asa turns his head and frowns at him. He looks like he wants to say something but can't make up his mind what.

"A serious conversation?" Kass nods at Tir. "About what?"

"About Frankie. We need to figure out who her father is."

"I don't see what difference it makes," Asa mutters.

"Hey." I slap lightly at his muscular chest. "It does to me."

He frowns. "Of course. I just meant, for the powers-that-be, it won't make a difference."

I shove at him and he sits back. "I'm serious."

"Yeah, let's be serious." Rook grins. "Do angels turn people into pillars of salt or piles of *fleur de sel*? Is there a difference? Does it depend on the angel's salt preferences?"

"What the fuck." Asa glares as he moves to kneel on the bed beside me. "Okay, look. It sounds pretty much like the same thing to me. Or you're relying on an ancient scribe of miracles to tell you that Lot's wife became a pillar of salt and then was reduced to a pile as she crumbled, and what the exact structure of that salt was? Be thankful someone thought to taste what was left of Lot's wife and determine that it was salt."

"Yuck. That's cannibalism."

Asa heaves a sigh. Shoves a hand through his golden hair. "And this is a serious conversation, how?"

"It's about to get serious," Tir says, hands balling at his sides, "once we stop ignoring the elephant in the room in favor of fucking and kissing and being silly."

"Oh, I'm silly, am I?" Rook mutters.

"The elephant?" Asa echoes.

"Yes! The fact that she brought me back!" Tir snaps, then turns to gaze directly at me, his voice softening. "You brought me back from the dead."

Back to that...

"You sound so sure," I whisper, tucking my legs under me. I'm wearing someone's overlarge T-shirt and my bare thighs are kind of stuck together because...

Oh... Kass. On the stairs. Right...

"She said she took the iron arrowhead out of your chest," Asa says, "and that stopped the poisoning, allowing you to heal."

"My heart stopped," Tir says, and I shiver, because he had been so still...

"You don't know that. She doesn't know that. She's not a doctor. And only an ECG can tell you for sure that a heart has stopped."

"Shut up, Asa. I know I was dying. Kass had hit me with his magic, making my blood run like a river. My breathing stopped. I could feel my heartbeat slowing."

"You still can't know for sure," he says stubbornly.

"I'm not God," I whisper. "I can't bring people back, whatever I turn out to be. Angels don't have such a gift. Right, Asa?"

He doesn't immediately reply. He's frowning at the far wall, or the closet, or something in his own head. Eventually, he says, "Not normally."

"Oh, great. Real helpful, pal," Rook says.

"But even the possibility of it being true is dangerous," Asa goes on. "Kass was right when he said last night that nobody must ever know."

"And if it's true, if you can really do such a thing... It's probably dangerous for you, too," Ryu says. "We don't know how this may be affecting you."

"Don't do it again," Asa says. "You must not attempt to ever do it again."

"What," I snap, "I may be able to bring you back, but you think I'll sit and watch you die?"

"Yes. That's exactly what I expect you'll do. This sickness... this exhaustion, Frankie, I have a feeling it's not caused by any wound. If you really brought someone back from the brink of death without using the elements, then you used your own life force."

"Shit," Tir breathes.

"All of you," Asa says, "promise that if one of us were to die, you won't let her bring us back."

"Damn you all," I whisper, close to tears again. What is it about these guys that makes me so emotional? "I can't make such a promise."

"Then," Asa says softly, "we'll have to hope that you don't possess such a gift. Giving death is bad enough. Giving back life is a disaster."

"Spoken like a true angel," Rook says but he looks troubled.

"No half measures. Bossy as all Hell. Sometimes you worry me, Asa. What the fuck are you anyway?"

Asa shakes his head and gets to his feet, reaching a hand down for me. "Breakfast. And then we will shower together."

Damn...

————

This time showering with the guys is strangely chaste.

A sentence I never thought I'd utter in my life.

It's me, though. I'm showering with Kass and Rook and I'm sort of keeping them at a distance. They do come inside, and this time I barely protest. The girls' showers are empty this time around, so I don't really have any arguments.

And I'm... out of sorts.

Becoming a habit, isn't it? I think to myself.

"Everything okay, Sweetheart?" Rook asks. He's standing under the spray in the stall next to mine. His staff is retracted and placed on the stall partition, looking innocuous for such a deadly weapon. He's dripping wet, his long black hair clinging to his shoulders and strong chest, his cock half-hard, and...

What were we talking about?

Oh right. "I'm fine."

I really am. We had breakfast brought to the room by Kass and Ryu from the kitchens, and I feel stronger. No lingering dizziness. The wound on my side is healing fine. My stomach has settled.

"What's on your mind?"

I give a short laugh. "What do you think?"

"You're still wondering what you are."

"Bingo."

"You're the Holy Grail, baby girl," Rook says softly. "The ultimate weapon. You're Cain and anyone who attacks you turns to dust. Well, salt. Good choice of condiment."

"Why? Why am I the ultimate weapon?"

"Because it seems you can choose who to annihilate. You're not a mindless bomb. And that's without counting the other thing." He winks and jabs a thumb over his shoulder toward the door, as if that's a synonym. "Resurrection. "

I shiver. "I collapsed a building once."

"Power needs to be trained. A weapon needs to be used."

"Stop talking bullshit, Rook," Ryu says.

"It's not bullshit and she knows it. So do you. She is all that. It's not a secret anymore."

"She's also a girl," Ryu says softly. "Remember that."

"Oh, I remember she's a girl." Rook leers at me. "Very well, too. I remember her tits, her ass, her—"

"For fuck's sake, demon." Ryu is scrubbing himself viciously with his hands under the spray, and I'm momentarily distracted when I catch glimpses of his body.

"You're right," Rook says, turning to see what I'm staring at and grinning widely. "Mmm... yeah. So what do you need, Darling?"

"I need to talk to my family."

In private.

———

The guys grumble and whine like little boys when I tell them I want the room to myself for a while again. Not for long, though, even if they declare they will be standing outside the door until I'm done with my magical call.

I understand that they won't leave me here alone, but do they all have to wait outside? I mean, I feel bad for Asa who's still healing, but couldn't they leave one person outside and the rest go... do whatever it is guys do? Play Scale-ball. Or jog. Or eat. They like eating.

It's just nerves. I'm going to ask some questions and I'm afraid of the answers.

I'm also afraid of how vulnerable I feel when faced with my family, of all the emotions welling up. I love them. I miss them. I wish they'd ride into this forsaken college and save me, carry me back home, back in time, when I was a little, innocent girl who knew nothing of magic and hadn't manifested any terrible abilities.

Funny how you can be a strong, independent woman but when surrounded by your family you turn back into the child you used to be. It's unnerving. And not helpful right now.

Granddad doesn't respond to my ping. Busy, busy researching about me, or is he in danger and hiding because of me? I try not to worry.

But Aunt Mia replies right away to my call, and her form shivers in front of me, a holographic image of her and my uncles standing behind her.

They seem to have been in the middle of some outdoor activity. Is that... a stadium?

"Honey, hi! How are you? Are you feeling better?" Her sweet face fills my vision. "The boys are playing Scale-ball with a school from across the country, it's a big match! Tell us how things are."

Talk about male interests my guys don't seem to share...

Such a normal activity, going to the stadium with their children to watch them play. It shouldn't hurt. That sting in my heart has no business being there. Of course, the world goes on turning outside of this college and of course, my younger cousins don't even know what's going on with me.

"Sweetling," Uncle Sindri says, moving closer to the center of the image. "What is it? Is there any development?"

"No," I lie, "yes..." But I can't tell them about Tir's suspicions. So I grab onto something else. "Is it possible that my father was an angel?"

They exchange glances. "It's possible," Sindri concedes. "We hadn't considered it, to be honest, especially since your power manifested. It seemed more..."

"Sinister?" I supply.

He winces.

"We did think it looked more like a demonblood power," Uncle Ashton says. "Your granddad thought the same."

"Ah. That's interesting..."

"Then again, your granddad initially thought your father might be a dark Fae," Uncle Jason says. "A *pukha* perhaps. Or a weredragon."

"A *weredragon*?" I repeat dumbly.

"I know, right?" He grins. "He never explained why."

I swallow hard. Wipe my hands down my sides. "Someone told me about a book, back when you guys first met at the Academy. There was a book where you read about a void of power and a counterbalance in magic."

"I found that book, Honeybug," Aunt Mia says. "I gave it to Emrys to read. We were trying to figure out what a Queen Witch could do."

"That's right," Uncle Emrys says. "We knew about the balance. It was written. *"Closing the circle will give the Queen Witch enormous power, thereby upsetting the balance. She will need a counterbalance to stop the world from falling into chaos."* We thought the counterbalance was the White Queen, and that's partly why she was allowed to live. But the void is still there and everyone thinks..."

"Everyone?"

"Well, the higher-ups think it might be you."

I stare at his handsome, earnest face. "How can it be me if I'm not even a witch?"

He nods. "Good question. We didn't know that back then."

"Is that why you decided to raise me?" Bile is rising in my

throat. "Because I might be useful? Because you could control me, control…" I swallow down bitterness. "The Holy Grail?"

"Daughter. Don't ever say that."

"Another war like the one that Lucifer provoked. The arrival of a powerful being. An elemental force that is emerging. An imminent threat."

"You are our baby *daughter*." Uncle Emrys glares. "We love you as much as Juliette. In your heart, you know that. We never thought you had any particular powers. Being the White Queen's child doesn't even mean you would turn out to be a witch, let alone anything else."

"But there was a strong probability."

"You can't believe that we—"

"I don't *want* to believe it!" I all but shout. "You think I want to believe it? You're my family. But if I'm this impending threat, then… Then we should stop communicating."

"No. Why?"

"Because you need to distance yourselves from me. Or you may get hurt."

"Honey, Frankie, no. You're our daughter, just as much as Julie is. We have to know that you're okay. You can't stop talking to us. It was bad already when you had to go away with Granddad, this… this is awful, I…"

"I'm sorry. Unless I figure out a solution, I won't put all of you in danger," I say more quietly.

The last thing I see is my aunt's stricken face before I cut off the communication. I fumble with the magic, striking sparks off the furniture and walls.

Lying down on my bunk, turning my back to the room, I pull the blankets over my head and allow myself to quietly cry.

16

TIR

"Should we wake her up?" Rook says. "She seems distressed."

By the time we re-entered our room, we found Frankie fast asleep, lying on her back on the bunk, and we're now all standing around her, like I imagine the seven dwarves standing around Snow White's bed might have been.

Or was it her coffin?

I frown. "Of course she's distressed. She's dreaming."

She's curled up on her side, pale hair spilling over the pillow and down the side of the bunk bed. She looks... small, like this. Fragile.

"Nightmares are a bitch," Ryu says. "Talking to her family seems to have triggered her."

"That doesn't surprise me," Kass says.

My family doesn't cause me nightmares. My time in the Wild Hunt does. The transformation I had to endure. The violence I had to accept and enforce and pretend to enjoy.

"She's saying something," Asa says.

"Something about monsters?" Kass mutters.

"She dreams of the men she's killed with her scream," I say.

Rook gives me a dark look. "And how would you know that?"

"I've seen it," I admit softly. "I visit her dreams."

"What the fuck," Ryu breathes.

They're all staring at me now with dark frowns on their faces.

They hadn't known. Of course not.

"A dreamwalker." Rook whistles. "Now that, I didn't see coming. Tell me more."

"What's there to tell?" I mutter, irritated.

"You, fucker," Ryu hisses. "Did you—?"

"I didn't walk your dreams, fox, so you can relax. Or any of you." I glare at them. They glare right back. "Why the fuck would I walk your dreams? Do you think I enjoy walking other people's nightmares? That it's my favorite hobby? I stumbled across Kass' nightmares when he first arrived, and trust me, I wouldn't like to get back in there. No, I've done my best to keep well out of your heads. But I *had* to walk her dreams." I shrug. "It's why they sent me here."

"If you wanted to spy on us—"

I snarl. "Why, are you hiding anything more, kitsune?"

He shrugs, still glaring. "My memories," he finally says. "They're private. What's left of them anyway."

Fuck. That leaves me without a retort.

"We were all chosen for our abilities," Rook says somberly. "We knew that."

"We knew nothing," Ryu spits the words. "I never expected..." He clenches his fists, brow furrowing deeper.

"Her?" I suggest.

A nod. "And you," he admits. "Us."

Us.

Such a big, gravid word. I gaze at her and let out a

controlled breath. I remember how she touched me, in so many ways, carnal and emotional and... and how she cared enough to bring me back.

I can't fucking get over it.

"She's changing us," Kass breathes.

True. She has been changing us since we met her, and we have been changing each other, and my thoughts are a goddamn jumble, a knot I can't untangle.

"And how does she feel about killing all those people?" Rook asks.

"Regret. Guilt. She's afraid of herself," I say, *whisper*, because it strikes right at the very fucking core of me.

Like I'm afraid of myself.

And it makes me want to save her even more.

"She doesn't just kill people." Rook cocks his head to the side. "If you're right, that is. She can also bring them back. I mean... that's so insane I've been trying not to think about it too hard."

"Tell me about it," I mutter and rub the back of my neck. Tension has gathered there, radiating pain up my scalp.

Ryu bends over her, lifting a hand as if to touch her, but his hand just hovers over her brow. "How does that work? She can kill many with one scream. Can she bring them all back?"

"I don't think the two work in the same way," I say.

"How would you know how any of that works? It's not the usual elemental magic, is it?"

"Are we still thinking she's half-angel?" Kass glances from me to Asa. "For all we know, you were just passed out and she gave you the kiss of life."

I grind my molars, struggling to keep my voice from rising. "Fuck you. Are you calling me a liar?"

"I'm calling you an idiot. There's a difference."

"I know what I know." I bow my head and cross my arms

over my chest—more like clutching at myself because I feel like I'm fucking sinking into quagmire.

And shouldn't I feel different after coming back from the dead? What about an epiphany, a realization of the meaning of my life? What about seeing the faces of my loved ones while I floated toward the light?

Why was her face the only one I could see, even with my eyes closed and life ebbing out of me?

"Angels. Yeah, we are hanging onto this condiment hypothesis," Rook says.

I huff out a breath. "*Condiment* hypothesis?"

"Yeah. That she turns people to salt. But tell us, angel," Rook says, "what about the mark of Cain? Doesn't it turn to salt those who'd attack her? Having a demon daddy makes sense to me. The mark of the beast? Seed of the serpent? Ring any bells?"

"What are you saying?" Asa asks.

"That your idea of her being an angel is not bulletproof. Maybe you want her to be an angel, like you. As for the resurrection claims, you know what I think about them."

Asa's handsome face looks gravely pensive. "Rook—"

"And who's to say that there isn't a demon out there with the power to bring people back from the dead, if it's true? After all, it's a thin line between angelblood and demonblood."

"That's heresy," Asa mutters.

"Is it? I'd say it's the plain old truth. Not all demons were born as such. Many are old elemental gods and even more are angels who fell from grace, as you well know."

Asa sighs. "What are you implying?"

But before Rook replies, Frankie stirs on the bed with a soft sigh, and we all freeze.

A few heartbeats pass.

"Haven't you ever asked yourself why you are called *Nephal*?" Rook hisses at Asa.

"It's just a clearance level."

"Seriously? *Nephal*. Nephilim." Rook throws his hands up in the air. "Offspring of fallen angels and human women. Ring any bells?"

Asa scowls. "I'm an angel in Heaven's service."

"Yeah. Intriguing, isn't it? And irritating, too, Asariel *Nephal*."

"It's just a name."

"If you say so, handsome."

"Wait a sec... what are you two talking about?" I mutter. "Isn't he a seraph?"

"Debatable," Rook says.

"Shut up," Asa grumbles.

"You don't seem so sure you're a seraph anymore, are you?"

"Shut. Up!"

"You don't even talk like an angel. Or act like one."

"But I remember Heaven! I remember being a seraph, even if... Fifth Heaven is not as it was. We're not close to the Divine anymore. Deals are made with Hell. The authorities govern the choirs with a steel glove. Information is scarce, hard to come by. We're not supposed to ask questions."

"What if they've gaslit you? What if the authorities are lying?"

"It's heresy to speak such words."

I'm staring at the two of them. My mind is still caught on her, on her face, on the memory of her hand on my chest, and they're talking about whether Asa is an angel or not. Like, what the fuck?

The truth is never heresy. The truth should never be hidden.

The truth. The question of whether Frankie could bring the dead back to life was theoretical until now, a possibility to examine. But now I am certain of it, and I think the others are seriously considering it for the first time.

We look at Frankie, and I bet we're all thinking the same thought: if she brought me back, if she has such a power, the truth should never come out.

What do you do with that kind of power? How do you manage it, how do you stop yourself from using it all the time, and what's the cost? Every magic has a cost. Demonblood uses your blood until you have no more to give. And elemental magic pulls life force from nature. Witches draw it from other supernatural elemental users.

And angels?

"We draw from the Glory," Asa says, and shit, I apparently said all that out loud. "And if the Glory is not available, if you're performing magic against Heaven's orders or simply have no access to it... then you draw from yourself."

He'd said that before. That's something we need to talk about more, but right then Frankie stretches and yawns. Like a kitten. A very sexy kitten.

Kraish, I want her like crazy and I'm doing my fucking best not to take it personally that I'm the only guy in this group she hasn't gotten down and dirty with.

I watch her in wonder, my dick and I in agreement on how much we desire her, and as she mumbles something, still half-asleep, more memories slam into me.

Of how she brought me back.

How I was drifting away in a dark tunnel like a bottomless well with only the hint of a light at its end, the light being her face, and I thought... I thought I heard her voice.

Her voice calling me back somehow.

She called my name.

No, not this name, not *Tirius.* Some other name, a magical sound, a concept. The concept of who I am.

Yeah, that, a word that fits the shape of me.

Like the word my mother's womb must have spoken to make me.

Don't they say that the divine Glory is, in fact, the language that can make and unmake the world?

Fighting a shudder, I reach down to lift a pale strand of hair curling on her cheek. I don't quite understand these feelings she has woken up in me. Not sure I want to understand or know them, or if this is going to be the worst mistake I ever make. The final mistake, the one to end me.

When she turns into my touch and the ice around my heart cracks right through, I know this is what Hell must be like.

Then why do I like it so damn much?

———

"Are you sure you're well enough to do this now?" I demand, following her through campus, the others following behind us, caught in an argument about... condiments? Fuck Rook and his obsession with that word.

"Yes." She cuts me a withering glance. "How many more times are you going to ask me?"

"As many as it takes to make sure you're not going to drain yourself instead of resting."

"I've rested enough. There are people to see and things to be discussed."

We're making our way to a small amphitheater where apparently the demons like to have their business meetings— which means we're probably about to walk into an orgy, not that I give a damn but Asa might have a coronary—and I have my bow slung over my chest, my quiver and arrows over one shoulder. My knives are in my belt. I'm ready.

And yet I'm not.

She feels more distant now that she's awake and recovered. A nasty thought, because I can't wish for her to return to being bedridden, even if she had been sweet in her dazed state.

She'd forgotten to hate us for a while, but now her head has cleared.

The world is harsh, set in black and white, and she's right. The only thing that should matter is forming coalitions within the College in order to survive the passing of days, at least until Heaven and Hell come to an understanding and new orders come through.

Putting distance between us is the right thing to do, I tell myself. *Do the same, T.*

Fucking do it.

But I can't. It's too late. My head is fucked up. I don't know what the Hell I'm doing. Putting one foot in front of the other seems to be the extent of my planning for now.

Talking with Kalissa and Greyson, deciding what to do about the Fae gang, dealing with the renegades paid by fuck-knows-who to kill our girl, it's all way over my head right now and I'm drowning in that shit.

The beast writhes underneath my skin, as confused as I am. Is this a fight or a fuck situation? It feels like something else entirely and I don't fucking know how to deal with it. Fighting and fucking is all I've known since I was sold to the Hunt as a child.

What do I do now that I've put myself in an impossible situation?

"Tir?"

"Hm?"

She gives me a faint smile. "We'll get your earrings back."

I frown at her, opening my mouth to say something, not even sure what. I'm so fucking out of my depth it's not even funny, because she doesn't look mad right now, only worried.

"Are you all right?" she asks, and that breaks through my strange daze.

"Of course." I manage a sneer, glaring at the school

building, now standing in front of us. "And I don't care about the earrings. Let's just get this over with, make sure the demons won't be lurking around to stab us in the back."

"But you said they were important—"

With a growl, I stalk toward the building, because how can I explain to her that the earrings aren't important compared to her well-being, and that they're about my past, a past I have to leave behind, at long last. "Coming?"

"Coming, coming, sheesh... Wait up!"

That's how we enter the small amphitheater, with me in the lead, and thank fuck for that, because when the attack comes, I'm in the frontline.

Danger, my mind blares at me, *danger, protect Frankie.*

"Ambush!" I yell. "Stay back! Stay the Hell back!"

I see them coming from the corner of my eye, shadows with glints of metal and fire, and my power bursts through me. Unslinging my bow, using it as a staff, I swing it around, letting my magic flow through it. I'm aware of my vision shifting, snapping to black and white—so fitting for this world—and my horns are a welcome weight on my head. I know I look terrifying, and that's what you need in a battle.

That's who I am.

I strike the attackers with all I have. I draw the breath out of their lungs, I break their limbs, I smash them against the walls as I enter a familiar dance of death and pain.

Violence distilled in my blood, pushed into me until it's all mine. The attackers start to trickle around us, avoiding confrontation. I'm going to wipe them out for trying to even get near her, cut them up and scatter their pieces to the four corners of the earth.

But Frankie appears by my side, swinging wide with her knives. Despite having walked here just fine, she seems unsteady.

And she breaks my concentration because now I'm concerned she may get hurt.

"Rook! Kass, dammit, where are you?" I yell. "Take her away from here."

"Got my hands full, pretty boy," Rook calls back. "Take her yourself."

Fuck.

"I'm not going anywhere," she hisses and keeps fighting with her knives. She still doesn't allow herself to use her power, and I bet she won't unless she's truly cornered.

Not letting her get cornered again.

With a curse, I grab her and swing her up into my arms.

"Run!" Asa shouts, "take her to safety!"

Now I can see what is keeping them back: it looks like a whole army of assassins has poured in from the top of the amphitheater rows, and Rook and Asa are all that's keeping the door free for us.

I take off running, racing past Ryu and Kass fighting right outside, running down the corridor, heading for the exit of the building.

"No, no!" She struggles in my arms. "Put me down, I want to fight."

"You have been unwell," I snarl. "They have this under control."

"No, Tir—"

"Do you want to scream and kill them all?"

She falls quiet then.

"So let me save you." After saving my family, this is the only good thing I get to do.

She doesn't take the chance to point out again that this is a lull before the storm, before my orders come in, before I trade her to return home.

Finding the exit, I burst out, dodging two attackers—figured they'd post their people at the exit, too—and put in an extra burst of speed, clutching Frankie to my chest.

Where to?

No safehouse. No hidey hole to slip into.

So I run and run, ending up somewhere behind the arena in a cluster of trees, small enough for me to determine right away that no ambush is waiting for us here.

Pressing my back to a tree trunk, I wait, just in case.

After a moment, I glance down at her.

She's still curled up in my arms, gazing up at me with those velvet-dark eyes. She lifts a hand to my face, then higher, to my horns. "You said once that this isn't glamour."

"It's not." I lick my lips, try to catch my breath. "The Wild Hunt changed my nature, from Seelie to Unseelie. I'm not the same anymore. I can't go back and somewhere deep inside my mind I knew it."

"Tir..."

"They sold me," I blurt out.

Her brows draw together. "What?"

"My family sold me in exchange for a blood debt. They told me they had no choice. I was the oldest of the children, it was the only way. And I accepted it, to save them."

I don't know what I expect as the answer to this truth, the truth I've denied all this time. I'm laid bare, welcoming a strike.

But she only says fiercely, "I'd have surrendered myself rather than give you up."

And that may break me just as surely as a barbed word would.

I stare at her. Pieces are falling into place. This strange ache in my chest when I think of my family is starting to make sense.

"You really would," I whisper.

"If I were your parent, I would. If I were your sibling, I would."

"And what about you, right here, right now?"

She swallows hard. "I would," she whispers so low I barely hear it. "I would."

Sliding down the rough bark until I'm sitting on the ground, I kiss her. I suppose it was inevitable from the first time I saw her.

I expect her to shove me off, but she doesn't. She kisses me back and winds her body around me.

This time it feels like Heaven.

17

FRANKIE

*W*hat's wrong with me? What is it about broken boys that makes them so irresistible?

Okay, let's be honest here, self. They were irresistible from the start, when they appeared to be heartless, selfish bastards. Don't go looking for excuses now for wanting them.

Yeah, but this is more than lust. This is more than attraction.

My heart is engaged.

Oh, no...

I tried to keep away, to keep feelings from growing, but I never stood a chance with these guys, did I? They're devastating. It doesn't matter that nothing has changed for them, that their missions are still running, that they're still going to give me up without a backward glance.

Knowing they have valid reasons, good reasons, dammit, reasons that I'd have embraced if I was in their shoes, doesn't change this mess.

They hold me, and kiss me, and protect me, and confuse the Hell out of me, when for them it's all straightforward.

Let them break my heart. There's nothing I can do about it.

I'm done fighting it.

I can't anymore.

I wind myself around him, the only one of the boys I haven't touched that way yet, the only one I haven't slept with. The one I brought back, from wherever he was when my power erupted.

The Fae who welcomed me to this College and started weaving this web of lies that fell apart the moment I showed who I am.

He kisses me as he carries me into the dorms and up the steps, never stopping. My nipples stiffen, my body tightens with my need of him. Where our lips meet and our tongues clash, he tastes like clean air after a rain, but the more we kiss, the deeper his taste runs—like mulled wine and ripe berries with a hint of smoke.

My fingertips dig into his muscular shoulders, the back of his corded neck, tangle into his soft hair.

This is addiction. I'm addicted to them.

He's still kissing me as he comes to a halt outside our room. Kissing me as he kicks the door open, though he breaks the kiss to glance around with a frown. Checking for intruders.

He then kicks the door shut, and all but throws me onto his bunk, climbing after me. His pale hair is in his glittering eyes, his cheeks feverishly flushed, all the darkness pulled out of him. I hadn't realized when he lost the horns and the claws.

But now he's here, with me. His hands move over my body reverently, desperately. First, my shoes and socks come off, then he tears at my clothes, his breathing coming in ragged pants. He doesn't need claws to shred them, he's so freakishly strong, tearing at my shirt, my pants, buttons popping, seams screeching as they give way.

I reach up to his face to stroke his jaw when he leans over me, gaze intent on my breasts, confined in the practical black cotton of my sports bra. His lips are pulled back, and his sharp teeth are bared. He looks like he's about to eat me, the most beautiful bogeyman on record, and I almost laugh at the thought but then moan instead when he trails a hand over my breasts, tugging at the cloth. His long fingers brush over my stiff nipples, sending a jolt of arousal right down my middle.

I'm already soaked.

Can't help it.

I'm so helpless when it comes to them, and it makes me mad, but it feels so good.

He reaches under my back, snapping the clasp of my bra. Then he's pulling it off me, and I lift my arms to aid him lay me bare.

I don't expect foreplay, not sure I even need it right now, but when his hands return to my breasts, stroking and massaging, I shudder with pleasure.

He's frowning a little now, toying with my nipples, his gaze flicking from them up to my face as if cataloging my reactions. Studying. Learning.

I reach up almost blindly this time and trace his sharp cheekbones, his chin, his mouth, dipping a finger between his lips, tracing those sharp teeth.

That seems to snap whatever trance he's been in because suddenly foreplay is past and he's tearing my panties off.

"Tir," I pant, impatient now. "Please."

He doesn't undress, though I tug on his shirt. He simply unzips his pants and slowly pulls out his long, thick cock. "*Arawn,* how I want you."

I can see it. Plenty of big, engorged evidence right there.

With his other hand, he reaches between my legs, fingers trailing over my folds, then dipping into me, making me gasp. "So wet. You want me, too."

This time I do laugh, a breath of a sound. "You couldn't tell?"

But his eyes are blazing bright now and he smiles for a

moment, soft and unguarded under the rippling foliage of the trees, and God, he's beautiful.

Then he does a reverse push-up, lowering himself over me, and his cock is already pushing into me even as I wrap my legs instinctively around his lean hips.

Oh God...

His mouth falls open as he pushes into me, a stunned expression on his handsome face. I stare up at him, my thoughts grinding to a stop as his thick cock fills me up, inch by hard inch, making my legs tremble and my back arch.

Oh.

My.

God.

My breath leaves me as he inexorably drives home, his cock bottoming out inside of me. He grunts, looking as stunned as I feel. His chin-length hair slides forward to shadow his face, but I want to see him, see his expression and the look in his eyes.

See the whole of him.

So I tuck his silky hair behind a pointy ear and he turns his face into my touch, kissing my palm. His hips flex.

We both moan. I love the guttural sound coming out of him, rumbling out of his broad chest, and it turns me on even more, if that's possible.

"The others," I murmur as he starts thrusting into me, "we should make sure they're okay—"

"Frankie," he groans, the sound like that of a wounded animal, "*Kraish,* Frankie..."

The others, I think, and *what am I going to do when this is over and reality smashes back in?*

We rock together, clutching at each other, instinct taking over, all thought processes suspended once more as we grind against each other, rutting.

My heels dig into his glorious, hard ass, his cock twitches

inside me, his breathing catches, and his gaze shatters like a sky of broken stars.

My back arches until my spine creaks, and a shout escapes me as pleasure slams into me, my body seizing. I clench around his thick cock, and he gives a strangled shout of his own.

He thrusts once, twice as I clench and clench, and it's too much and I'm falling apart, shaking on the bed. His eyes widen, his cock jerks, and he falls on top of me, catching himself on his elbows.

We're both breathing hard. I still have my hands on his shoulders. I slide them to the back of his neck, basking in the pleasure still coursing through me, milder now, sweeter. He shifts a little and a breath leaves me as I tighten again around his girth, aftershocks of bliss racking me.

His eyes are crystals, refracting the light as he gazes down at me, full of wonder. "You do want me," he says again. As if he can't quite believe it.

I smile. I feel him. I feel him and somehow, it's as if I feel all of them, inside me, around me, inside my body, inside my mind. Air and fire, water and earth, and a glow that has to be Asa. They are a part of me, and I can't puzzle it out, only bask in it. I feel complete. I feel whole.

I feel cherished and wanted and like I'm good enough for the first time in a long time, maybe in forever.

They're here, I think, and turn my face to the door to find them standing there.

And then tears start sliding down my cheeks, cool like rain, my chest growing tight.

"I can't do this anymore," I whisper.

Tir frowns down at me. "What? Why?"

Because now it means something to me, sex with these men means something to me, something important. It's not just hate sex, not even mindless, meaningless pleasure, no. It's an expression of my feelings for them.

I think it but can't say it, even as his arms come around me and he pulls me against his body. I only cry some more for what could have been but won't ever be, along with the future I'd barely dared imagine for myself growing up.

————

"Frankie!" Asa crowds Tir as he carries me to our room. "What the Hell? Is she hurt?"

"No." Tir draws back just enough to look at me. "At least I think not. Frankie, are you hurt?"

I shake my head but can't stop those damn tears from falling. His steps pound inside the stairwell, then we're inside our room and he gently lays me on his bed.

"Fuck, Tir, what did you do?" Ryu demands. "Did you break our girl?"

Our girl.

Now I'm crying harder.

"Fuck," Kass says, sitting on the bed beside us. "This day is going to Hell. First the ambush and now Frankie is crying."

I feel his touch on my hair.

I want to grab him and bury my face in his chest.

I want to pull them all around me and let them cocoon me in their strength and warmth.

I don't know what I'm thinking. I've always been an independent girl, even more so since I went to live with Granddad. Had to be, when my curse was revealed and my everyday grind consisted of self-defense and self-control.

Relinquishing control is scary.

Wishing to do it, willingly, even more so.

"Shall I bring you something to drink?" Kass offers. "Or maybe chocolate? Girls like chocolate, right?"

I hiccup around sudden laughter. My eyes leak some more.

God, I have to stop.

"My cock is like chocolate," Tir rumbles. "Maybe she wants some more of it."

"Your cock made her cry," Ryu accuses. "No more cocking. What do you say, girl? I vote for chocolate, I—"

"Quiet. There's someone outside the door," Rook says, his voice tight.

Suddenly, they're all turning away from me, while Tir sits beside me, hauling me against his chest. I wipe at my traitorous eyes, trying to see through the film of tears.

A fist bangs on the door, and we all jump a little.

"Open up!" someone yells. "Are you alive? Dammit. Open this door!"

Saved by the bell.

Or rather, by the demons.

It's Kalissa.

18

FRANKIE

"*A*dar Raksa Greysill." Kalissa dips her head at Rook in acknowledgment as she enters, followed by three demons.

"Wait... Raksa?" I whisper, shock snapping me out of my crying fit, and I twist around in Tir's arms. "Rook isn't Rook's true name?"

"Didn't sound very demonic, truth be told," Tir says and pulls me onto his lap, my head resting on a muscular pec. Through the soft fabric of his T-shirt, I can hear the steady thrum of his heart and it steadies me. "My bet is that at some point, he wanted to travel incognito, and the nickname stuck."

"A famous Hellhound," I breathe.

"Does that turn you on?"

I choke on laughter, wiping the last of the tears off my cheeks. "Why would you say that?"

"Just wondering."

"All of you turn me on," I admit, and it's his turn to chuckle.

"I seem to be interrupting." Kalissa runs her eyes over my naked body appreciatively. "Hello, my pretty. Feisty girls do give me a thrill."

I lift an arm to cover up my breasts a little, heat spreading over my face. I'm not into girls myself, though Kalissa is sexy, I have to admit. "You're not interrupting anything."

Tir's cock stirs against me, his pants the only barrier between us, reminding me of what we did and that Little Tir is still happy to be pressed to me.

"Look how she blushes." Kalissa gives a throaty laugh. "Oh Lucifer, I need to get my mind out of the gutter."

The boys say nothing, standing by the bed, all folded muscular arms, raised eyebrows, and bad attitude.

"She's ours," Kass says after a beat. "If you were having any naughty thoughts."

And I should be protesting I can make my own choices and speak my mind, but God, I like the possessiveness in his voice and his words.

See the point about the scary desire to relinquish control to them.

To let them take care of me.

Shit.

"I see how it is," Kalissa says, smirking. "Laying claim on her, are you?"

Are they?

"I'd do the same to this pretty weapon," she goes on, "if she'd let me, but I'll settle for a compromise."

My heart lurches in my chest. Here comes reality, folding back in. *A pretty weapon...*

"State your request," Rook says. "And then go."

She grins, steps closer to him, and lifts a hand to his face. I want to grab her and shake her for trying to touch him.

But he just takes a step back. "Keep your hands off me," he says, voice cold.

It makes me turn away to hide a smile.

Looks like harsh reality and the heart are two different dimensions that never touch. How can I be jealous on the heels of her statement, the implication that the boys are claiming me for my use, not for myself?

And yet there you have it.

I'm insane.

Certifiable.

Curled against Tir's warmth, settled against his powerful body, the other four men looming over us, I realize I wouldn't want to be anywhere else.

"I'm here to ask for a collaboration," Kalissa says, moving away from Rook to stand right in front of me. "Many people here at the College are trying to kill you, like they did just now."

"Did you have anything to do with this last ambush?" Asa demands.

"No, I swear it." She lifts both hands. The three demons accompanying her linger by the door, casting us dark looks. "I only came to parlay."

"Then parlay."

"I want to help protect Francesca. The demonic council will reward me if I prove I looked after their interests. I talked with Greyson and the shifters are of the same mind."

"Don't act like you and Greyson know what the Houses," Rook growls. "I wouldn't trust her, Frankie."

"Oh, no, of course not." Kalissa winks at me. "You'd rather trust a notorious psycho killer instead, would you? A man with a history of violence as long as the shadow he's cast on the conflict between Heaven and Hell. A man without a conscience, who ended up falling out of grace and is about to sell you to the highest bidder so he can carve a cozy little life for himself here on earth."

Dammit, I hate when others speak my worst fears out loud.

Rook's face is carved out of granite. Flawless. Uncharacteristically expressionless and pale. Gorgeous and forbidding. The only indication of any emotion is a vein beating at his jaw.

"So you want to protect me," I say in the silence that has descended after the last echo of her words has faded. "To please the House of Fire. And so do the shifters."

"Yes, that's the gist of it."

I nod. Sit up straighter, fully aware that my chair of office is Tir's lap. But first things first. "Give me back my pendant," I say. "And give Tir his earrings back, too."

"Are you serious?" Kalissa mutters. "We're talking life and death, and all you care about are trinkets?"

"Call it a token of trust. *My* trust." I gaze at her pretty face, the dark eyes, and lush lips, and wonder if, like Rook, she's using magic to make herself prettier or if demons just tend to be that pretty.

Seems like a contradiction of sorts.

But whether they are descended from ancient gods or fallen angels, they do have a claim to extra-good genes, don't they? All supernaturals tend to display that unnaturally perfect beauty.

Kalissa's smile looks fixed with Superglue. Her gaze also stays on me for unnervingly long minutes and I look right back, refusing to show her any weakness, any fear. She knows enough to guess most of it anyway.

Finally, she turns to her followers and snaps her fingers. "I kind of thought you'd ask for these items," she says as one of them, a tall and skinny guy with spiky dark hair hands her a small box. "Cute symbol on your pendant, by the way. That of your knitting club?"

"Don't knock knitting till you try it," I say, though I tried it and suck at it. I reach out with the hand not currently hiding my nipples. "Give it to me."

With a small roll of her dark eyes, she opens the box and takes out my pendant. She clutches the chain tightly in her fist for a long moment, as if reluctant to let go, then lets it drop in my outstretched palm.

It hits my skin, cool and heavy. Heavier than I remembered. I lift it in my fingers, turning it around, making sure it's the one.

"And his earrings," I demand.

"Whatever you say."

"I don't want them," Tir breathes.

I twist about to look at him. "Tir..."

"Most important jewelry to a Fae," Kalissa says.

"Not to me," Tir says. "Keep them, demoness, as a token of my mistrust for you."

"As you wish." Her eyes flash. She snaps the box shut, gives it back to the skinny demon by her side. "I hope you're satisfied, Francesca."

"I am." I'm not sure how wise it is to antagonize her, but against my side, Tir's heart is now beating way too fast. Something else is going on inside his head.

"Good. Then as a measure of our mutual trust and understanding, I will have two of my people outside your door, and they will follow you from a distance when you go out."

"The fuck," Kass snaps. "That's not trust, that's mistrust. You can't just—"

"Fine," I say. "Your terms are accepted. And in return..." I glance around at these men who stole my heart and don't even know it. "You'll protect these emissaries, too. No harm is to come to them."

I see them start and turn incredulous gazes at me. What, they think they are the only ones who can be protective?

"You're setting me a near-impossible task." Kalissa frowns. "Keeping you safe—alive—is already hard work, but..."

"But what?"

"If their handlers want them dead, there's hardly anything I can do. The sigils on their bodies can be activated from outside the College, outside the dome. Not to mention, I'd be dividing my attention on too many fronts, which could put your safety in jeopardy."

"No," Asa says, "not acceptable."

"Her safety is above all," Kass says. "Not ours."

"It's a bad idea," Ryu argues, "you shouldn't—"

"Do it," I say, returning my gaze to Kalissa, hardening my expression. "These are my terms."

I dare any of them to disagree again. Their eyes are wide, fixed on me, hands loose at their sides. Have they really never had anyone fight for them before?

Well, that's changing now.

I'm too far gone in this game of hearts. Might as well go all the way before the end finds me.

———

The moment the door closes behind Kalissa and her guys, I twist around to face Tir. "Your coming-of-age earrings. What was that about?"

He shakes his head. "It doesn't matter."

"The Hell it doesn't." Rook braces a hand on the upper bunk and leans over us. "They're fakes, aren't they?"

"Fakes?" I frown at Tir whose cheekbones have turned a dusky pink and who won't meet my gaze. "But why?"

"Coming of age earrings are normally bestowed on a Fae by their family." Ryu kicks at the metal foot of the bed. "But yours didn't bestow anything on you, did they, Tir?"

I'm frowning hard now. "But..."

"I was sold before I came of age," Tir finally says, teeth gritting. "That's all."

"But you wanted the world to think that you went through the ceremony," Ryu says, "that... what, fairy boy? What were you trying to prove?"

"That I was going back," Tir snaps, untangling himself from me and getting up. "That I'd leave the Wild Hunt someday and go home."

Dammit, I think I might start crying again.

"Maybe you still can," I whisper.

"There is no way back," he hisses. "They wouldn't want me back. They never sought me out. Fuck, I was a child when I was sold and deep inside I guess I'd always hoped... I'd hoped they were broken up about giving me up, that they'd do anything to have me return, but I never found a message."

"A message? Where?"

"At the haunted crossroads where the Wild Hunt stops. There are messages left sometimes, or small gifts for the Dogs, or the Hunters. Sometimes they are requests for help with revenge, and sometimes... they're notes from those you left behind. I looked... for a long time, hoping... Always fucking hoping."

"Tir..." I want to find his family and yell at them, hurt them like they've hurt him. "Oh no..."

He comes back to me, grabs me in his arms again, and I wrap myself around him. "I've clung to the past for too long, to what could have been. I've never had what I have now." His eyes are clear, letting what looks like raw truth shine through. "With you."

19

RYU

*T*he scent of sex is heavy on the air. The room is stuffy, and I can smell her cream and his cum, sweetness and musk rolled together. It should offend my sensitive olfactory sense.

But it excites me instead.

I gaze at Tir's bowed head, the glittering hope in his eyes, I gaze at Rook with his long hair loose about his broad shoulders, Kass with his strong body propped against the bunk bed, Asa shoving golden curls out of his squared-jawed face, definitely the most muscular cherub I've ever met...

... And my gaze inexorably returns to Frankie, because no matter how this newfound attraction to the guys affects me, she's been my drug from the moment I met her.

She's curled up against Tir once more, naked, splendidly curvy and sexy, giving off vibes of sadness but also acceptance.

Of Tir?

Us?

Herself?

Acceptance. Tir's story certainly is food for thought. If he can let go of the past... maybe so can I. Maybe I can find a reason to stay in this world.

Maybe I already have.

Finding a job in today's world feels difficult. I studied the present so I could fit in, but I don't. I'm a man from the past, frozen in time. A time traveler of sorts. A relic.

But if I got to be with her... with them...

And how the fuck do you picture that happening? a voice in my head snarls. *Or do we believe in miracles now? What's next, coming back from the dead?*

...oh, wait—

The renewed banging on the door startles me so fucking bad I almost shift fully. As it is, I feel my claws burst out and my tail swish as I spin around. My ears flick.

"What the Hell," I breathe. "Who the fuck is it now?"

Another bang. "Open the door. It's Greyson."

Greyson, the shifter leader.

"Fuck him," I say.

"Come in," Frankie says at the same time.

Dammit.

The door swings open and the wolves step inside, invading what I'm quickly coming to think of as our sanctuary. My hackles are up for too many reasons.

"Do you mind, pal?" Rook drawls. "We were having a moment here. A heart to heart."

"She said to come on in," Greyson says and frowns—at me. Of course.

I glare back and resist the urge to spit at him.

Foxes and wolves. Never getting along. Especially with an asshole like him. Especially with my bloody history with wolves.

With the way they killed my fox family.

He's my eternal enemy, independent of demonblood. This

is an elemental hatred that he made worse by his fucked-up personality. Let's face it, I'd have hated him no matter what.

"Did you need something?" I ask, my voice dropping to a low growl. "Like Rook said, we were having a moment."

"You can have your moment later," he snaps. "I'm not playing games, fox. I'm here because Kalissa said you'd be interested in an alliance."

The four werewolves standing behind him—*four, motherfucker? Just how insecure are you?*—growl. He chose his biggest, meanest gangsters to flank him, which just shows what kind of person the asshole is.

"You bullied us. Bullied her," I accuse, jabbing a clawed finger at him, my words distorted because my teeth are longer now, my canines sharp. "Not to mention quite a few of your buddies attacked us and tried to kill us. Kill her. Now you want us to be buddies?"

"Ryu... Let him say his piece. Please?" Frankie sounds... resigned? Disappointed?

And you think she'd want to be with you? that same smug voice in my head says. *That any of them would?*

But before I do or say anything really fucking stupid, a heavy arm settles over my shoulders.

A scent of blood and rust, and Kass drawls in my ear, "We got your back, *amico*." And then out loud he says, "Yeah, we're not big fans of you, Greyson, as you may have guessed. So state your request and fuck right off."

His warm breath ruffles my hair and warms my neck, sending shivers through me. He's tall and strong and solid, and feels good pressed to my side.

So now I'm flustered on top of everything, of all the emotions knocking around inside me, the anger and hatred and the lingering confusion and the goddamn longing for a life I can't ever have.

Just great.

Worse, I find myself leaning into Kass, accepting the strength he's offering.

Acceptance, that word again, *acceptance...*

Drawing a deep breath, I release it and force my hold on my shift to relax. My claws slowly retract, though I can still feel my tail twitching against the back of my thighs.

Frankie thinks it's important to play nice with these fuckers, and she's most probably right. We can protect her on our own but the more people she has on her side, the better.

I don't trust Greyson further than I can throw him—though I bet I can throw him quite far with all the rage he wakes up in me—but it looks like protecting Frankie is in his interest right now. I can trust him to do what's in his interest, the selfish dick.

"We're going to add our people to Kalissa's," Greyson says. "Keep an eye out for any attackers."

"What about your people who joined ranks with the assassins?" Frankie asks, her voice cool. She is sitting there like a queen, not ashamed of her naked body.

And why should she? She's a sex goddess.

But Greyson, who's standing in front of Frankie, legs spread, hands in his pant pockets, is staring at her unabashedly.

The fucker is ogling her.

"Take your fucking eyes off her," Tir rumbles before I open my mouth or throw a punch.

"She's buck naked," Greyson says with a grin I need to wipe off his ugly mug.

"And you're a dead man if you don't take her fucking eyes off her." I step toward him. "You said your piece. Now take a hike."

"Not before Frankie here tells me if she agrees with the alliance."

"Like I told Kalissa..." Frankie shrugs. "As long as you protect all six of us, not just me, then I'm in."

That... still hasn't sunk in. That she'd ask that. Demand it.

Set it as her only term, her prerequisite, her *sine-qua-non* condition.

As if we matter. As if we count for anything. Us, her kidnappers, her heartless evildoers. As if we mean *something* to her.

"Deal." Greyson smirks, still looking at her, damn him. "We'll protect your toyboys too. This is a high-stakes game and we won't lose."

Fucker.

Turning on his heel to go, he halts. "By the way, who are the guys you have guarding the door?"

"None of your business," I grind out. "Just fuck off."

With a shrug, he goes, and by then everyone's eyes are on me.

"What was that about?" Rook asks. "What guys? Did Kalissa already send her demons as she promised?" He glares. "Ryu, what did you do?"

"It's just a small illusion," I say. "Figured seeing two burly guys guarding the door might put some attackers off, at least, until Kalissa posts her demons."

Kass claps my back with a snort. "That's good thinking!" Then he frowns. "Wait... just wait. You can do that? Maintain a perfect illusion without even being there? How do I know when I talk to you that you're not an illusion?"

"You can touch me. If I'm solid, then it's no illusion."

"That's... that's good." His frown eases and he actually winks. "I don't mind touching you more often. Now I have an excuse."

Leaving me kind of breathless and torn between laughing and kissing him.

Damn these guys.

Why do they have to be so hard to resist?

Why does the dream of a future, a dream of going on instead of giving up, seem less distant when we touch?

―――――

"So alliances have been forged," Rook mutters, sitting heavily on the bed next to Tir and Frankie. "A good day's work. We should celebrate with some booze. Champagne and strawberries, and maybe some whipped cream to—"

"What we should do," I say, "is take a look at this pendant Frankie just got back. Let me see it, girl."

Truth is, I need a distraction from my ever-circling thoughts, or I wouldn't almost snatch it out of her hands. She looks a little startled, and I try not to stare at her breasts but they're so pretty and *oh fuck...* now I'm hard.

"I should get dressed," she says, realizing my conundrum, and there's a chorus of *"Oh no, fuck no, why?"* from all of us.

Yeah, including me.

"We need to sit down and think," Kass says as I perch on the desk with the pendant in my hand. "Throwing some clothes on could help. Honestly, I can't fucking think when I'm looking at you, girl."

"Or we could fuck, instead," Rook says. "Just a thought. I hear it helps with thinking."

Kass cuffs him on the back of the head. "Rook."

Frankie grabs the blanket and hauls it over herself a little too quickly. "Um, not right now?" she squeaks, her face going a lovely shade of red. "I mean, we just..."

"Yeah, you and Tir just fucked. We surmised." Rook grins and runs a finger down Frankie's arm. "You both need some time to recover. I respect that. Though there are spells to get your energy back up instantly, or I could just striptease for you if that—"

"We have to study the pendant." She scrambles out of Tir's lap and off the bed, almost falling to the floor in the process, and wraps the blanket around herself.

Rook blinks. "I fucking swear, I've never had so many

people run away from my charms in my long life. Have I developed warts on my nose or something?"

"No, Rook." She bites her lower lip in a terribly distracting way. "You're gorgeous. You all are. But I'm trying to sort through my feelings right now... and I need a break."

Rook's dark brows draw together. "But sex—"

"More sex is not the answer," she says firmly.

"But are you sure? You never know. We could try—"

"No."

He pouts and I want to laugh, but oh boy, even pouting looks good on his handsome face. From certain angles, it has an androgynous quality that turns him from handsome to pretty, and right now he's downright cute.

The renowned Hellhound, famous butcher of the battle of Adesh... cute.

Shaking my head, and fighting a grin, I focus on the pendant. The symbol, as Frankie had said, is a flower inside the circle formed by a snake biting its tail.

I turn the small pendant this way and that. It glints in the light, made of silver, perhaps, or platinum. It's heavy and doesn't feel like iron. Its light sting on my palm tips the balance toward silver. I may not be a werewolf, but all shifters are affected by silver to a smaller or greater extent.

No clues here so far.

"Wait, what's this?" A small indentation on the side of the coin-like pendant against my fingertips. I dig a little into it. "Can you open this?"

"Open it?" She frowns.

"I had a locket," I tell her. "With the photos of my family. What if it's a locket, too?"

"It's too small," she argues, doubt lacing her voice. "Too thin."

"Photos are thin," I say, pressing my nail into the indentation. "Damn..."

"Let me see," she says and after a moment, I hand it back to her, taking the opportunity to draw her between my legs.

She comes willingly, leaning back against me, and I draw in the sweet scent of her hair and skin. I slip an arm around her, looking over her shoulder as she examines the rim of the pendant, running a finger over it, thinking I've never felt so at ease in my skin as I have here, with her and the guys.

"It's not possible," she's murmuring. "I never noticed anything, and I've worn it all these years. If there was a way to... oh!"

It clicks open.

"How didn't I see this before?" she whispers.

It feels like a symbolic question, a ponderous universal question mark on everything and anything that has always been there and we never noticed.

Like how my heart is pounding with excitement in my chest, how my dick aches sweetly, so hard in my pants. How her skin feels like satin under my fingers. How the presence of the men around me feels like an embrace.

Right now, I can't recall why I wanted to end this life.

I've never felt more alive.

The pendant clicks open and inside... no photos. That's my first thought, startling me enough to make me conscious of the fact I'd been expecting to see my family's faces. And yet the pain of losing my locket isn't as sharp as it was a few days ago.

Focus, I tell myself.

Inside, there's an engraving. Engraved letters, a few lines of text. An alphabet I'm not familiar with.

"What is this?" Frankie whispers. "I can't read it."

"Let me see," Rook says, getting up from the bed and sauntering over. He props an elbow on my shoulder, leaning casually against me like Kass had done before, and frowns over Frankie at the small locket. "Nah, not a demonic script."

"You know all demonic scripts? I hear there are hundreds of them."

"I've studied them," Rook says. "Don't look so shocked. I wasn't always a soldier."

I stare at him. He's still a mystery. All of us have shared our life stories except for him—well, and Asa, but Asa is a whole another kettle of fish. Angelfish. Whatever.

Speaking of whom...

"Asa, come here." I don't beckon because I have one arm around Frankie's middle and Rook is leaning on the other and I don't want to move. I'm... comfortable. Warm. Surrounded by them and I like it. Way too much. "Take a look at this text. Is it some angelic alphabet?"

He stalks over to us, blue gaze intent—he's always so intent in everything he says or does, so focused and serious, it's actually frigging hot.

Good Lord and Inari Lady of the Fields... I've got it bad, don't I?

He stands in front of us and takes Frankie's hand, lifting it so he can look at the pendant lying on her palm. Kass and Tir also come over, standing by his sides, to see.

"So... is it?" I ask after a small eternity, unable to hold back my impatience any longer. "Is it angelic?"

"There is no angelic script," Asa says.

"Come again? You don't send messages? Don't write down notes?"

"Heaven has other ways of recording. This is cuneiform."

"Cune-what?"

"Cuneiform is the oldest human alphabet, used to write down ancient languages such as Sumerian, Akkadian, Hittite and Aramaic."

"And...?" I give in to the urge and wave a hand in a gesture for him to go on, slightly dislodging Rook who's still leaning on me. "Why is it important?"

"It's not. But it is sometimes used by angels when they absolutely need to write something down."

"Ah."

"Also, by demons." He glances at Rook. "I wonder why you didn't recognize it."

"Who says I didn't? But it's not a demonic script, like I said, and in any case, script is one thing, language another. The language it transcribes isn't demonic and it's not one of the two angelic tongues I'm familiar with. Can you read it?"

I turn my face to stare at Rook some more. "Just how many languages do you speak?"

"Many. I know, right?" He grins cheekily at me. "I'm more than just a pretty face."

"Way more." I can't help but laugh. And when he leans in and brushes his mouth over my jaw, I shiver pleasantly.

"Why, thank you, gorgeous. Let's revisit this conversation, preferably with fewer clothes on, at another time. Asa, spit it out, my man. Do you know what the text is saying or not? I'm starving."

"Again?" I gape at him.

"What do you mean, *again*? It's been ages since we last ate. My stomach has no recollection of any nourishment."

"Like a cat," Asa mutters. And then he frowns as if something doesn't compute. "A cat that likes to take over my dog's bed..."

"*Your* dog's bed? Since when do you have a dog?"

"I... don't." Asa blinks, then frowns. "I..."

"Asa." Rook pulls away from me and I almost reach for him, to draw him back against me. "Forget about animals and talk about the fucking text!"

Asa blinks again. Then he says, "I shall separate your soul from your body and carry it away to a garden where it can live in peace."

"That sounds ominous," I say. "Why are you threatening us? ...Wait, *that's* what the text in the pendant says?"

"Yes."

Ominous indeed. And that's me saying it, a person who had actually fucking wished for death.

20

FRANKIE

I trace my fingertip over the engraved letters, still annoyed at myself for having missed the pendant's little secret all these years. I never thought to look beyond its surface, the symbol on it, and the fact that it came from my mother.

Truth be told, I had only started wearing it since the last incident, after Granddad started moving us around every two days, and I was afraid to lose it.

I don't even know why I had held onto it so hard. Granddad hadn't seemed to think it mattered much. He'd looked at it at some point, said *right, it used to belong to your mother,* and that was that.

Never had I ever seriously thought it had belonged to my father. Did he give it to her? Or did she rip it off his neck as he fucked her?

I feel sick thinking about how I was made. There wasn't any love involved, I'm sure. Or luck. My mother had a plan, it seems.

To come back somehow.

And for that, she made *me.* Her weapon. Her unsuspecting

tool. What did she expect from me, to take over the world? To rule, with her by my side? To, I don't know, just kill everyone opposing me and craft for myself a throne from their ashes?

Or salt piles. A throne of salt crystal, haunted by ghosts.

I shudder.

Ryu's arm tightens around me, pulling me back against his chest. Rook places a big hand on my shoulder, Kass tucks a strand of hair behind my ear. Meanwhile, Tir trails his fingers down my arm and Asa is still cupping my hand in his. They're here, with me, touching me, and I take comfort in their strength, their presence, even if I can't see how they can help me in this fucking mess I'm in.

I've made up my mind not to fight my feelings for them— not that I have a choice, not that I ever stood a chance—but that doesn't mean I'm not aware of the conundrum.

Their missions.

My mother's evil plan.

My terrible power.

"So..." I swallow hard, determined not to cry again. "What is he? What is my father, based on this?"

"Still sounds like a demon to me," Rook says.

"A killer," Ryu says. "Is the mention of a garden tongue-in-cheek?"

"Sounds like something a Fae might say, all twisted up in riddles," Tir mutters. "Like something *I* might say."

"No shit," Rook snickers.

"Or something *I* might say," Kass says gravely.

Damn.

Silence spreads. Then Asa pulls back. "It's none of the four races. I thought I knew that symbol from somewhere. I never expected to see the sigil of one of the High Princes on this pendant."

"High Princes?" Tir blinks. "Wait, are we talking about angels again?"

"Archangels." Asa's not looking at me. His gaze is fixed on the pendant in my palm, dark and undecipherable.

"What, you mean like Gabriel and Michael and all those dudes?" Tir scrunches up his nose. "Do they even have dicks? How do they make babies if—?"

"We were all made in the same image," Kass says, "though seraphs and cherubs and thrones do seem to favor a different shape—"

"See why I don't think Asa is a seraph," Rook says. "He's too much of a dick to be a sword of fire. Then again, swords... Hm..."

"The dicks of the angels," Ryu mutters. "Sounds like a good name for a TV show."

"Guys..." My heart is thumping so hard my ribs ache. "It's not funny."

"No," Kass says, "it's not. So what's the verdict?"

"Asa..." I whisper. "You know who it is, don't you?"

His gaze finally snaps to mine. Silver flames seem to flicker in the dark cores of his eyes. "It's Azrael."

———

Azrael.

I find myself pacing about the room, stumbling over the two mattresses laid out on the floor where Rook and Ryu sleep, thumping my hip against the desk and the chair set before it, knocking into the bunk beds.

"Frankie," Asa says. "Stop."

All of them have begged me to stop, more than once. It's just...

Azrael?

Fucking Azrael?

"Angel of death," Asa says and I realize that he's talking with

Tir, his back to the wall, arms folded over his broad chest. "The psychopomp. Helping souls cross over."

"I thought Samael had that job."

"You're not up to date. Azrael took over a long time ago."

"Angelic politics isn't really my thing," Tir says, "though many in the Wild Hunt like to discuss it around the campfires at night. Then again, the Hunters will discuss just about anything. We love us some good gossip. Hunting is tedious business at the best of times, gory at the worst."

"Foolish Fae," Asa mutters.

"Complicated cherubs," Tir retorts.

They're kind of... grinning at one another? But I can't decide what their exchange means right now, because I'm still stuck on... *Azrael*.

Ugh.

"That... *thing* that is my father is not an angel," I mutter, "that's a demon. Rook was right."

"The boundaries between good and evil are thin," Rook says, and I glance at him in surprise. "The line between what we perceive as good or bad isn't the same for everyone. And death is a natural thing."

"He kills people!"

"No, he only collects souls," Asa says. "Azrael doesn't cause their death. He only taps the person on the shoulder and accompanies their soul to another sphere. He's called the King of Skulls but he's not the Grim Reaper himself. He's not *death* himself. He aids the transport of souls and is attracted to pain and mourning."

"Wait, he gathers all souls? All over the world?"

"No, of course he doesn't do that for every soul. Only selected souls."

"Is that supposed to make me feel better?"

"Why do you feel bad about it in the first place?"

"He's... a monster."

"All angels are," Rook says cheerfully. "Come to think of it, all of us are. We're not human. We're not normal."

"How can you be smiling?" I demand. "My mother seduced and... and reproduced with an archangel of death to have a child for... I don't know what. Leverage against Heaven? Or... or to kill people like it's nothing. Oh my God, that's why I kill people with my scream. Daddy dear's gift to me is the gift of death."

They all fall quiet. Asa doesn't insist that Azrael isn't death. Because that doesn't matter. What you pass on to your children doesn't have to be what you are, except in part. They gaze at me, their faces grim.

"Pillars of salt," Ryu says quietly. "Asa called it."

"*Fleur de sel,*" Rook muses, but he doesn't even smile.

I'm not smiling either. "Tell me about my father."

Asa shrugs. "He's an archangel. Powerful. A conduit for Heaven's energy and decisions. Impartial himself, following orders, guiding souls." Asa is frowning so hard his brow is deeply lined. "He likes cats."

"Wait... are you serious? Asa—"

"I don't know why I said that. It's from a tale someone told me..." He's frowning even harder, if that's possible.

"Don't trust Asa's memories," Kass says. "It's obvious there's something off inside his head."

Asa opens his mouth, closes it again. "Maybe the vampire is right."

"*Stronzo,*" Kass says, which I'm pretty sure is a swear word, but he says it fondly. "We'll get to the bottom of who *you* are, sooner or later."

"That's what I'm afraid of," Asa whispers. He glances at me. "On another note, if you are an archangel's daughter, then bringing back someone from the dead might not be so far-fetched after all."

Oh, great. I can't... I can't yet wrap my head around these new revelations and their ripple effect on my life, as it is. But now it makes sense why I'm so dangerous, why everyone wants a piece of me, why these guys were sent to fetch me for their individual authorities.

And understanding it isn't helping me.

"Frankie..." Asa comes to me and puts his arms around me. "Hey..."

I realize I'm shaking. Full-body tremors.

I also realize the guys, my Wonderboys are now around me, all five of them, joining the hug that puts me in their middle, their arms weaving together to form a wall.

To protect me—from the world. From my origins. From myself.

Nothing and nobody can protect you, I think. *This isn't some spell you can break. Some curse you can lift. This is just who you are.*

And still, I close my eyes and let them hold me up, wishing we could stay that way.

21

FRANKIE

"*A*re all angels men, then?" Kass asks a long while later. We're piled up on the mattresses on the floor, all six of us. "Dick jokes aside."

And it's not sexual, this piling up together, or not overly so. I've thrown on panties and stole an overlarge T-shirt from Asa, and I'm just snug and comfortable, pressed in their middle, their warm, solid, big bodies cushioning me from all sides.

"I love dick jokes." Rook reaches over Tir who's currently lying on his side beside me, one arm draped over me, to stroke my cheek. "And dicks. But also pussies, in case it wasn't clear."

"It was clear, don't worry." I roll my eyes a little, my mouth twitching.

"No," Asa says. He's lying at my other side, an arm around Kass' shoulders, Ryu sprawled over them. "Angels... they are sexless. Most of the time."

"Do they choose to become sexy then?" Ryu sticks out his tongue, lifting his head to shoot me a heavy-lidded look. "And sex other people up?"

"I... don't know," Asa mutters. His other arm is around me, warm and solid. "I don't know who decides what they do."

"The plot thickens," Rook drawls, "just like my cock."

"Your cock?" I ask.

"Yeah, that part of my anatomy you're currently lying on? The hard, long, thick rod?"

"You mean your leg?" I wink at him.

"I mean the part that is about to detonate like a nuclear head if you keep writhing on top of me."

"I'm not writhing."

"No, but you will be if I put Rooky inside of you."

"Rooky?" I gape. "Your dick has a name?"

"That's its pet name. Its real name is Raksa Warhead."

"Dear God." I'm laughing again.

"I'm supposed to protect her from everyone, including you," Ryu says, "and probably from Warhead, too. There goes my reward."

"I hope the rewards you asked for weren't that important," Asa says.

We all turn to stare at him. Is he serious?

"You're a bit of an asshole, you know that?" Ryu says.

"I am being serious."

Ryu rolls his eyes. "Well, there's the answer to my question."

"You think we'd embark on such missions if the rewards weren't important?" Rook mutters.

"Rook has a point," I say. "I mean, we know you want to return to Heaven, Asa. It's important to you."

"Yeah, but Heaven is the one who will have you, Frankie," Asa says. "Nobody can stand in its way. So I hope the rewards weren't that important, because you will never receive them."

Twisted sort of angelic logic but... logic nevertheless.

"Excuse me," Rook says. "The fact that there are agreements between Heaven and Hell tells me otherwise. The Houses cannot be underestimated."

"Heaven just wants peace," Asa says.

"Bullshit. Heaven wants power."

Asa sighs. "Yes. It does."

"And you're not a seraph," Rook goes on. "You remember things. As if you've had a human body."

"I do have memories of Heaven, too."

"Do you remember, really?"

"It's hazy."

"You don't know what you are," Rook barks. "And you don't know what you want. You're no different from the rest of us, Cherub."

"I'm not a cherub and—"

"Let's see what we all wanted from this fucked-up mission, then," Rook says grimly.

"Do we have to talk about this?" Ryu mutters.

"Don't look at me," Kass frowns. "You all know my reward was to be Brody. Let him rot."

"My reward was returning to my family," Tir says. "Still not sure how I feel about that."

"Asa's reward was becoming a seraph again," Rook says, "or... becoming a seraph in the first place."

Asa is glaring at the far wall.

"And mine," Rook continues, "was to live a life on the human plane. A good life. Strike off my record, give me some cash, a place to stay. A second chance." He frowns. "Or a first chance. Whatever. A chance to see what it's like to not always fight. Shallow, I know."

"No, Rook." I shake my head. "Nobody is saying that."

"Look, I've been fighting since I can remember. A child soldier. Yeah, demons are born, too. Everyone has to start from somewhere. Sent to fight wars on Earth, missions in Hell, forays into the lower planes of Heaven. Always maiming, slashing, crushing, killing, except for days camping out inside the vast libraries of the Second Heaven, doing crash courses in dead languages, warfare, and torture resistance. So shut your mouth."

"Hey," Tir mutters, "I didn't say anything. Though you never said you were a genius. Shit, man."

That was Rook's education? Crash courses in how to decipher enemy scripts and withstand torture without breaking?

Holy shit.

Rook continues as if he hasn't heard. Maybe he's talking to himself. "You're a demon, you're supposed to enjoy this. It doesn't matter if you're a succubus, a *raur*, or a djin. If you're new or ancient. If your magic is related to violence or just mischief. All of us, lumped in one basket. Your heart is black, you're a demonspawn, you're evil."

"My uncle Emrys said something of the sort," I whisper.

That gets Rook's attention. "He did?"

I shrug. "Quite a few times. Tends to come up in his tales of his youth. He also hated inflicting pain. Rook..." I have to half-climb over Tir to cup his face. "I'm sorry."

His deep voice drops lower. "What for, Darling? My past isn't your fault."

"And yet I *am* sorry, and I wish I could have been there to help. Or at least give you a hug."

"I'll have that hug now, how about that?" He opens his arms, and kicks at Tir to make way. "Come to daddy."

I giggle. "*Rook.*"

"Come to me, Sweetheart. Save my soul."

"I can't do that," I whisper even as I roll over Tir who groans, and fall into Rook's arms, on top of his muscular body. He wraps me up in heat and peppery spice. "I can't save anyone."

"You don't realize you're a balm to a man's soul," he breathes, burying his face in my hair, his arms locking around me so tightly I can barely breathe. "To *my* soul, or what's left of it, just some shriveled black scraps."

"Don't say that." I breathe him in. "I'm sorry you were hurt.

Sorry that all of you suffered. I wish I could take that past away."

"Being around you makes it easier," he says. "You're our angel. Sorry, Asa, but you're not soft enough to qualify."

Asa gives a rumble of a laugh.

"I'm Azrael's daughter," I whisper, pulling back a little to study Rook's handsome face. "Not some cuddly cupid."

"And yet cuddling is happening."

"Azrael's and the White Queen Witch's daughter," Tir says. "A force to reckon with."

"Only it will be the death of me," I breathe.

"Speaking of death..." Rook frowns. "That was our fox's wish. His reward for this mission. So tell us, Ryu... Has something changed for you?"

Oh, Ryu...

"It's true. I had... wanted to die," Ryu says, his gaze going distant. "That was going to be my reward."

"Going to be?"

"I... might have changed my mind. It doesn't matter anyway."

I swallow hard. "How can you say that?"

"It doesn't matter because I don't want to succeed anymore." He scrambles over Asa who grunts and Tir who complains that everyone is climbing over him, and rolls beside me, gathering me against him. We're crushing Rook but he's grinning so he can't be in much pain. "I don't want to die, Frankie. Not anymore."

"I'm glad," I whisper and hide my face in his chest not to let him see me cry again.

————

Though I don't ever want to get up from the nest made from my guys' warm bodies, the banging on the door can't be ignored anymore after a while.

"Who the fuck is it?" Rook grumbles.

"Open this door before we break it down!" a male voice booms.

"I thought we were done with the stupid talk about alliances," Tir says around a yawn, stretching like a cat beside me, and my gaze follows the way his shirt rides up his chest, baring his hard stomach. I swallow hard, because last night may have been all about cuddling and non-sexual sleep, but this morning I honestly wouldn't mind climbing them like trees.

All of them, stirring and stretching around me, half-naked, muscular bodies and perfect, gorgeous faces, dragging my mind through the gutter. What's a girl to do?

If only the annoying banging would go away, I'd bang them instead.

I'm quietly giggling to myself, feeling quite unsteady and a little crazed, when Asa gets on his feet in one fluid jump and goes to open the door.

"What's so funny?" Ryu asks, smiling at me.

"Just... banging," I manage, dissolving into more giggles.

"Banging," he repeats. A crease forms between his brows. "That's funny?"

"It's..." I wave a hand, helplessly. I mean, he's sitting there, bare-chested, hard pecs and a six-pack and those shoulders and arms are honestly works of art, and his red hair is all mussed up, his green eyes bright... and words fail me.

"You're very bangable," Tir tells him, fake-serious, and *oh God...* dying here.

"No, you can't come inside now," Asa says right then, and I turn to find him talking with two men standing right outside. "What do you want?"

"Are you seriously asking me this? I just said the dean sent us. You're skipping classes, not answering the dean's summons, and you have been accused of inciting the incident in the grand auditorium."

"The Hell?" Ryu jumps to his feet and joins Asa at the door. "We didn't incite anything. That wasn't us. We were attacked there."

"All the same, you need to say that to the dean, not me, and one doesn't just ignore the dean's summons. Not if you want to stay in the College."

"It's not like she can throw us out. There's a fucking magical dome over the College, if you didn't notice."

"Trust me, everyone knows about the dome that Heaven placed over us. Who knows who's the asshole who organized it so we can't get out of here and we're trapped like rats in a maze while assassins roam freely."

I wince a little. At least, they don't know it was Asa.

"The assassins aren't after your lily-white asses." Tir rolls out of bed—well, off the mattress on the floor—and joining them, throwing an arm over Ryu's shoulders. "So, kindly fuck off with your ridiculous little fears."

"The Hunter," the guy breathes. Looks inside where I'm still sitting on the mattress with Rook and Kass. "The vampire and the Hellhound. What's this, a pajama party? Or an orgy?"

"What it is, it's none-of-your-goddamn-business," Tir says pleasantly. "That's what it is."

"You'd better answer the dean's summons this time, Hunter."

"And you'd better run before I catch you," Tir bares his sharp teeth, "and show you how the Wild Hunt tears its prey apart. It's an art form. It can get quite messy. Abstract art, I guess you'd call it. Or even funerary art."

A curse, and then I hear steps moving away.

I hide a smile.

"That was a little over the top," Asa says. "*Tears its prey apart?*"

"Over the top?" Tir says. "You've obviously never seen a Wild Hunt from up close, have you? It's a bloodbath. It's a fucking gory massacre."

Gathering the overlong T-shirt around me, I'm slowly getting to my feet, trying to ignore Kass who is stroking my leg, because this dialogue happening in front of me is pinging all kinds of signals inside my head.

It's obvious that Tir isn't okay, that flippant attitude and choice of words isn't like him, he's reliving something horrible inside his memories and I need to go to him—

But the world darkens at the edges, and I can't find which way is up.

"Frankie!"

Hands grab at me, guiding me back down to the mattress. God, this is embarrassing.

"I'm okay." I don't shake them off just because they feel so good on me, but I rub at my eyes and wait for the darkness to recede.

"Are you sure?"

"Yeah, just a head rush."

"We need food," Rook says.

"You always need food," I mutter.

"You're lucky to have me around. Left to your own devices, you'd starve."

"Frankie... Since you brought me back," Tir says, staring at me, "you haven't been okay."

I shake my head. "Don't say that. I'm really good."

"First the infection and then what your cousin gave you," Rook mutters. "When are you going to tell us what she gave you? What was it that made you so sick?"

"It's..." The words *none of your business* stick in my throat. "It was nothing."

Hate sex turned into meaningless sex and then into something more. Or maybe it had been something more all along. I don't know. Thing is, like sex, my feelings for them are real.

If this is a trap, then it's closed its jaws on me already.

"Nothing?" Rook's easy smile falls. "You were sick for days. Puking you fucking guts out."

"Rook," Asa starts but it seems there's no stopping Rook once he's lost his cool.

"I thought you were going to die," he goes on, his voice rising. "We're locked in this College, courtesy of tall, blond and handsome here, unable to reach a hospital, and you were white as a ghost, no, whiter than, and I thought you were going to die in my arms, you…"

"Yeah? Afraid to lose your asset? To lose the cozy life promised to you if I croak? Is this what this is about?" Funny how anger returns so easily after all. I guess as long as fear rules me, anger will define me. "Don't worry, I'm okay, like I said."

"What the fuck did she give you? I'm not letting her back here ever again if you don't tell me."

"You don't get to order me around!" I shout.

"Frankie," Tir whispers.

"Was it poison?" Rook demands. "Did you want to die, like Ryu here?"

"Poison?" I can barely breathe, I'm so furious. "It was just a morning-after pill! Okay? Happy now?"

He blinks at me, midnight-blue eyes and long black lashes, and his face flickers, the ruined half flashing like a warning sign. "What?"

"A morning-after pill." I swallow hard, anger still heating me up like the wick of a candle, about to catch fire. "I've had unprotected sex. With all of you. I had to take the pill and devise some form of contraceptive."

I can't read his face. I mean, I can, he looks furious, but why? It's as if my anger transferred itself to him—but no, wait, he was angry from the moment I almost blacked out, his rapid-fire questions about the reason I got so sick and what my cousin gave me seeming to fuel his feelings.

Or reveal them, tearing down any pleasant, placid façade he had going on.

"Rook," I try again. "You asked, I answered, it's no big deal. I really am okay now, I'm—"

He grabs the desk and throws it against the closet. The crash has me flinching back, and I swear I feel the impact in my bones. Jarred, I fall against Kass who wraps an arm around me.

"Sh," he says. "It's all right."

"Rook." Tir takes a cautious step toward him, hands lifted. "Hey. Relax, man. Calm your tits, yeah? Everything's cool. What's the problem with—"

"Fuck your speech, trickster!" Rook is wreathed in shadows and flames. "Fuck all of this. Fuck promises, fuck hopes, fuck feelings, okay? It never works out. It's all shit."

I'm on my feet before I know it, black spots swimming in my vision, but screw that. "I need to get out."

"Frankie," Tir starts, "wait."

"Going to pee," I tell him, grabbing someone's sweats and pulling them on as I head to the door. "Leave me alone."

But he follows after me and I don't give a damn.

I need a minute to gather myself.

"*W*hat the fuck just happened?" Ryu frowns. He takes a step toward the door and glances at the ruined closet. Stops. "Think she'll be fine with Tir?"

I say nothing. I can't pretend to entirely understand these men and their intense, fiery emotions—but it feels as though I should be able to. As if it's all right out of reach. And sometimes I get moments when it all makes sense, when I know I've felt that, been through the gamut of all the emotions a person can feel.

My head is pounding in time to my heart, a dull ache in my temples and behind my eyes.

"Rook..." Ryu turns to the demon. "Man, you lost it for a moment there. What the fuck?"

I turn to look at the demon who is standing in the middle of the room, eyes glittering, mouth set in a flat line. His long hair is tangled around his face.

"You destroyed the desk and the closet," Kass grumbles. "Ruined all my clothes, and for what? Can't undo any of that."

Ryu plants himself in front of Rook. "Talk. Why?"

"You heard her," Rook mutters, pushing some dark hair out of his face. "She asked her cousin for a morning-after pill that made her sick."

"So?"

"I do get it," Kass says, "though you can't lose it like that, man. But yeah, morning after pill... the fuck."

"Right?" Rook mutters. "Are you as annoyed as I am?"

"Ah, I get it," Ryu says. "Right. That sucks."

I stare at them. "What am I missing? Morning after pill... What the fuck is that? I didn't cover it in my study of humans. Didn't seem relevant."

"It stops her from conceiving," Rook growls.

"Conceiving... as in babies?"

"Yeah!"

"Right. So why were you so mad?" I frown at the trio in front of me. "And why do the rest of you agree?"

"I couldn't really tell you why," Ryu says.

"I could," Rook says. "Because I fucking thought about it. The thought of making a baby with her should have me running for the hills, but instead, the thought made me... feel happy. And then the thought that she made herself sick to avoid having my baby made me so angry. Tell me I'm crazy. I'm insane. I know it."

The other two nod glumly.

"You're shitting me," I breathe.

Rook grunts. "I'm telling you the truth. Have you ever thought... of having a family? Children."

"Being with someone who actually likes you...and wants you," Kass says.

Ryu nods. "I had all that once. And I never thought I'd ever have them again, but she makes me hope for things... wish for things I shouldn't."

"I've never had a family," Rook says. "But fuck, I sure as Hell would like a chance to try. Try for a family, kids or not. Know what I mean? It's not... Look, I get it. This isn't the right time for any commitment. She did the right thing. And yet..."

"Yeah, that," Kass says.

"It's a caveman thing," Rook says.

"You sure acted like one," I mutter.

"We're fucked," Ryu says. "Fucked in the head. Going apeshit over her taking the pill when we have nothing with her, when we're only with her because we have to. This isn't going to work out."

"Which part?" I inquire politely, because they're right, this is crazy.

Kass laughs. "No part. Any part. It's all a fucking mess."

"Plus, she hates us," Ryu says.

"No," Rook objects, "she doesn't. Not anymore."

"Well, she should!" Kass grouses.

"That's not the point, and it's not even the worst part," Ryu says quietly.

I turn to him. "No?"

"No, the worst will come when we have to give her up, and then live with that knowledge. The knowledge that we gave up the best thing that ever happened to us. The best person we've ever met. The girl who cares for us."

The girl we care for in return, I think, frowning at them.

Feelings.

A white dog running through the sprinklers on the green lawn.

A cat winding around my legs.

Sunlight warming my skin.

A face I know.

Pain.

It always ends in pain, that's all I know. The memory of the Divine Throne and Heavenly Choirs is fading and I'm fully aware that, unless this situation is resolved fast and Heaven gets Frankie to do what it wills with her, I won't make it back home.

The only question now is... where is home?

And how can I just give Frankie up? Even if duty demands it. Even if it's to save the world.

———

Going to my knees to pray won't work here. My head is all over the place. I leave the guys talking in quiet voices and step out of the room.

"Going to check on Frankie?" Ryu asks and I don't contradict him.

I simply don't reply at all.

Outside, two muscular guys lean against the wall. They don't react as I go past them. Ryu's illusions, I realize. Not bad. They look solid.

Each one of these guys has such gifts. All I have are confusing memories and use of the divine Glory—but it's not mine, that power. I borrow it, use it like all angels.

Who am I?

What am I?

How long was I in Heaven?

How long until I get back?

Heaven feels like it's high up in the sky. Historically it was spoken of as being above the clouds and the stars. Hell was said to be under the ground, along with the fairy mounds where the Fae and maybe also the vampires and the shifters used to live. Inside tombs and under hills.

Places we couldn't reach or visit while alive.

Now that the supernatural has entered the human world, it's clear that things aren't quite that way. Heaven and Hell aren't elsewhere. They are right here. Parallel universes reached through magical portals, many of which now stand wide open, allowing the races to circulate without impediment. Different planes of existence, now mostly mashed together.

Yet I remember... I remember song and light and freedom unlike anything else. A feeling of rightness and joy. So different from the twisting, aching feelings that have taken over my body and mind in this College.

And I need to ask. Ask who I am. Surely the answer is simple. Am I a seraph or not? Are they hiding something from me? Just a reassurance that this is normal from being in a human body would be enough.

There is a small storeroom by the stairwell. I break the flimsy lock and step inside. It will do. With the door half-closed, I have just enough space to kneel.

So I do.

My knees hit the floor and I struggle for focus when all I can hear are Ryu's words.

"The worst will come when we have to give her up."

My stomach churns. But we have to give her up. That's the whole point of this mission. It's what I volunteered for. To save the world.

I have barely started my oration when the light around me flickers and brightens, blinding me. Well, that was quick. Expecting Daliel, I say nothing, waiting for him—it —to verify it's me and give me permission to voice my request.

But the presence before me is too strong, buffeting me like a fiery wind. That's not Daliel, and when I lift my head, I can't help but jerk back.

"Malakh Raziel," I whisper as the archangel towers over me, his head and shoulders going through the ceiling, turning the mortar, bricks and concrete into glass. "*Urun-en.*"

"*Umbar umsa.* State your business." He is silent for a few heartbeats. "You seem surprised to see me. You asked to speak to me directly last time."

I manage to bow my head again. "I hadn't expected you to show up every time I request an audience with Heaven."

"I decided to oversee this mission personally. We are about to close the talks." His face looms closer, its luminance hurting my eyes. "She appears to be more dangerous than we thought."

"How so?"

"There's a rumor about her father being an angel. An archangel. Is there any truth in it?"

I stiffen. This isn't what I had planned on talking about. "No. It's just a rumor, I'm sure." And then, as gears turn inside my head, "Who told you that? Was it the librarian?"

"You do seem to know about the rumors. I would appreciate it if you informed me instantly the moment you discovered new information, *Umbar*. Why did it take you so long to call for me?"

He thinks I called him to share our discovery about Frankie's father.

"The librarian knew Frankie's mother personally," Raziel goes on. "Did you know about it?"

His Glory intensifies, scorching me. "We all know who her mother is," I say. "That didn't seem important."

"*We* judge what is important!" he roars, the voice emanating from his open, black mouth like a hurricane, and I almost fall back on my ass from the gale his words unleash. "Not you!"

"*Urun-en*," I whisper. "As you say."

Meanwhile, outside the door of the closet-like storeroom, two students walk by, lost in conversation, but they can't hear us. Raziel triggered a silence protocol the moment he appeared.

And a good thing, too. I've been so frazzled it just slipped my mind. A frazzled angel on a deadly mission, distracted by four guys and a girl who coincidentally is the target of his mission.

Heaven help me.

I should self-flagellate for this.

Recite a hundred Hail Marys at the very least.

But Raziel, Great Archon of Heaven, diverts my attention by bending over me, making me feel small like an ant, his face blurry and constantly shifting.

"It's almost over," he booms. "We will be taking her away soon. You shall receive your reward, Asariel. A place in Heaven."

I start. My body tenses, every muscle locking down. "What? When?"

"You will know when it happens," he says, voice cold and sharp like a blade. "Tomorrow, most likely. You shall receive your orders to lift the dome and let Heaven in. What is time to an angel?"

I always knew this was coming and yet I never thought it was now. Like death, I think. You always think it's out there but never here.

"And what will happen to her then?" I ask.

"That is none of your concern."

"Will she suffer?"

"If you refer to her power, she will be imprisoned in a cage where she cannot use it, its bars made of divine fire, imbued with the power of Heaven, its lock—"

"And for how long?"

The enormous face bent over me seems to settle briefly into tense lines. "For as long as she lives, which may be forever. I don't understand why you pose these questions, *Umbar umsa*. I thought your mission was clear from the start."

It was.

But my head isn't clear anymore. Nothing is clear. My own emotions keep tripping me up, but as I lift my head, outside the small storeroom, I see a girl with long blond hair and dark eyes.

It's her.

Musen.

And the emotions I've been trying to keep at bay become an avalanche and crush me.

"I..." She's coming out of the girls' bathrooms, Tir in tow. They're talking. They haven't seen me. Three guys follow close by, probably Kalissa's guys. Watching over her, as I should be doing. And all I can see is her. I can't breathe, my chest tight, my heart hurting. Can't speak.

Can't do it.

"It would be like killing her," I whisper. "No, a fate worse than death."

Raziel is silent for a few beats. "You know what she is. She's a weapon. She can't be allowed to roam freely."

"Maybe there's a way to take away her power."

"There isn't. It doesn't matter. Heaven wants her. Demands her. It is your duty to obey."

Shakily, I find my feet. Standing up, I take a breath. "No. You can't lock her up."

Another incredulous pause. "Are you refusing to obey?"

"I am saying, there may be another way."

A glint of interest. "What do you have to bargain with? Are you defecting, Asariel?"

"I want you to consider other possibilities."

"There are none. Do you want to be obliterated? This is your only chance. Make your choice. Live on earth as a human or become a seraph."

"Become one? Am I not one?"

The glowing face shifts. He's toying with me like a cat with a mouse. "Ah. You are catching on, as the humans say."

"What...?"

"You were in an accident. Your soul rose to Heaven but if you refuse your orders, you will go right back where you were when we found you, when Azrael touched you."

Azrael. The angel who engendered Frankie, who has given her this terrible power.

"I can't obey," I grind out. My nails are biting into my palms. I realize my hands have curled into fists. "I can't hurt her."

"Do you think that by dying you will stop the wheels from turning?"

"At least, I won't be the one who has set the wheels into motion."

"This is foolish."

"Is it? I requested the Raziel Protocol. If you kill me, you can't lift it for at least a few days. Lots of bureaucracy in Heaven."

Raziel blazes. "You really are going to disobey Heaven. And what would a few days gain you?"

Me? Nothing.

But maybe she will have a chance to figure this out and somehow escape.

Slim chance.

A chance nevertheless.

It's a weird sensation, a spur-of-the-moment decision. Truth is, it may feel like one but I know deep inside that it's been a long time coming. Since the moment I met her, probably. Since the moment I had the first doubt, the moment she pulled the first smile out of me.

A heavy decision.

But at least what I am makes sense now.

Going back to death makes sense.

I wasn't meant to be an angel.

Azrael was wrong to guide my soul that high up. A mistake in the angelic strategy. I wasn't meant to rise.

Might as well end it now.

"You have made your decision, I see," Raziel says. "We should never have trusted a newly arisen for such a mission. Rest assured the same mistake will not be repeated."

"Good luck with that," I whisper, closing my eyes. Angels

are not exempt from erring, according to the holy books. And I've certainly never been much of an angel anyway.

"You will be removed from your duties," Raziel goes on.

I think of kissing Frankie, of her body against mine. I think of the guys lying on the mattresses with me just this morning. Of how accepted they made me feel. And how alive.

How they made me ask all the right questions. How to let myself be.

Then a shadow falls over me—a man stumbles through the door, a blade flashing in his hands—and he thrusts it into me.

My heart stutters. A strange feeling. A pain shoots through me, seizing my body. My muscles don't obey me. I sink back to my knees, then topple sideways. My head thumps against the floor. All I can see is the wall in front of me.

So this is what being removed from my duties meant...

So this is the end, I think, for me, but not for them...

The wall fades as it all rushes back in—a life. My life. I had a life on earth and it flashes before my eyes, behind my closed eyelids. I had a dog, Jerry, and we fed a stray cat that used to wander into our garden. I had a girlfriend, Dinah, she had a cute smile but wasn't sure she was ready to settle yet. We planned to travel. I worked... for the police.

Paranormal section.

Dealing with supernatural crimes and the mafia of the Four Houses.

Never thought I'd deal directly with Heaven.

There was a case of a family being threatened by the vampire clan. They owed money. They had a beautiful little girl and when they came for them, I was on call.

I tried to save them. Save the girl, at least.

It was done. I stepped out of their house...

A car crashed into me. Threw me up into the air. It felt like flying.

An accident? Who knows.

It's all falling into place. I'm falling. Still falling. Still feels like flying.

And then I hear her voice in the present, screaming. "Asa!" Screaming my name before it all fades to black. "No!"

There's something I should tell her, to stop her, not to let her... do what?

Then that thought also goes out like a candle, and it's dark.

23

FRANKIE

"Asa! No! Asa, can you hear me?"

Something had called me, made me go looking for him. Strangely, he was inside a storeroom and I heard what the angel told him, but all of a sudden, a man rushed into the room and now Asa is lying on the floor, blood pooling around him.

Just as cold is spreading through me.

No...

Then the presence of the other angel tugs on my senses and I whirl around. "Anything you want to say to me?" I snap.

Silence greets me.

"Bring him back!" I demand.

The huge face is immovable. "He made his choice."

"His choice? What choice? Is he dead? Did you kill him? How? The College is closed off! Nobody can get in or out. You're just a projection."

"You think we don't have people on our payroll?" He nods at something—someone. A man is sitting on the floor, looking down at the blood on his hands.

"Heaven is planning on taking you away tomorrow," Raziel says. "But Asariel decided to buy you a few days."

"But..."

"He did put a crimp in the plans. With his death, the dome won't lift until the details of his demise are recorded and a replacement chosen. But Heaven has time, Azrael's daughter."

His presence fades. Sort of fizzles out.

Fuck him. Fuck him so hard.

I can't speak. My throat is too tight to breathe.

"Asa." Tir falls to his knees beside me. "What's wrong with him?"

"He's dead, he's..." I choke. "No. I won't let this happen. I'll bring him back."

"But he said you shouldn't—"

"I don't care."

"Frankie—"

"No! What use is such power if I can't use it to bring Asa back? Who cares what he said? I can do this."

"Frankie! Tir!" Rook, Ryu, and Kass are running toward us. "We felt something, is... Oh fuck, Asa."

"That angel killed him," I say, realizing I'm sobbing. "Used that man to kill him."

The man in question is shaking. "Please, don't hurt me," he's babbling over and over. "It was a job. I was promised a good position on the Fae council—"

With a growl, Tir grabs him and hauls him out of the storeroom. "Fuck right off. If you ever come near us again, I'll rip your head off your goddamn shoulders. I'll deal with you later."

I don't even look to see if he leaves.

Asa is lying on his side, one arm curled by his face, the other over his middle. His eyes are closed as if he's asleep, but like with Tir, I know. His chest isn't moving. He's still, too still to be alive.

I trace with my fingertips his pale lashes, his strong jaw, his soft mouth, and I want to wail and rage, but *no*.

No, this isn't over.

I'm not ready to part with any of them.

Not when I just made the decision to let them into my heart, no matter what.

Not when he died to give me a chance to escape and live.

My heart is breaking. I feel it cracking inside my chest.

"Frankie," Kass breathes. "He said you shouldn't. It may drain you completely. What if it kills you, too?"

"I don't care." Closing my eyes, I reach for the spark inside me.

It comes more easily to me now. I've trained it a little with the small spells the guys taught me. Still, I'm not exactly sure how I did it with Tir. I only remember the heartbreak, so similar to this one, and the despair.

I reach for Asa's soul.

That bright flame.

It's still hovering over him and I reach for it. I reach for life, for energy, and I feel four more bright flames around me. They support me, sustain me, as I reach for him.

Come back, I think. *Asa, come back to me. To us.*

A great wrenching sensation tears apart the inside of my chest.

Pain.

It's familiar. I've been there before.

Come back, come back, I chant inside my head, placing my hand over Asa's chest, over his heart. *We need you.*

Was the first time real? Was it a coincidence? Maybe Tir hadn't died, like the guys theorized.

Asa is dead.

Raziel confirmed it.

No doubt this time around, not about him being dead. The

only doubt is whether I can do this, whether I can call him back.

"Asa!" I whisper, "Asa, please…"

The pain is rising in me, all-consuming.

I realize my boys have put their hands on him, too, and on me. We're a circle, and it gives me strength. Emotional support. I'm not alone, and neither is Asa.

"Come. Back!"

When he draws a breath, I'm not really expecting it, the sound hitting me like a shot. I'm bowed over him, I realize, my hair loose, curtaining my face, the hands on my shoulders and back keeping me from sprawling over Asa.

Then he draws another.

I sit back, my own breathing labored, my chest aching. "He's alive."

Their eyes widen, brows shooting up. Green, gray, blue eyes fixed on Asa's recumbent form. Rook grins. Kass is pale but his mouth is trying on a smile. Tir is trembling. Ryu grabs Asa's hip and shakes him. Rolls him onto his back.

"You brought him back," he says, and this time I nod without hesitation.

Can't deny it.

Once might have been a coincidence, but not twice. Not this time.

Holy shit, I brought him back!

Asa. I finally let myself lean against him, rest my head on his shoulder. Funny how I couldn't bring myself to do that when he was dead, but now he's alive, I'm ready to lie on top of him, smother him with everything I feel for him.

I'm not even surprised when Kass shifts and pulls Asa's head on his lap, stroking his forehead, or when Tir casts a small spell and directs air to waft over Asa's face.

After an endless moment, I sit back and tuck my hair behind my ears. If my cheeks are wet, I don't give a damn.

"Are you all right?" Ryu takes one of my hands in his, green eyes concerned. "You're so pale. How do you feel?"

My chest is a mass of pain and I'm dizzy, but it doesn't matter.

"I'm fine," I say, even as the darkness draws on me, trying to pull me under. I gather my thoughts. "But we may have a problem."

"Yeah," Rook says, "now Heaven will know what you can do the moment they see Asa sauntering about the College."

"So we have to keep Asa's return a secret," I say. "Hide him from Heaven."

Until we figure out what to do.

———

"Oh, piece of cake," Rook mutters. "Hide a resurrected angel from Heaven. *Pff*. Easy-peasy."

Yeah, it's easier said than done, hiding an angel from Heaven. Also, he may be alive but he's dazed and it takes Tir and Rook to half-carry him back to our room.

I also need to be carried as my legs won't hold me. The world keeps fading to black. Ryu carries me to our room, eases me down on top of Kass' bed.

"I'll go and bring us some food," Tir says.

"First good idea you've had in ages, boy," Rook says, but his grin looks a little forced.

"Easy," Ryu says as Rook and Tir place Asa down beside me. "He will have to stay in here. He won't contact Heaven, or answer any summons from them. Nobody sees him, nobody hears him. Like a ghost."

"I've seen ghosts," Kass says.

"In a manner of speaking, vampire. Also, what the fuck do you mean, you've seen ghosts? Like actual ghosts, or are you being very metaphorical right now?"

"I've seen ghosts. Not sure my imagination wasn't playing tricks on me. That was after Brody went down and when you have a bond with another vampire, when you've sired them, sometimes you catch glimpses of their thoughts, so maybe…"

"Brody was broadcasting ghosts to you? How romantic… not."

"The breaking of that bond… made me sick for a while."

Rook slides an arm around Kass' back. Says nothing.

I'm sitting on the bed beside Asa. It feels familiar, from when he was injured, protecting me. He's done it yet again.

"He stopped Heaven from taking me away tomorrow," I whisper, stroking silky golden curls out of his face. "And I still don't know if it was worth it. I'm still the weapon everyone is afraid of. Still a force nobody knows what to do with."

"I have a few ideas what to do with you," Ryu says and his dark, heated gaze scorches me.

I snicker. Shake my head. "I bet you do."

"Going to get that food," Tir says. "No sex until I come back, okay?"

"You really think that's what I'm about to do after bringing Asa back?" I ask incredulously. "Have sex?"

"Why not?" Tir says softly. "Living life is the only thing one can do."

And then he slips out of the room and is gone, leaving us to contemplate his words and mine.

Ryu laughs softly and comes to kneel at my feet. Takes my hand. "I think we'll take it easy for now."

"Yeah, you look shaky, Darling." Rook sits beside me on the bed, slipping an arm around me. "Maybe you should lie down."

"We should have put him on the mattresses, I whisper. "So we can all lie together like last night."

"You liked that." Kass smiles, coming to stand behind Ryu.

"I think we all did," Ryu says.

Kass eyes Asa's long body. "We can move the angel. He's not that heavy."

"He's not awake yet." Ryu leans forward, frowning. "Is that normal?"

"Probably. Hard to come back from death. I think Tir said he felt like shit for days after you brought him back."

"He never said that to me," I breathe.

"Those first days weren't conducive to confessions of any sort," Kass says.

I hated them then. It's not that long ago. I *thought* I hated them, but once I got to know them a little, once they told me why they were doing this, my hatred dulled like a once sharp blade corroded by understanding and the affection that crept up on me, hiding behind lust.

I want to bask in their presence, their warmth, the fact that they are all still alive and here, with me, no matter the cost, no matter the future.

Weariness is weighing me down, though, and I lean against Rook. A yawn cracks my jaw.

"What shall we do?" I whisper, more to myself than for anyone else's ears. "We got Asa back, but if Heaven wants me now, if they reached a decision, then what's going to happen? Asa bought us a few days, but afterward the dome will lift, if they don't find a way to do it sooner, and then..."

"We have to prepare," Rook says. "The moment the dome is lifted, we take you out of here, hide you."

"And then?"

"One step at a time, Sweetheart. We won't let you be a prisoner, a lab rat, a tool for Heaven, or anyone else. We'll take you far away, give you a new identity. We'll think of something."

"Travel in South America," Ryu says. "Visit Peru."

"Visit Bangkok," Kass mutters. "And Tokyo."

"I've always wanted to travel," Rook says, tugging me to my feet. "Come on, my pretty, you look about to fall over. Let's get you on the mattress, and then carry that lug of an angel beside you, how about that, for starters? Eat the food Tir brings, get our energy back, and then we can strategize. Though I see one problem..."

"Only one?"

"Well, I'll need a passport. For all that traveling we're planning." He cracks a wide grin. "And then we're off."

24

FRANKIE

*T*ir comes back with a tray loaded with food. It's getting to be a habit, I think as he places it on the mattresses and we all gather around to eat. Only Asa isn't partaking as he's still out, lying behind me on the mattress, but I see the steady rise and fall of his broad chest and it's such a relief.

I mean, okay, I may be twisting about every five seconds to check, but so what? Who can blame me?

The relief is such that I want to break down and cry again, but I won't let myself.

Because he's alive.

Kass leans against me, holding up a small sandwich. "Here, try this, it's not bad." He's sitting cross-legged beside me, dressed in a black tank top and sweats, and smells deliciously of soap and male musk. "Don't try the sausage rolls, they suck."

"Was that an attempt at a pun?" Rook mutters, sitting across from us, his mouth stuffed with food.

"Only your dirty mind would go there right now," Ryu says, elbowing him.

"My dirty mind goes to all the dirty places, all the time. It lives in a gutter."

"We noticed."

I eat the sandwich Kass gave me. I feel... woozy. That's the word. I don't want to worry the guys, because it's nothing a little rest won't fix, I'm sure. Even chewing and swallowing feels draining, but I should eat to get some of my energy back.

"Hey Kass, why do you always wear those high turtlenecks? And why were you so touch-averse at first? Was that Brody's doing?"

Kass stiffens beside me. He looks down at the chicken wrap in his hand and frowns. "No, that's... That's something else."

"What?"

"None of your..." He swallows hard, puts the wrap back on the tray. The color drains from his face. "I just can't..."

"Hey... hey." Even as exhausted as I feel, I can tell this conversation is skirting around a trauma and that he's not ready to open that can of worms. I catch his hand. Squeeze it a little. "Let's just eat."

He nods, a grateful look in his gray eyes. "Yeah."

"Hurry up and eat before Rook inhales everything." Tir nudges him from his other side. "He's a real incinerator."

"You should have seen me in my youth," Rook says around a small waffle he's stuffed into his mouth. "This is nothing."

"Since when did you say you've been fighting in Hell's army?"

"Oh, I seem to recall a big fuss about a Napoleon trying to take over the humans. French was suddenly in fashion among demons. It was annoying as fuck."

"Napoleon?" Kass blinks. "*Che cazzo?* Are you fucking with us?"

Didn't Tir say he was older? But I don't say anything.

"*Ceci n'est pas une pipe*," Rook says. "No, wait, that's not what

I meant. I meant it's all true. *C'est vrai. Liberté, ordre public.* That's what he said. Napoleon, that is."

"My man, that's old. You're ancient."

"And wise, which is why I appreciate the finer things in life. Like good food."

"You think the food here is good?" Ryu chuckles. "Are you insane?"

"Wait, are you saying there is better food to be had?" Rook licks his fingers. "I'm listening. I want a list of places to eat once we get out of here."

Tir and Ryu exchange a quick glance I don't miss. Yeah, to get his wish he'd have to deliver me to the House of Fire. And he probably will. Liking me doesn't mean he won't do what's best for him, fulfill a dream.

"I still don't get why food is so important to you," I whisper, nibbling at my little sandwich, not really hungry.

"Well, I've been eating army rations most of my fucking life, and let me tell you, when I say that's Hell, I mean it. Who's in for a dinner of skinned, raw rat fillet with cockroach flakes? Anyone?"

I gag. "You're not serious."

His grin falters. "You're right. Usually, you had to catch the rat and eat it, skin and all. Cockroaches too."

"Oh, god."

"Look what you've done. You put her off her sandwich," Kass accuses, but it's mild.

"I'm not hungry," I whisper. Too tired to stay seated anymore, I lie down on my side, beside Asa's outstretched form, placing a hand on his chest. "How did you end up a Hellhound, Rook?"

"Recruiters grabbed me. They needed someone small enough to crawl through air vents and tunnels and the narrow wells in the lower Hells. I was a scrawny little thing. Always hungry. And that hasn't changed." He laughs softly but there's a haunted look in his dark blue eyes. "I tell you... I would have killed for a crust of bread back then. And I did kill. They kept telling me how resilient I was. But it was fight or die."

"Oh, Rook..."

"It's okay." He visibly shakes the dark cloud off, takes another bite of his egg roll. "This... this I'd have pillaged a city for. So don't knock it. And for what it's worth..." He swallows his bite, lowers the roll, a flush on his cheeks. "What I have here with you, guys... With you, Darling... I'd ruin the world to keep it."

Aw, man.

I lift my hand off Asa's chest, reach for Rook's hand. He laces our fingers together. "If you do, you won't get to visit the world's best restaurants or ride rollercoasters or party till the dawn."

"Oh, you know what, Darling? I hear those things are overrated anyway."

I want to smile at him but can't. "You will give me up. Seeing how Heaven treated Asa... you won't be given a choice. Those contracts felt like choices but they won't hesitate to break them and take from you everything if you fail."

"Think we don't know that?" They all exchange uneasy glances. "The six of us pitted against the powers-that-be. I won't lie to you, Princess, that's a tough one."

"I know. And I don't expect you to defect for me."

"But the plan remains. The moment the dome lifts, we run—"

"I don't know if your plan will work," I whisper. "I'm sure Heaven will be ready for me to try and escape. They will have measures in place."

"You could—"

"No. I won't kill more innocent people."

"Assassins are hardly innocent," Kass says, "and Heaven and all the Houses will send more of them to kill you. Sleepers.

Fuck knows how many are on their payroll. Those people don't deserve your mercy."

"People like you? People who may not have much of a choice when it comes to doing bad things? Wouldn't you give them a chance to live?"

"Dammit, girl." Kass sighs. "You're not making this easy."

"That's because it isn't easy. And it won't get any easier. I'm a tough case, a weapon that shouldn't exist in the first place." I close my eyes. My hand, fingers still tangled with Rook's, rests on top of Asa's chest. "Thank you for saying you'll try to help me, though."

"You belong with us," someone whispers, and I don't even know who it was as I drop into sleep.

————

I slip through dreams, falling from dreamworld to stranger dreamworld.

Tir is there. He reaches for me, wraps himself around me as we fall. A Fae, distant descendant of angels, demonblood and angelblood fighting in his veins.

"*I will be your guardian angel,*" someone says. I know his voice.

Asa.

He steps out of the shadows as we land on our feet. Huge white wings stretch out of his back, but he's dressed in a formal gray suit and he has... blood spatters all over him.

Fear rushes through me.

The others follow him, all bloodied and wearing grim expressions on their faces. And they all sport wings, for some reason. My dreams really are a mess. Wings representing their Houses, I suppose—leathery dragon wings for Rook, eagle wings for Tir, black leathery bat wings for Kass, strange red furry wings for Ryu—or is that a cape?

Tir keeps an arm around me as they approach. His pale hair is blowing in a wind that doesn't touch me.

"Do you want this?" he asks and I don't know what he means.

"Explain," I say.

"Our deaths," he says, "our punishment if we help you escape, if we go with you."

God dammit, even in my dreams there's no escape from guilt.

"I don't want anyone else to die," I whisper. "Much less you. You should give me up and go find happiness and peace."

Suddenly they are standing around me in a circle and I'm at their center, naked and scared.

"No one can know," they whisper, chant, turning around me as if in a ritual dance. "No one can know."

"Know what? What do you mean?"

Their wings brush me with every step they take, soft and yet abrasive. My head is spinning.

"What you are," they say. "No one can know what you are. That power is too great for anyone to wield, but if you take control of it, you could be an archangel, an Archon of the High Spheres, a force that could bring Heaven to its knees. If you would just wield it without guilt."

"I can't. I don't want it."

"So powerful..."

"Don't leave me." My voice cracks. "I don't want this power. I don't want to be my mother's weapon, or Heaven's."

"What would you do?"

"I would give this power away," I whisper, "if I got to be with you."

———

The dream lingers at the back of my mind as the next day dawns and I decide to get out of bed. I refuse to stay in bed. I should get back to classes, back to research... Find out if there's anything else I'm capable of.

Anything else I should be worried about.

The guys have tried arguing with me not to get up, and now they are watching me take a few wobbly steps, frowns on their handsome faces.

Not everyone is here, though.

"Where's Asa?" I glance around. "And Rook and Ryu?"

"The guys dragged Asa to the showers," Tir says from his perch on the desk. He pushes off it to stalk toward me. "How are you feeling?"

I shrug. Tiredness drags me down. "He shouldn't be out of this room. He's supposed to be hiding."

"We threw a blanket over him. He's in disguise."

I can't help but crack a tiny smile. "He's incognito just because you put a blanket on him?"

"Yeah, well..." Kass is leaning against the bunk bed. "Any case, the only way Heaven will know he's alive is if he responds to a message from them. Otherwise, he might as well be invisible."

"Can't risk it," I whisper.

"You're right. We can't." Tir stalks over to me, leans against the wall. He keeps stealing glances at me, a frown on his face. "You okay?" he asks as I struggle to get up from the mattress, offering me a hand. "That was a heavy dream. All those wings..."

He was in my dream, walking its streets and dangers, and he remembers it, probably better than I do.

"Did you see...? *Oof.*" He grabs me and I lean against his hard chest. He smirks down at me.

"Sure you don't want to lie back down?"

"Positive." I draw a long breath. "Did you notice anything interesting?"

"You're blushing," he says. "And you smell fucking good. Both very noticeable things."

"I meant in my dream." I snicker a little but he's right, there was a heaviness to the dream that lingers over me like a black cloud.

"Everyone was bleeding." His smirk fades. "All of us..."

"Except for me." Now he said it, this little haunting detail returns. They weren't just spattered with blood. They were *dying*.

I pull back from him, shuddering.

"Frankie—"

I want to throw up. I grab blindly for the bunk bed and lean against it. "No..."

"It was just a dream. A bad dream. You're not a prophet. None of that is going to happen. You should lie back down, rest. Bringing Asa back took a Hell of a lot out of you, even if you don't want to let it show."

"No." I shake my head, then regret it as bile rises in my throat. "I can't. Need to think."

Think of a solution.

He's right, I'm not a prophet, but the dream was so real.

"Frankie," he tries again.

"What will happen to you if you refuse to give me up? Heaven killed Asa without a second thought when he did. Will the Houses kill you?"

He winces, his gaze shuttering, going opaque. "Don't worry about that."

"Are you serious? How can I not...?"

"Shush." This time Kass slides his arms around me, and I snap my mouth shut, taking his strength and comfort. "Everything will be all right."

But it won't, will it? One way or another, we're screwed.

This thing between us is screwed.

I knew I shouldn't have invested my heart.

I knew it was a damn bad idea.

We stay here. If they kill them, I'll bring them back. Somehow, we stop anyone from taking us away from this College... if anyone does, I'll kill them.

Holy shit, I can't do that.

What the Hell am I going to do?

Before I manage to work myself into a proper panic, the door opens and the other guys walk in.

Rook saunters inside and grabs me around the waist, pulling me away from Kass. "Whoa, girl. You're white as milk. Shouldn't you be in bed? We thought to put you and Asa together side by side, snug as bugs in a rug, and—"

"No." I shake my head, put my hands on his broad chest and push. "I need to get out... out of here."

"Tir, what did you do to her this time?" Rook growls.

Tir shrugs his shoulders, mouth set in an unhappy line. "Search me."

"Kass? Did you upset her?" Rook sighs. "We were only gone for ten minutes, dammit. Frankie, wait."

"Where is Asa?" I look behind them, and there he is, leaning against the doorframe.

Alive.

He's alive.

I can't... "I'm going to class," I announce to the world in general, frustrated with my weakness, both physical and emotional, the wisps of my dreams chasing me as I grab my backpack.

"Now?" Kass asks.

And then I remember I need to probably get dressed and run a brush through my hair before I show up in any class. "Shit."

"Frankie, just... slow down." Kass grabs my hand. His dark

brows draw together. "You just brought someone back. You can barely stand, let alone go to class. What's wrong? Shouldn't we be celebrating getting not only Tir but also Asa back?"

"You don't understand." I turn my face away. "Of course I'm happy, I'm over the moon happy, you have no idea... But this is the power that will screw us over. And the way I feel..."

"What way is that?"

I shake my head.

"She means that she likes us," Ryu says softly, grabbing my other hand and tugging. "Don't you, girl?"

"You know I do," I whisper, my face warm.

"Frankie." Asa says, coming to haul me into his arms and he smells of blood and death, and I fall against him with a small sob.

"Asa... You're okay."

"I told you not to bring me back," he whispers.

"And I told you, you can't ask that of me. These powers I have... I don't think I can ever stop using them. They're connected to my feelings, you see. To my fear and... and what I feel about you," I finish lamely, because confessing to loving them, to falling for them so fast and hard makes me sound stupid.

"I'd ruin the world for this," Rook had said.

I'd ruin it, too, but if I kill again, I'm afraid my mind will shrivel up and die. For them, though... Would I do it for them?

And then what? We ride away together into the sunset? I'll always be hunted. And they will be, too...

There is no happy ending to this story.

———

"Franks! There you are," my cousin exclaims. "Been looking for you. I thought you'd be in classes yesterday and now you've already missed the first two."

Yeah, we're late and of course she'd notice my absence since I changed all my classes to be with her. I adjust the straps of my backpack, its weight comforting on my back. I even stuffed my Jungle Book inside, just because. I need it close.

"Jules, I..." I glance over my shoulder at my bodyguards. Ryu stayed with Asa, not that Asa was happy with that, so I have Rook, Tir, and Kass with me. "I'm—"

"I was coming to see you. Dammit, girl, you look like roadkill. What's going on with you? The contraceptive spell I put on you shouldn't affect you like that. Maybe I should remove—"

"Contraceptive spell, huh?" Kass growls under his breath. "You didn't say anything about that."

"I thought we agreed now is not the time for babies." I shoot him a glare. Then I turn back to Juliette. "It's not the spell."

"Then what is it?" She waves at the guys. "Did these hunks keep you up all night?"

Rook coughs, unsuccessfully trying to smother his laughter.

"No. That's not it, either," I say. "I just had... a stomach bug."

"Ouch." She winces in sympathy. "Those suck."

My cousin believes me, believes my lie. She's always trusted me.

The guilt monster really has it in for me today. It won't stop gnawing on my stomach lining for everything I do or am liable to do, from lying to my cousin to destroying the world or being the death of the men I love.

Jesus, there, I said it, all right? I'm in love with them. Head over heels.

I guess keeping a level head is out of the question now, huh? *Shit.*

She links her arm with mine and leans in as she pulls me in the direction of—I assume—our next class. I don't even know which one that would be. "I'm not sold on the stomach bug thing, just so you know. I think my theory is much more plausible."

"Oh boy. Julie..."

"I mean, having five gorgeous hunks with big dongs pleasuring you every night must be exhausting, like our cousin Mandy always says."

This time it's Tir who chokes on a guffaw. "Dongs."

"I don't know what you're talking about," I say firmly. "And I've never heard of a cousin Mandy."

"Sure you have. A distant cousin, for sure. Mandy's Secret Garden of Shifters? She's a witch living in a cottage in the woods with pets and herbs, caring for wounded shifters. She works for the Save the Shifters Organization."

"Never heard of it."

"It's out in the low country. Lots of woods. Lots of shifters."

It sounds like a dream. But I'm caught in this nightmare.

I gather my wits. "Julie..."

"I know something is going on, okay? Can't you trust me, tell me what it is? Maybe I can help, maybe Mom—"

"You can't. She can't."

"But Mom—"

"I bid you all a good day," a cool male voice says, a familiar, annoying voice, and I turn around to find...

"Cirdan," I mutter.

"Don't mind me, humans." He waves a disdainful hand at us and turns to Tir. "I'm here for Tirius Verdell. We have been waiting for your answer."

"Answer to what?" Juliette frowns at the Fae.

"Tir," I start, "you don't have to do as they say, you—"

"I accept," Tir says. He shoots me a cautionary look. "We need all the help we can get, every single person who'd have our back."

I scowl. "But—"

"No matter how it all plays out. The more allies the better, Frankie."

He's right, so I shut my mouth.

"We are pleased with your decision." Cirdan gives Tir a slight bow. "We will be waiting for you this afternoon, for your traditional speech to the group—"

"Don't wait up. I will come if I can, and I may bring friends with me."

Cirdan stops, arrested mid-bow. "As you wish, Tirius."

"What was that about?" Juliette whispers as Cirdan turns and walks away. "Did I get that right and your hunky Fae will be the leader of the Fae gang?"

"Yeah, it does look like it," I whisper.

"Wow. You've barely arrived, all of you, and you're putting your mark on the school. Imagine what you'll do by the end of the school year."

For now, I hope we'll make it to the end of the day, but I say nothing and let her drag me to class.

25

KASS

*T*ir is troubled. He isn't happy with assuming the leadership of the Fae gang. Then again, this whole situation stinks. College politics is a quagmire, and he will be tangled up in that instead of being there for Frankie.

With us.

The vampires seem to have mostly gone rogue, selling their black souls to the highest bidder. And even if Tir manages to control the Fae, even if the demons and the shifters really are on our side and manage to keep more of their members from jumping onto the dark side's bandwagon...

Yeah, there's still no clear path to winning this game.

I can sense the fear and sadness weighing Frankie down. Combined with the drain of bringing Asa back, it's small wonder she looks so pale and wan. It makes me want to wrap her up in my arms and lie with her in bed. Feed her morsels of slow-cooked meat and give her tonics and sweet port to drink. To brush her hair and stroke her body. Pleasure her. Take care of her. Make her smile.

Then again, that has been my fantasy since I first saw her.

Sorry, Brody. From that moment on, I knew deep inside that what I'd had with you had been only half a truth. Mostly a lie. The way I feel about her and about these guys just can't fucking compare.

Do I want Brody to die? No. But if someone wants to bring him back, it won't be me.

What if there's a good explanation for what he told Rook? What if he didn't mean it? What if he loves you? You know. "Deep inside."

A snarl twists my mouth.

Fuck him.

Fuck Brody and his toyboys.

Everything has changed.

Speaking of which, heading back to classes is surreal, I swear to God. Feels like fucking ages since we attended.

And after everything that's happened, guarding Frankie's back as she strolls through the paths of the College with her cousin, arm in arm, both with backpacks on their backs as if nothing is going on, is a mindfuck.

Rook has even whipped out a cigarette, seemingly out of thin air, and with a snap of his fingers lights it up. Tir is giving him amused glances. I watch the demon's sensuous mouth wrap around the end of the cigarette, the blissed-out look on his face as he draws on the smoke, and my dick hardens.

He's beautiful. Dammit, they all are. I wouldn't mind getting down and dirty with them, now that I feel I can trust them.

With Frankie in the middle.

Naked bodies and handsome faces.

These guys and this girl I've come to care about. I find myself thinking about them all the time, wanting to help them get over their struggles and also yeah, get naked with them.

Hey, I'm half-incubus. Can't blame a guy.

Though I doubt anyone in their right mind would fail to desire them.

"Heads up," Tir mutters. "Look at the welcome committee."

Fuck. It's the dean. Flanked by two gorillas. Well, guards.

We're muscular, but these guys are giving us a run for our money. Where did she get them?

"Coming to welcome back the prodigal sons?" Rook pulls on his cigarette, puffing out a ring of smoke.

"The black sheep, more like," I say.

She stops in front of us and puts her hands on her hips. Dressed in a power suit, dark eyes narrowed, she looks like a force to be reckoned with and I can't tell what her power is.

"Ladies. Gentlemen. How nice of you to leave your room at last."

"We live to please," Rook says, puffing out another ring of smoke.

She snaps her fingers and his cigarette flies out of his mouth and to the floor where she steps on it. "Blowing smoke in the dean's face is disrespectful."

Huh. Telekinesis. Without any obvious demonblood spell. Elemental magic, then. She may be a shifter.

"Hey, that was a good cigarette," Rook grumbles.

"You may think you're above God and the saints, emissaries, but you're still enrolled in this fucking College and you'd better answer my summons or there will be Hell to pay."

Worse than what is going on? I doubt it.

"Where are your friends?" she demands. "Asariel and Ryu. Tell them to join us right now as we go to my office to talk about the situation you have created."

"*We* have created?" Rook splutters. "Like you said, we're just emissaries."

The dean nods at Frankie who's tight-lipped and pale. "I should have known that doing a favor to your grandfather was a bad idea. Angels have their own agenda."

"My grandfather was only trying to protect me," she whispers.

"Speaking of angels. Where is Asa?" the dean demands.

"Asa is... indisposed," I say. "Ryu is taking care of him."

"He wasn't indisposed when he kicked out the person I sent to get you. Tell him to come. Now."

"Or what?" I mutter.

"I heard that, Mr. di Battista."

"With respect," I say because I was raised to be a fucking good boy, "there are people after Frankie. That's the whole reason we've been holed up and why Asariel is indeed indisposed."

"Is he injured?" She frowns. "I haven't been informed of any recent attack."

"And yet there have been many," I say. "Maybe your informants are slacking."

"See, all this you must tell me about," she decides, turning to go, gesturing for us and her gorillas to follow her. "How else am I going to fulfill my duty and protect you if I don't know what is going on?"

But her gorillas hesitate and one of them advances on us.

What the Hell is going on?

"Fuck," Tir curses, and I think I see a line of red blossoming on his arm. "Fall back! It's an attack!"

"Protect Frankie!" I yell.

"The fuck," the dean whirls back toward us, eyes wide, but I have no time to worry about her as both gorillas come at us.

Counting on the element of surprise, obviously, because why else would they think they'd get past us? Of course, Frankie is at the front of our group. Didn't think the attack would come from the dean's side.

I thrust my power at them, to slow them down as their blood rushes up to their heads. Tir is closer, and I see him moving into their path, punching and kicking, too late to draw a weapon.

Rook's hands are on fire, or so it looks like. He throws fireballs at the men. The dean ducks, then crawls out of the way. I think she's too stunned to think about using magic.

When you haven't been raised in battle, it's hard to switch on fight mode so fast. I wasn't raised in battle but growing up in a mafia family is pretty much the same thing. Always on edge, always expecting danger and the other shoe to drop.

I grab Frankie and her cousin and haul them behind me. Frankie has her knives out, but her cousin looks like she's about to throw up.

"No, Kass," Frankie starts, always wanting to be on the front line, always feeling responsible for whatever bad happens. That girl is killing me, in all the best ways.

"Stay back. It's you they want."

"Which means they won't mind slaughtering you to get to me! Don't—"

With s snarl, I pull out my lash and snap it, catching one of the gorillas around the neck. I haul him away from Tir and Rook.

Rook who's already jumping on the other guy, dispatching him with a knife.

No mercy.

I yank on my leash and the gorilla chokes, trying in vain to dislodge the lash from his neck.

Then he drops to the ground like a sack of potatoes and a ringing quiet spreads.

I spin back to check on the girls—on *my* girl, mainly—and find them shaking but otherwise okay. The cousin is clutching Frankie's arm like a lifeline, hiding behind Frankie's backpack.

I grin approvingly when I see the knife still held in Frankie's hand. And I'm glad she decided to stay back and not jump into the fray as she normally does—although granted, that might be because she was protecting her cousin, and partly because she's still wiped out from bringing Asa back.

Speaking of whom...

Ah fuck. There's Asa, Ryu on his heels. They're racing toward us, faces tight with worry. How did they know?

"Is Frankie okay? Are you okay?" Asa grabs me by the shoulders, then grabs Frankie, his gaze running over her. Finally, his eyes flick to the others. "Status!"

"We're not in the army anymore, fuck's sake." Rook bends to retrieve his knife from the dead guard. He wipes the blade on his pants but I can see a faint smile on his face.

"We're fine," I tell Asa, nodding at Ryu who's slowed down and is also taking us in, checking to see everyone is okay.

"You knew," Frankie whispers, grabbing Asa's arm. "You felt it."

This tug in my chest when one of them is hurt or in danger.

We have a bond, I think, ridiculous as it may sound. Since when do we have a psychic bond? That normally doesn't happen, except if the girl is a witch and we're her elementals.

Looks like this witch snagged herself an angel, too, but otherwise I shouldn't be so surprised. I should have felt it.

She does look surprised, though. Guess she didn't see it coming. Didn't fully accept it until now.

"Oh God, what did just happen?" the dean whispers, slowly unfolding from her crouch by the wall where she crawled. "Why...? That's blood."

"Your men attacked us," I say.

"But... they are trusted men. Have been working here for years. I can't—"

I shrug. "Welcome to our world."

———

The dean's office is large, her desk big enough to host entire council meetings. It's ornate, carved of mahogany, reminding me of the mansion I grew up in. Two dark doors loom behind, probably leading to other offices. Two armchairs stand in front of the office, and I lead Frankie to one of them, while Rook leads Asa to the other.

Neither of them complains that we make them sit, a testament to their exhaustion.

"I still can't believe my men attacked you," the dean says, eyes wide, sinking into her leather office chair and folding her hands on top of her polished desk. "I've worked with them for so long, I can't believe they made a deal behind my back. I wonder what they were promised and who is paying them."

"We still don't know that," I say. "Heaven and the Four Houses want Frankie alive, but someone out there wants her dead pretty badly, and…"

A sharp tug in my chest. Magic. My contact with the House of Water, my handler, as Frankie very well put it, is pinging me.

I have to answer sooner or later but I ignore it for now.

"You really are a motley crew," the dean says on a sigh. "And you're so young. You make me feel old."

"Not all of us," Rook says. "Appearances can be deceiving, trust me."

"And the rest of us feel too old already," Frankie whispers.

I spare a glance for Asa who is sitting in the chair not occupied by Frankie. Didn't get much of a chance to check he's okay since he and Ryu came to the rescue earlier. He looks… haggard. Much like Frankie. A knot forms in my throat knowing he really fucking died. We almost lost him.

If not for Frankie…

She managed to send her cousin off on the way to the office, promising to talk to her later. She's sitting stiffly, still with her backpack on. Even with the dark bags under her eyes, she looks beautiful. More beautiful than ever. She hasn't complained at all, but her tiredness really worries me.

Asa's words echo in my mind. His warning that we shouldn't have let her bring anyone back again. That it sucks on her own life force. I wonder how that works in reverse, when her scream kills people. Does she get a boost of power?

I can't contemplate not having Tir and Asa back with us.

Dammit.

Another ping in my chest.

What's so urgent, I wonder? I hope Heaven hasn't already told the Houses that they won't be getting Frankie. I mean, what other outcome was there? We were just putting off the inevitable.

"Fuck," Rook mutters, pressing a hand to his chest. A glance at Tir and Ryu shows them wincing, too.

A general alert? What the fuck? We exchange dark glances.

"I don't know who to trust," the dean is saying. "The two men you just killed—I thought they were on the side of justice. And I promised your grandfather I'd take care of you, but now it looks like I can't do much to keep my promise."

"It's okay," Frankie says. "I don't think he foresaw this. He thought nobody knew I was coming here, but somehow everyone knew before I even arrived."

"Who leaked the information? Who could have been?"

"I wish we knew," I say. "Too many possibilities. She had assassins going after her for years. It's obvious the Four Houses and Heaven have known about Frankie for a long time."

"They didn't know what I am exactly," she says. "I didn't, either. But now the cat is out of the bag."

"I wish your grandfather had told me more," the dean says, leaning back in her chair. "What are you, then?"

Frankie frowns. "The White Queen Witch's daughter, of course."

"Yeah, of course, but..." The dean frowns. "He mentioned incidents but never told me why you had assassins coming after you. I was hoping you could tell me."

"I think it's time to end this meeting," I say, pushing off the wall I've been leaning on, a bad feeling souring my stomach. "We are behind on our classes and we take our education very seriously."

"Yeah, that's right." Ryu steps closer to the chair where

Frankie is sitting. "We probably have tests coming up and stuff. You know how it is."

"I mean..." The dean is still frowning. "I don't know why your grandfather thought you'd be safe here of all places."

"Because he trusts you?" Frankie says.

"You saw I can't look after you. Not if you don't tell me what your powers are. Why suddenly everyone is after you."

"There's no 'suddenly' in any of this," Frankie says, frowning. "I appreciate your concern and I promise to tell you anything that happens, but like Kass said, we should be in class."

"Class can wait, Azrael's daughter. We should talk more about security measures—"

"And how do you know who my father is?" Frankie scrambles out of her chair, panic written all over her face. "Oh, shit."

Ryu grabs her arm and hauls her against his side while drawing a *shuriken* from his belt. "Stay back."

"Frankie, wait." The dean rises, face distorting. I don't know what animal she is but we can't stay and find out.

Something's off, she shouldn't know so much about Frankie, Frankie hasn't even talked with her grandfather about her father and what we found out, or anything else. How much does the dean know?

"Let's go!" I grab Asa by the arm, pulling him to his feet, trusting Ryu to haul Frankie out of here. "Tir, Rook, move it."

"Not so fast," the dean says as we reach the door of the office, her voice distorting.

Then the two doors at the back of her office fly open and men pour inside, an avalanche of them, falling on us.

Fuck.

26

FRANKIE

I can't trust anyone.

Anyone except for my guys, I amend as we turn to face the men coming at us.

Shifters, I think, at least most of them, turned into their animals, and the dean is shifting, too.

Into a fucking tiger.

Holy shit. I grab for my flimsy knives, my heart thumping hard. Using my knives is against the College rules, I think randomly.

As if murdering people isn't.

There's a lion among the shifters. A few large wolves. And the tiger, of course.

We're in goddamn trouble.

"Go, go!" Kass shouts, pushing us back, toward the door. "Let's go!"

The beasts leap at us and for a mind-freezing moment, I think this is the end. Silly to have worried about so many things if a tiger is going to tear my throat out now. I open my mouth, a scream building in my chest—I'd kill again, despite my resolution not to, but no time for that as I'm dragged sideways by someone—

Asa's sword sings as he pulls it free of its scabbard and swings it against the tiger—

I throw my knives, one after the other, at the wolves jumping at us—

"Frankie." Ryu. It's Ryu hauling me sideways as the lion roars and leaps.

Shit, shit.

Rook's staff extends and he swings it around, hitting a wolf and sending him flying against the desk. Tir's unstrung bow serves as a staff, too, which he swings the other way, catching another wolf. The smack of the wood hitting flesh is thunderous.

As is the roar of the tiger Asa is fighting.

Cursing, I cast about for a weapon to help him. He's unsteady on his feet and the tiger is huge. Screw the dean. All this time she was waiting to ambush me? *Bitch.*

Kass cracks his whip at the tiger, managing to draw her away from Asa, his magic pulsing, distracting the beasts. We have magic on our side, I think, we should be winning.

But two men are standing at the back of the room, hands raised, and they seem to be pushing back on the Wonderboys' magic, putting out the fires, releasing the air, stopping the blood flow, tearing through the illusions Ryu throws.

Fire catches on Tir's clothes, and with a curse, he pulls his T-shirt off. With a loud curse, he wrenches the air from around one of the men and the man chokes, falling to the floor.

Ryu is half-shifted, his face contorting, his jaw too long and his mouth filled with sharp teeth. He claws at the lion who inches back. There's blood on his shirt.

The situation is getting hairy. The door, we have to get to the door...

It bangs open, and people pour inside. I grab Kass' arm, and pull him back, certain these are also assassins set on slaughtering us.

Don't scream, I tell myself, *don't scream*—though why not? Why not kill all these assholes? It's just... will I miss my guys again this time? Can I really control my power or was I only lucky the last two times?

But then I see Kalissa, and she nods at me as Fae and demons burst into the room. "We got this. Get out of here, now. Rook, get them out and keep her alive."

"I don't need you telling me that," Rook grumbles, throwing flames at a wolf trying to bite him, then shoving the howling wolf off him and turning to us. The room stinks of burned fur and spilled blood. "Let's go!"

Tir throws an arm around me, lifting me off my feet and running for the door, the others following. I sling an arm around his neck, a leg around his hip, and hold on for dear life as we race out of the melee.

All they have to do is slow the beasts down until I've hidden somewhere on campus, and then...

Well, then we'll see. One step at a time. I rest my head on Tir's bare, warm shoulder, drawing in his scent that's blending with the stench of acrid smoke, and I tell myself to be grateful we at least made it out of that office alive.

Granddad won't be too happy when I tell him about the dean's betrayal.

Then I wonder if I really want to talk to him, tell him about my new power. It's not that I don't trust him. I trust family. And I know I have to tell him eventually. But truth is, what can he do except worry more?

———

We run through the College. I'm still in Tir's hold and I wish I could still my thoughts and see clearly what we should be doing. I don't even ask him to put me down, aware that we're doing better time this way, his long, assured strides eating up the distance. His nipple hoops are hard pressure points into my side. His scent is sharp like jagged glass. His hair tickles my hands where they're wrapped around his strong neck.

Funny how you focus on small details like that when the world goes to Hell.

"Where are we going?" I ask. "Tir? Where can we go?"

"The arena," he says. "We'll barricade ourselves below. Safest place on campus."

"Move," Kass barks and leads the way, followed by Rook, then us, Asa and Ryu bringing up the rear. "We don't know who else might be compromised."

Just about everyone, I think as we make our way through the campus and to the huge arena in the park. *Anyone could be an assassin. Anyone could turn at any time.*

As long as I roam free, there will be no shortage of attackers, hopeful for one reward or another. And as long as I am a weapon, there will be no lack of powerful people wanting to use me.

I could run. I could hide. But what about the boys?

If only I could protect them...

"Asa!" I call his name. "You shouldn't be here with us. You should be in hiding."

"There is no point," Asa says. "They know I am alive."

"How?"

"The dome is still up. And only I can break the protocol and take it down."

"Shit." I cling to Tir, twisting my head to look at Asa. "That sounds pretty trusting and short-sighted on their part. Why would they give such power to you?"

"They thought they had me under their thumb. Never thought I'd question who I am and what I really want. "

"But surely Raziel himself can undo the Raziel Protocol... right?"

"He can unravel the spell," Asa says. "It will take him at least a day and a night."

"A day. That's all we have?"

"Two, tops."

There goes any chance to attend class, I think, kind of randomly.

But not that randomly, I suppose. Deep inside, I realize I was excited to live a normal life for a while. Be a student. Talk with my cousin. Date gorgeous boys. Laugh and party and feel safe.

Feel free of guilt.

We reach the arena and Kass leads us through an underpass that leads to what has to be changing rooms and storerooms under the bleachers. We race through the dark passages, lights automatically flickering to life as we go, illuminating the corridors and gray metal doors going past us.

Finally, Kass opens one of those doors and we burst into a changing room. We all stop in the middle of it. I struggle in Tir's arms and after an endless moment where it's almost as if he's forgotten where he is and what he's doing, he lets me down on my feet.

A couple of gym mattresses are stacked against one wall, as well as some equipment—face guards and gauntlets for Scaleball I assume, as well as someone's forgotten dirty sock. The lockers are old and covered in small graffiti.

Rook closes and locks the door. He stays still for long moments, one hand braced on it. I wonder if he's listening out for pursuers or if he's lost in thought.

What a mess.

Trying not to think at all, I put down my backpack and check out the place. Another door opens at the other end and walking there I find another locker room, and then the bathrooms. At least, we have water and won't die of thirst.

The whole place smells funky, stinking of old sweat, old plastic, and male deodorant.

Though now it also smells of five hot guys, their yummy scent overlaying the stench.

Finishing my quick tour of our new abode, I return to find them frowning, some seated on the bench, some standing. Rook has pulled a mat to the floor and is sitting cross-legged on it, winding his long hair back in a knot.

"What's wrong?" I ask when nobody speaks.

"Well," Kass says. "House of Water won't leave me in peace. I have to take this call, guys."

"Same," Tir says, a hand on his chest, and the others nod. "We should see what they want, why they're all pinging us like crazy."

They look worried.

"Then take your calls," I say. Makes sense that their handlers would want to talk to them with everything that's happening. "We have to know what Heaven told them, if anything, right, Asa? And I need to talk to my granddad."

27

FRANKIE

*T*hey don't protest. I carry their worried faces in my mind as I slip into the dark bathrooms and sit on a small bench there, reaching for my magic. I cast my thought out to my granddad, using my power like a line.

The spell evades me at first. I try to recall how I did it last time—I've only tried it, what, twice so far? Also, I keep thinking of the boys and that muddies the connection, I guess.

Focus on Granddad, Franks.

When his kindly face appears at last, I heave a sigh of relief. "Granddad!"

"Franks! Why didn't you call me sooner? I tried reaching out to you but nothing got through. I've been so damn worried."

"I'm sorry."

"What happened, Honey? There's been a lot of movement in Heaven, or so my ears there tell me."

So I tell him my news.

Not your average everyday account, that's for sure.

I tell him about my father.

My new-found abilities.

And the dean's betrayal.

Granddad wipes a hand down his face. "My God. I hadn't expected that. I can't trust anyone anymore."

"I said the same," I whisper.

"Franks, setting the dean aside for a moment... rewind." Granddad actually mimes rewinding something... a tape? "Did you really say you can bring people back to life?"

I fight a wince. "Yes."

"Are you sure?"

"Oh yes." I nod, flashes of the pain I felt seeing Tir and Asa die pinching my heart. "I am sure. Nobody else knows apart from me and the boys."

"*The boys,* huh?"

"Granddad..."

His voice becomes serious once more. "Listen, Franks. Something like that never stays under wraps for long."

"You're right. Asa says Heaven must already know he's back because the Raziel Protocol he implemented is still in place. So Heaven must know about me, if they hadn't known before."

"You brought back the guy who locked you up in that thrice-damned college?"

"Oh God... He's a nice guy."

"I bet he is. About to deliver you to Heaven, isn't he?"

"No," I say fiercely, "he isn't. None of them are."

"Are you so sure?"

"Yes," I insist, even as a tiny doubt nibbles at my certainty.

"Daughter of Azrael. Of course it makes sense," Granddad muses. "Had we known sooner who your father is, we might have predicted this power of yours."

"You never thought to take a good look at my pendant," I mutter, annoyed with him even though we had examined it together.

"Your pendant? Your mother's trinket?"

"It's a locket, Granddad. It used to belong to Azrael."

He frowns. "You mean the answer was under our noses all this time?"

I almost laugh at the indignant tone. "Yes."

"Such power over life and death. No wonder everyone wants a piece of you. No wonder Heaven is displeased. Only Heaven is supposed to manage resurrection. Death, well. That's the easy part. Killing, I mean."

"Easy for you to say, perhaps," I whisper. "But if this is because of my father... because of Azrael... does that mean that he can also bring people back?"

Granddad is quiet. Then he says, "Archangels can bring people back to life sometimes, if life just left them. Restarting the heart, gathering their soul back."

"I didn't know."

"Not common knowledge. Like I said, Heaven would want such secrets locked down, not known outside. But bringing someone back... there is a price to pay. You give some of your soul to that person."

"What does that even mean?"

"Your soul is your spiritual energy," he explains. "It's what keeps you alive as much as your body. The more you give away, the closer you get to death."

"Angels don't die, do they?" I think of Asa, lying there lifeless, and swallow hard. "At least, that's what I thought."

"It depends on their lineage. And you aren't an angel, Franks. At best we believe you may be an angel's daughter. We don't know if bringing people back could kill you sooner rather than later."

"It doesn't matter," I whisper. "I don't know what to do. The dome will be down soon... Heaven and the Four Houses will swoop down to claim me."

"The moment the dome goes down, I will be there, and so will Mia and her conduits. We'll take you away."

I hate when he calls my uncles "conduits" though they are

that, too. But above all, they are my uncles, and the men my aunt loves. "And then what?"

"I don't know. We'll buy you some time."

I hesitate. "Are you really going to oppose Heaven?"

"Been doing that for a while now." He finally smiles. "And for my family, I'd do that and more."

"I don't want to get you into trouble, Granddad. You, or Auntie and my uncles."

"You were trouble since you were born," he says, still smiling. "The good kind of trouble. Keeping me on my toes."

I blink, my eyes hot and wet. "Right."

"You have to keep me updated on what's going on, Franks. And if you develop any other abilities, you have to tell me, all right? We need to know all the parameters before we act."

"I feel like a nuclear head about to explode," I whisper. "Everyone's afraid, and I don't know how to stop from taking people down with me."

"You're not going down. We'll do everything in our power, I prom—"

"Don't," I breathe. "Don't promise me you'll save me. Tell me... wouldn't you lock away someone who is a danger to others?"

"You're not that, Frankie. You are learning to control your powers."

"It doesn't matter," I say bitterly. "It doesn't matter if I do. Nobody cares about that. The powers-that-be care about what I can do. My potential. And no matter what I do, I'll get people that I love killed..."

"That doesn't change anything for me," Granddad says, his voice steady. "I will still be there. We will be there to try and save you."

I know he will. I push myself up from the bench, then lower myself to the floor. I see it playing out in my mind's eye, my family arriving to save me only to be caught in a bloody battle and I shudder.

Breaking the connection, I stay there for a while, trying to think of a way to keep my family from getting hurt and keep from being taken away, too.

And the boys?

What will the boys do? What have they decided? What bone or punishment will be thrown at them to sway them away from me?

Eventually, I make myself get up. I need to talk with them.

What I don't know is that things are about to get infinitely worse.

Of course, it was mentioned before and I should have seen it coming, but I think none of us did...

———

The boys look... gloomy. I can't find another word for it. They look like someone told them their cat was run over or something.

"What's up?" I ask.

They shake their heads. All of them.

Okay, this is weird. "What happened?"

"Nothing... nothing," Ryu says.

"You are lying to me. I thought we were done lying to one another. Is it bad news? Did something happen to your loved ones, or... or did you get new orders?"

"Nothing," Tir says, and I realize his face is very pale.

"Something scared you." I turn to Rook. "Is it something about me?"

Rook shakes his head, not looking at me.

"Tell me," I insist.

"Jesus. Frankie, let it go, okay?" Kass snaps.

"How can I just let it go? You all look unhappy."

"Well, that's the state of things. Unhappiness. Things aren't exactly going our way right now."

"I see." I push the hurt down. "Fine. Don't tell me."

You see? the voice that sounds so much like mine screeches in my head. *Why didn't you listen to me? Why did you decide to give your heart away?*

Shut up, I tell it. *It was my decision. And I won't regret it.*

Are you sure?

"Anyone see a first-aid kit?" Ryu says. "I seem to be bleeding all over the place."

Shit.

————

Ryu is bleeding, Tir is singed, though that's too light a word for the red burns on his back, but being Fae I hope he'll heal quickly. Kass moves like he has broken ribs. Rook refuses to let me check him over so I suspect he's wounded, too, and Asa... He's quiet, staring down at his hands.

I hate this. This strange, sudden awkwardness and stiffness between us. How can I fix it if they won't tell me?

Did the powers-that-be threaten what is dear to them? I know they said that it's not the same as before—Kass with Brody, Tir with his family, Ryu with those he lost, Rook with traveling the world. Even Asa who's been longing to return to Heaven seems now unsure about the wisdom of it.

But you can't turn feelings off just like that. I should know. I've tried.

I find a first aid kit, wouldn't you know, and start cleaning out the cuts on Ryu's arms and sides. It looks like claws tried to rip him apart, and my heart thumps heavily as I bandage him. He's so quiet.

Everyone is still so quiet.

I don't get it.

I touch Tir's shoulder, and he jerks away. I try not to take it personally, but oh boy, it's a struggle.

"Just going to put some burn cream on your back," I tell him, and at least he just goes still and lets me do it.

They all drift away from me again once I'm done, not an easy feat given how much space their tall, muscular bodies take and the cramped little room we're in.

The sinking feeling in my stomach grows.

"Okay, guys." I put my hands on my hips. "I know I'm making your life hard by being *me,* but... can you at least talk to me?"

"It's not you." Ryu is studying the view from the small window of the changing room, and I can testify that it's not as exciting as that.

"You don't make our life hard," Asa says.

"We like you being you," Rook mutters—from the other side of the narrow room, pressed to the wall by the metal door.

"Well, you're not acting like it right now. Just... tell me what I did. You're mad at me, and I don't know why."

They only shake their heads. Stay quiet a bit more, gazing at various inanimate objects—the walls, the mat, the bench, the door.

Dammit.

"Okay," I grate out. "Don't tell me. It's not like you owe me the truth or anything."

And that only makes their frowns darker.

Still no reply.

The tension in the room is palpable. The boys are all but vibrating with it, hands clenched into fists, broad shoulders taut. I can even hear them breathing harshly.

What in the world happened? Why won't they tell me?

"Fine, be that way." Refusing to acknowledge the prickling at the backs of my eyes—what the Hell, did they have a meeting and agreed to ghost me now?—I pull my book out of my backpack.

Cradling it to my chest, I take a breath. It's like holding an old friend, a confidante, a bosom buddy who knows my secrets.

Sitting on the bench, I leaf through it, trying to calm myself.

Here Mowgli is talking to Kaa, the snake—and in the margin I have scribbled my annoyance at Juliette for a fight we had regarding Aunt Mia. I can't remember what the fight was about exactly. It was so long ago.

And here Mowgli is in the monkey palace—and in the margin I have drawn a monkey with a face like my cousin Kellen's. Obviously, I'd had a grievance. It makes me smile.

In the part where Mowgli talks with the bear Baloo, I have written an extensive note on how being a girl sucks because of periods and stupid boys, and in another part where he runs through the jungle, I have written a tear-stained little essay on how I feel so alone sometimes, even surrounded by my family, because nobody knows what it's like to be the villain's daughter.

Aunt Mia had found me after that, I recall, and hugged the Hell out of me. Told me how loved I am. Dried my tears and made everything better.

"This can't go on," Ryu mutters, turning away from the small window. "What will you guys do?"

I glance up, torn from happy memories. "I'm sorry, what?"

"It will be fine," Tir says.

Ryu whirls on him. "How do you reckon that?"

Asa is quiet, scowling at them.

"The moment the dome goes down, we escape," Tir says. "We run like Hell and hole up someplace."

"Yeah, that was the plan, wasn't it?" Rook gives a strangled laugh. "Fucking Hell."

"We're going through with it," Tir says, turning to glare at all of them. "Any objections?"

"*I* object," I say. "No."

Asa finally reacts. "No? What do you mean, no?"

"*I* escape. *I* run and you stay. If I am gone, you are safe."

"You forget that our Houses won't let us just stay here and, I don't know... continue with our studies or something." Tir bares his teeth at me. "We run with you."

"You will live a life on the run?"

"There is no other choice!"

"You could renegotiate, tell that you'd made a mistake—"

"We fucking can't, Frankie!" Kass snarls. "Fucking dammit."

"Shit." I jerk, glance from one to the next. "Now will you tell me what happened?"

"You wanna know what happened?" Rook steps closer to me, his face flickering. Handsome. Monstrous. Scarred. Beautiful.

I jump to my feet. "Yes."

But Rook grabs me and wrenches the book from my hold, pages ripping. I cry out, reaching for it, but he pulls it apart.

He pulls my book, my journal, my *friend* apart.

"No..." Tears of shock slip from my eyes as I go after the book, but he keeps tearing at it, turning his back to me. "No!"

"This is what happens when you hang out with the men sent to kidnap you. Monsters, like us."

"Dammit, Rook," Tir says, "stop—"

"This." He turns my book into confetti and when I reach for it, he shoves me away. "This is what happens."

Shoves me right into Kass' hands, who wraps a hand around my neck. "What do you think happened, Frankie? What do you think they ordered us to do the moment they realized what you can do?"

They're all on their feet now, crowding in around us.

I choke. Try to pry Kass' fingers from my neck. "Let go."

Asa takes a step toward us, his hands curled into fists. "Kass. Stop."

"Scream," Kass breathes in my ear. "Scream now and end it all."

No. No!

Tir and Ryu approach us, too, eyes narrowed. None of them moves to get Kass' hands off my neck.

My heart is banging about inside my chest. *You trust them,* I remind myself. *You trust them with your life. Right? Decide if you do or not. If you want to kill them or not.*

You can't turn feelings off just like that. Remember? What if the choice they were given was impossible?

Then Tir tears Kass away from me and punches him. "What the fuck do you think you're doing?"

"Following my fucking orders," Kass grunts and slashes at Tir's arm with sharp claws as I stumble to the side, gasping.

"We all got those orders," Rook growls, "and you don't see us choking the life out of her."

"No, you're only destroying her things and waiting for her to catch on. So clever. A prelude for things to come?"

Rook grabs and shakes him, his eyes bleeding to black. "Shut your mouth."

"Stop. Kass, Rook... just stop. Shit." I cough, my throat aching. "Holy shit."

Nobody moves to touch me again. Just as well.

I glance at the ripped-up pages of my book on the floor. Glance back at the boys.

That silence from before blankets us again, suffocating. They're waiting to see if I figured it out, I realize. And I think I have.

"You were ordered to eliminate me, weren't you?" I croak, rubbing at my neck. "All of you?"

Their tense faces are my answer.

They were told to kill me.

Like I said, I should have seen it coming. They, too.

"Then do it." I take a breath, open my arms. "You should. I shouldn't be allowed to go free."

"Frankie," Asa says, just my name, yet it's like a moan of pain.

"Only think of a way that won't get you punished. If you do it..." I swallow against the lump in my throat. "Agree you will all say you did it. They can't prove who it was. Maybe that will work."

"You really think we'd do that," Kass breathes.

I frown at him. The imprint of his fingers burns on my throat. "Yes."

Kass hisses. I flinch when he stalks back to me, when he lifts a hand to my neck again. "Is that what bothers you? That we'll be punished? Is that what you heard when we told you we were told to eliminate you?"

I swallow against his fingers. They caress my skin and it hurts, already bruising. "But—"

"Goddammit." Kass' hand releases my throat and falls to my arm. He buries his face in my neck. "Dammit, Frankie. No."

"We'll think of something else then," I whisper.

"Think of what?" His eyes are full of torment when he lifts his head. "I wanted to see if I could hurt you. But I can't do it. There's no fucking way in Hell." His arms go around me, hauling me back against his tall body. "Can't face a world without you."

I break. I fall apart. My knees buckle and Tir sweeps his arms around me, holding me up. I'm pressed between their bodies. "I can't do it, either."

"You must. I'll be your downfall," I breathe. "Your death."

"This was our choice," Kass says, his voice cracking. "To take on this mission. This isn't on you."

"You are the reason we smile every morning," Tir tells me. "You're the reason we want to live. *Kraish, elenyi,* I've spent my life hating who I am, hoping time would turn back, and I don't wish for that anymore."

"I don't want to end it all," Ryu says, coming to join us. "Not anymore. I want to see the future. With you."

"Told you, Darling," Rook says as he throws an arm over Tir's shoulders. "You changed my mind about everything. I know the world won't give me what we have here. Come here, give us a hug." He hesitates. "Sorry about your book."

I slap at him, my breath hitching. I want to slap them, kick them, I want to scream at them. For tearing up my book, for bruising my neck. For bruising my heart.

Asa comes last, his eyes troubled. He stands on my other side, tucking a strand of hair behind my ear. "I wasn't asked to end you, which probably means that the Houses are going behind Heaven's back to do it. They've realized Heaven is about to get you. For the record... I would never hurt you, Musen. I didn't know it when I arrived here, but I know it now."

I'm crying now, ugly sobs, because I almost lost my trust—in them, in my assessment of their character, of their feelings. Almost. I got what I've always wanted, this normal, happy life with these hot men. Almost.

And yet if they do this, if they refuse to end me, they're dead.

I look at them through my tears and my heart is full.

So what if it's cracked? I have this, right now, and if it's all I get, then it will be the last happy memory I'll keep, whatever fate throws at me next.

My heart is full, and I want them. I want them more than I ever have, but it's different. Deeper. Stronger. It takes over my body and soul.

Then Tir kisses me, drinking my salty tears, turning the emotion into lust, and I fall into them, not caring right now if we all live or die.

28

ROOK

*F*or days, it's been like watching events unfold through water, through a thick lens distorting everything. Distorted battles, distorted touches, voices coming and going.

The order to kill her made me goddamn dizzy.

Goddamn crazy.

I always thought that seeing red was an expression, but I swear my sight fucking turned crimson.

Shredding her book. Coming so close to hurting her bodily.

Only I wasn't the one who lost control. It was Kass. He almost ended her life... and she could have ended mine, ours, with a single scream.

She didn't.

Guilt is a vise around my heart, but the anger, the helplessness, it's even worse.

If I killed her, I'd have killed myself next, I know that.

Even telling her about our orders would have been Hell, and I'm glad Kass was the one to break the news. We knew it might come to this. But until I got my orders, I wasn't sure I'd be so ready to give it all up for her.

Now I know.

Now we all know.

I'm not quite sure I get it, I think as we all come together around her. Not sure how this love thing works. I've had friendships over the years, I've had lovers. I've lived a long, dangerous life. Sex has been my number one diversion, and also a need. But this thing with her, with them... It's not the same.

Not one fucking bit.

For starters, in the past, I'd never hold back and let another kiss her, touch her. Wouldn't have taken pleasure in watching like a voyeur but also in giving my spot, taking pleasure in seeing two people I care for together.

Two or more. I grin when Kass starts kissing her neck while Tir tastes her lips.

It looks like an invitation for everyone to join in, and yet I still hold back. So unlike me. I watch as Ryu starts running his hands over her, as Asa strokes her hair—a hair fetish? Who knew?—and nuzzles her.

Fuck, I'm hard as Hell.

And right now, everything is sharp and in focus, everything clear.

You'd say it's my incubus nature.

But it's more than that.

Much more.

For the first time in my goddamn life, I know what I want. Who I want it with. I'm a damn seer. I can see the fucking future.

A bit too late for that, isn't it, Raksa? The future you see is improbable, not to say impossible. A bit too fucking late to discover love, and all that jazz.

With a low growl, I finally join in the tangle of bodies. Ryu is tugging them down, to the mattress on the floor, and I grab two more and throw them down beside the one already there.

Then I haul them all down, down with me.

Let's get down and dirty, that's my motto.

And the weird lurch in my chest when I put my hands on them is starting to make sense...

Tir seems determined to get inside Frankie first, and I run an appreciative hand over his muscular ass, helping him pull down his pants. Kass is divesting Frankie of her shirt, his hands cupping her tits through her black bra, and Asa...

Asa whips off his shirt and my mind blanks out a little. I do notice that the wound on his chest is gone, a thin scar left behind. That's some quick healing.

But then Frankie moans and I'm done watching. I wanna play. I want in on this game that feels like much more than that, on this ritual of bonding and exploring of bodies and feelings.

I want into the family.

And right now, I very much fucking want *into* Frankie, or maybe into one of those muscular asses getting revealed as the boys drop their pants in a hurry.

Oh, yeah.

I'd definitely tap one of those.

All of those.

This is better than traveling, eating gourmet food, and drinking the finest Whiskey. This is Heaven, baby.

Even in the middle of this fucking mess, with trusted allies turned traitors, with ultimatums that will most probably mean our deaths, with Frankie in danger and these newfound feelings in the balance.

Asa pulls Frankie to him, cups her face and kisses her, while, to my delight, Kass turns to me and hauls me against him, pressing his forehead to mine.

"We're doing this," he whispers. "Really doing this."

"Fuck, yeah."

When his mouth slams against mine, I savor him, parting his lips with my tongue, tasting his mouth. I'm fucking torn, to be honest, between discovering how Kass tastes, how he feels against me, all hard muscles, his big dick hard and hot in his pants, and watching as Tir and Asa undress Frankie, kissing her mouth, her neck, her shoulders.

Fuck, her tits are glorious.

Then Ryu joins Kass and I, effectively distracting me. What's a demon to do when flanked by two smoking-hot hunks? My body has needs, immediate needs, and Rooky, the rascal, is so hard and heavy it does feel like a nuclear warhead.

I can pleasure all of them.

No problem.

Just gimme time.

"Come here, fox." I grab the back of his neck, haul him in for a kiss, too—why not taste all of them? Rooky is excited about this, dammit—growling deep in my throat when he aggressively kisses back, grinning against my mouth, not as reticent as Kass.

Then again, I like the reticence, the contrast between the violence and the incredible strength, and that odd shyness. Lowered dark lashes, a soft mouth, an uncertain look, all in a lethal body, and I'm a goner.

Such a goner for this fucking fox, so decisive in taking what he wants, even if he clearly has never been with a man before.

Damn these guys. They're scorching.

I grab hold of Kass' arm and drag him closer, in case he decides to change his mind and go off to bite someone, while feasting on Ryu's sweet mouth.

The fox is giving back as good as he gets, feasting on my mouth, exploring with his tongue, biting and licking. He's gripping my hip with one hand, my shoulder with the other, bruising, and I welcome the ache.

It answers the ache in my gut—in my chest—in my mind.

Sliding down a hand over his muscular chest, I pinch his nipple, rewarded by a hiss and a nip at my lips.

Then his hand slips from my hip to my ass, grabbing it and slamming me against his very prominent hard-on.

"Oh, yeah, good initiative," I growl against his mouth. "Love it. Come here, Kass." I haul him even closer, until the three of us have our faces almost touching one another. "Let me show you how we start off in Hell..."

Their hard cocks bump against my hands as I reach for them. They've both helpfully shed their clothes, so this is easy.

I wrap my hands around their cocks, press our bodies closer together... shove my weeping cock into the equation... and close my hands over all three.

A gathering of cocks.

A game of flushed, wet crowns.

A song of desire and need.

Kass gasps, grabbing my biceps, staring down where I'm pleasuring all three of us. Ryu reaches down to help me stroke us.

"Come on, kit." I grin at him. "Let's do this. Grip them hard..."

It's fun. It's pleasure. It's a prelude.

Kass groans, tipping his forehead to my shoulder. He's not new to being with men, as we all know, which makes that blush on his cheeks... endearing. He also obviously hasn't been with men in a long while, or with anyone, if his touch aversion is anything to go by.

Not until us.

His cock is long and veined, hot against mine. Ryu's is thicker, a little curved. No knot, I notice idly, like an actual fox would have—yeah, being a demon means I have experience with quite a few animal cocks, too.

Sue me if you like.

His green eyes are glued on our cocks, the way the skin slides as we move our hands over them, the pearly drops beading at the crowns. A bouquet of cocks.

Well, aren't I a fucking poet?

"*Minchia,*" Kass breathes, his fingertips digging furrows into my biceps, sweat dripping from his brow. "Yeah, there..."

He erupts first, his cock jerking in my hold. I admit I follow next, so taken by the sight I let go without a thought—because it's us, and there's no one I need to impress—and then Ryu swears and hunches over as he joins us.

We all come almost at the same time, a fountain of cum and heat.

It's perfect.

We're all three of us groaning, now hanging off one another, as the waves of pleasure drain out of us, when I sense a presence at my back.

I know who it is before turning around—that warm glow, that sweet scent, that feeling of rightness and arousal skittering down my spine.

Yeah, I'm still hard. Surprised? Let me introduce you to some incubus qualities. First one... we are hard, though not hard to please. Second, pretty boys and girls get us hard in an instant...

And there she is, naked and beautiful and damn hot.

Frankie.

Reaching for me.

Oh, yeah...

———

A hand outstretched, she's gazing at us, at me, lips red and eyes dark, and I drag the guys with me, closing the distance between us as I reach for her hand.

It's like a ritual dance, like those ridiculous courting dances birds do, like the medieval dances I saw people perform in the French villages in my youth, both of us flanked by two people, taking a step simultaneously toward one another, reaching for one another.

"Rook," she whispers as our bodies collide. She has bite marks on her neck, on her breasts, and it ignites my desire more. She smells sweet and wet. Asa and Tir are still fully hard, so I didn't miss out on them having sex while I played with the boys' pretty cocks.

I lick my lips. This is a buffet. A feast.

And she is my main course. My main goal. My heart.

"Come here, Darling," I whisper, overwhelmed by all this. "Let's fuck."

Her lips tilt in a grin. "Yeah," she says, "let's."

I tumble her to the mattress, pressing myself between her legs, Asa and Tir following us down, lazily stroking themselves.

That's when I realize we need to shift positions.

"There you are." I lift her to her knees and kiss her, feast on her tits, make her arch as I play with her nipples, licking and sucking them. I'm on my knees, too, and I pull her onto my lap.

She's so ready. I'm just putting off the pleasure of entering her. Using two fingers, I push into her and she cries out, clenching hard.

"Rook," she repeats my name, her voice strangled.

And that's when Asa and Tir scoot closer, bodies gleaming, cocks hard and flushed, putting their hands on her.

"Oh, yeah," I growl. "What are you two waiting for? Join in."

They put their mouths on her neck, her back, her arms. Asa settles behind her.

"That's what I'm talking about," I crow. "Tir, get behind him. Let's all join hands. Or bodies. You know what I mean."

Frankie snorts softly, and I grin at her.

"Where were we? Oh, right." I lift a hand to her face, stroking her cheek. "Gonna make you scream, my Sweet. You'll see."

"Promises, promises," she breathes, then gasps when Asa strokes her ass, Tir muttering directions in his ear. "Oh, God..."

Darkness flickers inside of me. Dark arousal rises, a need so vast it swallows me. I laugh out loud, my elemental magic shaking me as I absorb all this need from everyone around me.

I'm guiding my cock between her legs when Ryu and Kass join us, too, kneeling behind me, stroking me—my ass, my legs, but also stroking one another, judging from the sounds they make.

This is... this is what I've secretly hoped for, what I've needed. All of us together.

This feeling surging through me. More than arousal. More than need.

It makes my goddamn eyes prickle.

Gonna cry like a fucking baby.

I groan when Kass settles behind me, teasing my ass, trailing a knowing finger between my ass cheeks. "Yeah, do it. Do it."

When he groans in return, I'm sure Ryu is behind him, preparing to join us all, as I bade them, linking us in a chain of arousal and intimacy, a chain of passion and worship.

Pushing into her, I start the chain reaction. Her pussy grips me, so hot and tight, and the avalanche of emotions is drowning me as much as the pleasure wrung from her body.

This is it, I think. *If this is the end, then I'm ready.*

29

FRANKIE

I've never been in a situation like this. Five boys, five men I'm in love and lust with, surrounding me, touching me, touching one another.

Rook has his hand between my legs, making me squirm with arousal, toying with my folds, dipping his fingers in and out of me—and then Asa settles behind me, stroking my ass.

My brain threatens to short-circuit and burn down.

Asa... his hand joins Rook's at my pussy, dipping inside, drawing mewling sounds from my throat that don't sound like me. I'm writhing, a creature made of need. His fingers join Rook's inside me, then he draws my wetness to my ass, and then... then he dips a finger inside.

Stroking my ass from the inside.

My mouth falls open. I've never done this before, and... and didn't expect it to feel so good. I'm so engrossed in the sensations, a strange feeling of fullness although it's not the usual kind of fullness I'm used to, that I don't realize when Rook's fingers leave me.

I do realize it, though, when his cock takes their place, because *holy shit*... No wonder he calls it a warhead.

He spreads my legs wider, shoving at my thighs with his muscular ones, opening me wide, pushing his cock into me.

Wrapping a hand in my long hair, he tugs, pulling me forward, so that I lower my body, impaling myself on his hard-on.

A cry leaves my lips as his cock inexorably slides deeper into me, spreading me, filling me to bursting. Pleasuring me. I start to come even as he pushes deeper, shaking on top of him, moaning his name.

"Beautiful," he growls, his true face flickering in and out of reality, the shadow of dark wings rising on either side of him. "So damn beautiful."

I'm still gasping, clenching hard around his thick cock, my hips rolling as I milk more pleasure from it, when something big prods at my ass.

"Ready for me?" Asa whispers in my ear and I don't have time to do more than nod, when his cock nudges at my back entrance.

And pushes into me.

Oh, dear God...

It's another slow thrust, unstoppable and mindblowing as he fills my ass, stroking something so deep inside my core that I jerk in shock.

Damn... I'm poised on another orgasm, Asa's panting echoing in my ears, his hands on my hips stopping me from toppling against Rook's chest.

Rook who groans, pupils dilating, lips parting, teeth sharpening. Over his shoulder, I see Kass grimacing, cursing, rocking against Rook, and behind him I see Ryu doing the same.

The thought of all of them sinking into one another has me clenching again, coming again so hard I see stars.

My wail of pleasure has barely left my lips when Asa starts to move, rocking into my ass, Rook rocking into my pussy, nailing me between them. Their groans turn primal, harsh, torn from their throats as if against their will. We're all fucking now, rocking together, each of us breached in ways we'd never dreamed before. Breached, taken, owned.

Connected.

We are all touching, stroking, all of us connected in a grand circle of arousal and need, of pleasure and affection.

And as another wave of pleasure wells up in me, rising to engulf me, I feel a yank, a jolt in my chest. In my magic.

I grip Rook's arms, screaming as it all slams into me—the pleasure of another release, the blinding flash of magic, the feel of my men inside my mind.

Holy shit...

The chorus of groans and curses tells me the pleasure is going around, one by one my Wonderboys collapsing on top of one another.

Super domino, I think, and want to laugh but can't find the energy for it. Cards toppling.

A circle closing.

Rook has his arms around me, his face buried in my neck. Asa has claimed the other side of my neck, his breaths warm on my skin. They're both still pulsing inside me.

Behind Rook, Kass shakes his head slowly, like a wet dog, muttering something under his breath.

Ryu chuckles.

Asa kisses my neck.

Tir moans behind him.

The entire row of us ripples, and pleasure washes through me in a quiet wave.

God...

It takes us a while to start disentangling ourselves. I feel the movement as Ryu draws back, pulling Kass along, so that Rook jerks a little, hissing.

Then somewhere behind me, Tir moves, and Asa groans, his cock twitching inside my ass.

"All right, Sweetheart?" Rook mutters, still buried to the hilt inside me. "Not hurting you, are we?"

"No, it's... it's not that." I'm struggling to catch my breath. "Did you feel that?"

"The orgasm that hit us all like a freight truck?" He grins. "You bet."

"Be serious."

His grin fades. He rubs his chest. "Yeah. Yeah, I felt it."

"What was it?"

"We're connected." Ryu rests his chin on Kass' shoulder to gaze at me with wide green eyes. "And I don't mean only physically."

"Something clicked," Kass says. "Inside of us."

"I felt you all," Tir says.

"I felt all of us," Asa whispers.

"A witch and her conduits," I breathe. "I didn't think it would happen. But I've felt it..."

"...we've felt it before," Kass says. "It was bound to happen, to be finalized, sooner or later. It's..."

"...the path we chose," Ryu says, "the path we want..."

"...or fate," Tir whispers. "Who knows how destiny works, but I..."

"...want this," Asa breathes against my neck. "We're now..."

"... one," Rook finishes, tucking a strand of hair behind my ear. "If you want us, Frankie." He cracks a rueful smile. "Guess I'm asking a bit too late."

I shake my head. "The reason this happened is because I wanted it." I swallow. "I want it. It's you who should doubt this. Binding yourselves to me and one another... I'm the worst person to be around when you want to keep breathing."

"Our choice," Kass says firmly, and the others echo his words. "Our choice. We want this."

And so do I...

———

Well.... in a twist of fate I'd never anticipated, I'm now bound to five annoying, fabulous, sexy men.

Like Aunt Mia bound my four uncles to her.

What does it mean? What do I do now? It wasn't exactly on purpose that we fell in bed together. Not planned. Not with anything on our minds other than finding pleasure together.

I ponder this development—unexpected, but not entirely so—as we troop back to our room the next day. Rook scouted ahead as the other boys flanked me, weapons and magic at the ready, as we crossed the campus and re-entered the dormitories, everyone's eyes following us.

It's a relief to be back in our small room. It feels... like home, somehow. And I need to change clothes. My top ended up ruined, one of the seams torn, and my pants are stained with something.

Stains never made me smile before.

I end up pulling on one of Kass' black T-shirts. It's huge on me, and I like his scent on it. I focus on that as I take stock. My boys have been up and about since we came back, showering in groups, fussing over me. Tir is on guard right now, his gaze roaming over me, lingering on my boobs.

He doesn't even try to hide it. It brings heat to my cheeks as I remember what we did last night.

I glance at my bunk bed, my backpack sitting there, and recall that my book... is gone. A pang goes through my chest, followed by a surge of anger against Rook for tearing it apart. Funny, I'm angrier at him for destroying my book than with Kass who went for my neck.

That had been a frightening moment, though now I

understand their frustration and fear when they received their new orders.

Kill her or lose whatever you hold most dear. Kill her or lose everything.

Kill her or die yourselves.

I shiver.

Nobody's dead, I remind myself. Sure, they haven't refused their orders openly, definitively yet. Can the dome protect them for now? Will it stop the Four Houses and Heaven from punishing them?

I've lost my book, my adolescence, and my mental health support in one fell swoop. But what is that damage in the bigger picture? What does my worrying about the future, about my magic and the damage I can do to the world matter, when these boys... these five *men* have everything to lose.

And still, they aren't afraid of me. They have confidence in me that I won't harm them, that I will find a way out of this. They are willing to sacrifice themselves for me.

Maybe later today reality will smack me upside the head and wipe this stupid smile off my face, but I can't stop smiling.

Even when Tir says, "Ready for your training?"

"In sex?" I ask innocently, batting my lashes at him.

Rook laughs. "We've created a monster."

"Fight training," Tir says, not taking the bait. "You promised you'd let me train you."

"Did I? You already gave me a lesson in knife throwing."

"When you almost beheaded Asa? I remember. That was the only time, though. We've barely scratched the surface. And we need to train you in magic, too."

I snap my mouth shut, then, because he's right. It's necessary. Taking a deep breath, I nod. "Fine. Lead the way."

His face lights up. You'd think I'm giving him a present.

Looks like I did. He's a sadist, I think a couple of hours later, as I sweat in the park behind the arena, trying for the hundredth time to follow his instructions, observed by Rook and Ryu.

"Center yourself. Focus on the elemental power." Tir's voice cracks like a whip, my connection to him burning when he orders me to stop and try again, when he snaps at me for falling back on my knives and forgetting to tap into my power.

"I'm trying," I snap right back.

"I know." His voice softens. Then hardens again. The man is obviously used to commanding others. "Differentiate between your powers. Angelic is white. Elemental is... what color is it? Do you have a specific element affinity? Most witches do."

"I think it's blue," I whisper, twirling my knives.

"Air. Figures." He winks. "House of Air. Because we Fae are the best."

"No, idiot," Ryu calls out, "it's because she is also part angel and angels have an affinity for air."

"Because we Fae used to be angels."

"So you keep saying, though I can't see anything angelic in you, fairy boy," Rook says. "Frankie, remember I'm next. Nobody can teach you portaling like I can."

"Pull energy from around you, Frankie" Ryu says. "You're a witch. A witch princess."

"Don't say that," I whisper, clutching my knives. "As if I need to draw more attention to myself."

"You are who you are," Ryu says softly, coming behind me to pull me against his chest. He nuzzles my neck. "And you will do what you need to do to get out of this alive. The first step is learning how to use all this power at your disposal. You may be half angel, but you're also a witch. Draw from nature. Draw from other supernaturals. Draw from us. Don't hesitate. Not when you need to fight."

So I close my eyes and do as bidden. I don't want to draw from people, not unless there is no other way, so I focus on the world around me. The breeze in the leaves, the rich soil, the water running through the trunks, the fire of its living existence.

Yes, air comes more easily to me, but I focus on the grass around me instead. Rook said I hadn't drawn on it when I brought Tir back. Let's see if this time I manage.

Green energy, earth energy—but it's all connected, isn't it? Do they feel that as I do? Earth, but also water, and fire, and air, coming together to create that spark of life. I call it to me and it comes.

Turning, I throw my knives, and with them, my magic...

... at Asa.

Again.

He deflects the knives, only suddenly he's covered in green sprouts and branches that twine around him like a strangler fig, like a rope.

"She got you, buddy." Tir laughs. "She's getting the hang of it."

And Asa starts to glow—his skin, his eyes—and the branches explode off him, falling to the ground. "Well." He brushes an invisible speck of dust off his shoulder, mouth twitching. "Good work."

I grin. Progress. At last.

"I'll take over now," Asa goes on, and Tir glowers.

"What? No way. I'm her instructor."

"Only in elemental magic. I'm the only one who can teach her angelic magic. You can watch if you want."

"Isn't it all connected? She has to master her elemental power first." Tir's glower darkens. "You can't just take over."

Asa gazes steadily back at him until Tir sighs and shrugs.

"Hey, Cherub, remember we're next!" Rook calls out and waves.

Asa ignores him.

And thus begins my next chapter in torture... I mean, training.

Just great.

30

ASA

*A*ngels are God's hands. Which means they are his commands. They are the tasks set to them. They are God's words of command. Only the archangels endure. And the seraphs and cherubs and ophanim who are part of God's Glory.

The rest turn to dust the moment they are done. But there are also angels, millions of souls, who seek redemption and perhaps a second chance.

Reincarnation?

Perhaps.

It's been two days since the orders to kill her came in. Since we refused, since I was killed and she brought me back.

Since we had magical sex that bound us to her.

But Heaven hasn't found all that as satisfying as I have, or even amusing. I ignored the first pings, but now I have to take this one.

The call from Heaven I had been expecting.

I'm kneeling in our room, and from the corner of my eye, I catch Frankie and the guys entering. My mouth pulls into a smile. They nod at me.

They may as well listen in. Not like I have any secrets from them anymore.

"Auria," I say in greeting when the connection clicks and the angel appears in front of me. "What happened? Did Raziel get bored with toying with me?"

My handler's face glows faintly before me. "Asariel, twice dead and twice reborn."

"Listen—"

"You thought we wouldn't immediately realize you were back among the living? It doesn't matter how you try to hide from us. We are tracking you."

"Of course you are," I say in resignation. "And there's the Raziel Protocol situation."

"Lift the dome, Asariel." Auria's voice fills my ears like a trumpet blasting. "Lift it now."

I almost smile. "Let me think about it... um, no."

"Sooner or later, it will be lifted."

"I'd have later, then," I mutter, "rather than sooner."

"This is your last chance to ascend, Asariel. Lift the dome and deliver her to us before any of the other parties get her and we lose this race. You know this can't be allowed to happen."

"You still can't enter the dome." My voice hardens. "And no matter how many people you send against us, against her, we will stop them."

"We will up the stakes. Give her up and we'll give you what you want. Choose what you want. There can be no more delay."

"Does her father know about her?" I ask, changing tack. "Does he know you're asking me to give her to you? I bet he doesn't. Did you know that the Four Houses sent orders to terminate her?"

A pause. Auria's bright face shifts. "They know what she is. What she can do."

"No shit, Sherlock," I mutter.

"Who told them? There is a leak."

"A leak in Heaven," I say. "Not here. The dean was in on it."

"Everyone knows now who Frankie is, what she can do. You say the Houses ordered their emissaries to terminate her. Surely now you see the urgency, Asariel. You must break the protocol and let us take her to—"

"To safety? Really? You think I am that gullible?"

"You're a soldier of Heaven!"

"Not anymore," I counter. "I'm not even an angel anymore, am I? I'm reborn as the human I used to be."

Auria is quiet for a while. "It's not that simple. Once an angel, you can't just shed that divine spark of Glory."

"Sucks for you, then," I quip. "Still an angel and yet not obeying."

"It won't end well for you. You do know that."

I'm aware of the others gathering behind me. It makes me feel stronger. "It doesn't matter. I was supposed to be dead. This second chance at life was a bonus."

"If you don't give her up, then you must terminate her. We can't let her fall into enemy hands, we—"

"Enemy hands? Are you hearing yourself?" I give a bitter laugh. "We made peace. We are supposed to be at peace. Why is there still war in Heaven?"

"Not your place to question us, Asariel. We didn't start this war. And handing such a weapon over to Hell or any of its demonblood minions would be a grave mistake."

"Why do you feel so threatened?" I ask, since Auria seems to be in a talking mood. "Everyone says Heaven has the upper hand. More power. More defenses. Why this fear? What if she can kill people with her scream? What if she can bring people back? What's the big deal, anyway?"

"She's the Grail."

"Meaning?"

I hear Frankie making a wounded sound from somewhere

behind me, then Tir's soothing voice. Does she know what Auria means?

"She or her progeny," Auria says, "will have the potential to end the world."

A chill goes through me.

"Ending the world is surely a choice," I bite out. "And you can't see the future. Nobody can, no human, supernatural or angel."

"You can't know that. There are prophets."

"And you don't know her. Never bothered to get to know her, or you'd be aware she'd never do such a thing."

"Don't be naïve!" There's a snarl in Auria's voice that surprises me. "Everyone is attracted to power."

"You know nothing." I get to my feet, unfolding from the floor. "No, we won't kill her, and all your assassins won't reach her. We'll make a stand and fight. Besiege us all you like. This is war, all right."

Something like a chuckle sounds. "*You* want to take on Heaven? You and your puny friends? The Four Houses and Hell can't stand up to us and *you* will?"

"Funny, huh? My human side is much more reckless than the angelic one, it seems." I grin. "Go figure. Must be that finite life and looming death that makes me do this." I give him the finger." Oh sorry, do you want me to explain what the gesture means?"

"Hand her over, Asariel. Hand her over or kill her."

"We won't do it. That's my final say. Asariel, out."

31

FRANKIE

*T*he dean is locked up in her office, guarded by Kalissa's demons.

The dean's bespectacled assistant has assumed duties and his first demand was that we stay in our room with escorts outside, until he makes sure the campus is safe.

Laughable.

I'm still basking in the afterglow of our intimate time together, the new ease with which the boys take my hand, wrap their arms around me, kiss me.

I'm also exhausted from the training they all decided to put me through—Tir and Ryu for fighting with elemental magic, Asa for using my angelic power, Rook for creating portals, and generally opening holes in the magical layers of reality. Only Kass hasn't popped around to give me pointers, but I've caught him watching a few times.

For a few days, it seemed like we were falling into a routine. Like everything was fine.

But nothing has been fixed. Nothing has been solved.

And just now, as we were returning to our room, a guy came

running at us, and Asa threw us all inside the room and locked the door.

Awesome, right? Locked up in this tiny room with five hunks?

Yeah... Being cooped up inside the small room with five tall, muscular and annoyed men is a bit of a challenge.

They pace like lions in a too-small cage.

And they are avoiding the calls from their Houses. It's putting them on edge, not knowing their fate.

I know they feel fear.

I feel them. I didn't know you could feel the men you're in love with in your mind. Is this what a bonding feels like? Can you feel your conduits' emotions?

I want to ask Aunt Mia about it. She never mentioned anything like that. I wonder if it's normal, if it's the angelic side of me that causes it. Or, if it has to do with the men I'm connected to.

"Tell me of any new abilities," Granddad had said. Is this one of them? Does it mean anything? Does it matter to anyone but me?

And the more they pace and frown, the more anxiety I get from them and the darker my thoughts become.

Ryu is rubbing at his chest, standing by the window. They all gravitate toward it, a glimpse into the world outside this room, as much as they gravitate toward me.

"Is the House of Earth still pinging you?" Rook asks.

"They haven't stopped."

"Same," Tir breathes.

They stand, broad shoulders slightly hunched, jaws locked.

"What's the fucking point of hiding here?" Rook mutters. "We might at least fuck instead of standing around with long, gloomy faces. Who's in? Raise your hand."

"Rook..." I shake my head, a smile creeping up on me. "You're incorrigible."

"You love me for it," he says, "don't you?"

I nod. How can I not?

"So are we fucking? You don't look convinced. Let me convince you." Rook slings an arm around me. "Penny for your thoughts, Sweetheart."

"Maybe you should give me up."

He frowns. "No. Never say that again."

"My thoughts aren't worth your penny after all?"

"Not these ones. Erase them from your head."

"You will be hurt for disobeying." I swallow hard. "Last thing I want is your pain."

"I told you," Kass says, sliding a hand around my waist, "this is our choice."

"And that makes it all okay?"

"No. Nothing is okay. But refusing the mission, staying with you is also a choice. A choice we have made. A choice we'd make over and over."

"What he said." Tir comes to tweak a lock of hair out of my face. "So let's stop dicking around. Let's make a plan."

"Last I checked, the plan was the same as before," Asa rumbles.

Tir huffs. "That's right. The moment the dome lifts, we open a portal. But the question is, where to go?"

"Not to Hell," Rook says. "Seriously, don't. There's nowhere we're safe in Hell. Nobody should live there, ever. And you can't portal to Heaven without a tether."

"Faerie is tricky, too," Tir says with a frown.

"Vampires own a lot of estates," Kass says. "I'm trying to think of a place."

"What about in the shifter lands? The reserves outside the city. Lots of woods and hills, lots of places to hide." Ryu shrugs. "I know the area well. Lived there as a fox all this time."

"That could be."

"You still think we could outrun Heaven?" I mutter. "They'll be waiting, hovering over us like vultures, waiting for the moment the dome weakens to dive in. Not to mention the Four Houses. Waiting to pounce the very second the protocol is lifted."

"I don't see any other way," Rook says. "We're not giving you up, that's for sure. And it doesn't matter what we do. We could give ourselves up, put our neck out for our heads to be chopped off, that wouldn't help her."

"We need to get you away from their claws," Kass says. "It will buy us time to find a real solution."

""Kass..." I gaze into his grey eyes. "You think there is one?"

"Out there? You never know."

"Entire libraries didn't hold the answer to what I am," I breathe. "It would take a lifetime to search for a way to undo me."

Undo me. The words echo in my mind. Would it be possible? Is there a way?

"Frankie?" Tir cups my cheek. "What's the matter?"

I blink. "What if I could give this power back? I could ask Azrael. I mean, I didn't always have these powers growing up. Maybe there is a way to go back... back to having no magic."

"It doesn't work that way, Sweets." There's regret in Rook's voice. "No more than you can diminish physically and go back to being a baby."

"Why? What if I can reject my powers?" I search his midnight-blue eyes. "Find a way to block them, permanently?"

"Magical beings can't unmagic themselves."

"How do you know?" I drop my gaze to his chest. "And shit, how can I resent this power? If anything were to happen to any of you—anything else—then I can bring you back."

"Darling... you can't keep doing that. That's not how the world works and it will put a stop to it if you do it too often."

"Or kill you," Asa says darkly.

I jut my chin out. "I've done it twice."

"I know. But you must take energy and life force from somewhere to produce a life. Something died for Tir to live," Rook says.

"I didn't see anyone die."

"A part of you must have," Asa says. "Nothing comes from nothing."

I shiver. "And when I kill people?"

"Then that energy probably flows into you," Rook says. "What if for every hundred people you kill, you can bring back one person? Would that suit you?"

"Stop." I shake my head, my heart thumping. "No... I don't want that. I don't want this power. I don't want this terrible choice."

Kass growls. "Shut up, Rook. You'll make her sick."

"The truth is a sharp tool," Rook says quietly. "It may wound. But it also lances infected wounds and heals."

"It doesn't matter," Tir says. "She can't just give her power back. We said it. It doesn't work that way."

"You never know, though," Ryu argues. "She's a hybrid, like some of you, and hybrids are always virgin territory."

Rook starts laughing.

"What's so funny?" Asa demands.

"Virgin. She's definitely not a virgin, not anymore. She's—"

Kass' growl is deeper now. "Rook, shut your trap."

He lifts his hands, grinning. "Just saying. I think it's awesome she's not a virgin. I have nothing against virgins, mind you, but—"

"Rook," Ryu says.

"Okay, fine. Shutting up now. I'm..." Rook sighs. "Fuck, I guess I'm nervous. This is like going to battle."

"God, Rook is right to laugh. What's the point?" I rub my hands over my face. "While I am a weapon, I will be hunted. So what are we doing except putting off the inevitable?"

"Frankie..." Asa pulls me into his arms. "You're right. Maybe there is a way to undo your powers. Once we're out of here, we can work on that."

Pressed to his warm chest, it's easy to believe everything will be all right. But I fight the illusory sense of safety. "How? In the woods? Who will help us solve this?"

Dammit.

"Then maybe the vampire estates, like I said." Kass frowns. "At least there we will have access to libraries and the internet."

"And how do you propose to keep it on the down-low?" Rook asks. "Do you trust your family to help us, the family who betrayed you, no less, to put Frankie's safety above the House of Water and risk punishment?"

Kass' jaw works. "No, you're right. Hell. Is there any safe place for us to go?"

I wish I knew. Can't think of any place where we won't be found. We're not super spies with connections to the underworld and even if Kass may know people, I mean...

Is there anything Heaven and the Four Houses don't see?

A tug inside my chest tears me out of my spiraling thoughts.

Aunt Mia is pinging me. I want to take the call—I miss her, miss them all—but I hesitate. I said I wouldn't involve them more to keep them safe as much as possible.

But that was wishful thinking. They are my family. They're involved, no matter what, and what's more... what if she knows of a safe place to go? What if she can help me find a way to undo my powers?

———

My aunt's pretty face appears in front of me, her eyes wide, as if she didn't expect me to answer. "Honey? Are you okay?"

Guilt swamps me—predictably—at making her worry and her also predictable greeting still manages to make my eyes feel hot. "Yeah, I'm fine. Sorry I snapped at you and Uncle Emrys last time. I was so stressed out."

"Don't worry about it, munchkin," Uncle Jason says. "Emrys is damn annoying demon. We all snap at him."

"Jase!" Aunt Mia slaps him lightly on the chest. "We should encourage respect in the young ones."

Uncle Jason just winks at me and grins, a wolfish grin that matches his nature.

I grin back, feeling a bit better at the normalcy of this talk. It almost feels as if I'm back home with them. I'm standing at the desk by the window, but instead of the view outside, I have a full-screen image of my family.

It's time to ask the big, hard questions.

"Auntie..." I lick dry lips. "What would you do if you had a great power but you were hunted for it?"

"Asking for a friend, are you?" She smiles at me, that kind smile that accompanied me throughout my life growing up, letting me know I'm accepted and loved.

Only now...

"For myself, obviously. Did Granddad tell you anything? Anything new, about..."

"He said your powers are growing." Her smile falters. "And I know everyone is after you. I'm worried sick. We're ready to portal to you the moment it becomes possible and—"

"Nothing you can do," I whisper and I see her dark eyes fill with tears. "These great powers... I'd like not to have them anymore. I don't want them."

"Oh, Honey..." She turns away from me and Uncle Sindri puts his arms around her.

Great. I've managed to make her cry.

Uncle Ash gets in front of her, hiding her from me. "What can we do, Bug? How can we help? Say the word and it's done. Also, we'll be there, no matter what."

"I know." I swallow hard. "I'm truly sorry for doubting you even for a minute—"

"You *should* be sorry." He gives me a fanged smile, his vampire side showing. "Because we'd never give you up, girl."

Shit, he's right. How could I ever doubt my family? I'd blame this whole mess but it's my mistake. Just like I doubted my boys earlier on.

If nothing else, I need to trust my gut, my heart, when it tells me to have faith in the people who have proven their affection for me. A matter of self-confidence? Of feeling worthy of love? I grew up bathing in affection. Having a mother who only ever cared about her own agenda shouldn't be able to change that.

Shouldn't take away from the love I have in my life and the love I can give.

"Uncle Ash, is there any place safe I could hide in if I manage to evade Heaven's grabby hands—and the Four Houses', too? We've been trying to think of one."

"We? Who's we?" He frowns. "Frankie?"

"Oops. I thought you knew about the boys."

"The boys…" Uncle Jason's eyes narrow, glowing yellow like a wolf's. "Are we talking about the emissaries? Those standing behind you?"

Oops again. I turn around slowly and sigh. "Tir? What are you doing?"

He's waving at my family. And he's not the only one.

Ryu is wiggling his fingers.

Rook and Kass just look smug.

Asa is frowning.

I fight an urge to scream but also laugh like a lunatic.

Oh boy.

"They are your friends," Uncle Emrys says slowly.

"Friends with benefits?" I hazard. "But yeah. That."

Uncle Emrys' eyes start to blaze. "The Hell. I'm coming over right now. If they dared touch you—"

"She's not a kid, Rys." Auntie Mia shoves him slightly out of the way, wiping at her eyes, a determined look on her face. "Frankie, won't you introduce us?"

Uncle Sindri doesn't look happy. "But Mia—"

"They are helping her," my aunt says. "They care."

"They do," I whisper and proceed to introduce them. It's surreal. "This is Tir, Wild Hunt. Rook, Hellhound. Asa, angel. Ryu, kitsune. And Kass, vampire."

"*Piacere*," Kass says with a small formal bow. "It means, it's a pleasure."

"Italian?" My aunt's brows go up. "That's romantic."

"Romantic?" Uncle Sindri glowers from behind her, baring his sharp Fae teeth. "Romantic is tearing the world apart for someone, not an Italian accent."

"Oh my God, Sindri you're jealous?" Aunt Mia snickers. "That's so cute."

"I'm never jealous," Uncle Sindri says with great dignity.

"Can't romantic be both?" she complains. "Being Italian and saving the world?"

Kass laughs.

"I like your aunt," Rook says with a grin.

"And as for the tearing-the-world-apart-for-you bit, we're definitely on the right track," Tir quips.

"Yeah, working on that, Ma'am," Ryu says solemnly.

Asa gives a long-suffering sigh.

"You'll look after her?" Aunt Mia says. "Please? For us? We're so worried about her."

"Auntie!" I protest.

"We will," Asa says solemnly. "But we're doing it for us. Your niece is our bright light."

"Don't mind him," Rook says, "he fell into bad poetry as a child and hit his head."

"Not to mention, spending time in Heaven leaves a certain trauma," Tir adds. "It addles the brain."

"Actually, I think Asa put it exactly right," Ryu says. "She's a bright light. *Our* bright light."

Kass nods.

My face is too hot. "Guys..."

"Aw, how nice." Aunt Mia claps her hands together. "You seem so fond of her. You're all so cute."

"Mia," Uncle Ash growls softly. "Calm down. They're not kittens."

But she looks like she's planning our wedding already. I see white gowns flashing in her dark eyes.

I mean, she's not the type, really. She's always very dynamic and independent and heads all the meetings of the Four Houses' royalty. She had led the negotiations that brought peace among the Houses, even if it remains tenuous. I admire her so much, and I've always wanted to grow up to be like her.

I guess she does have a romantic soul. She did all she did for love, after all. Let her have her fantasy of a cozy future of me with these guys. It won't last long. She's practical, and she knows... she knows about me and how this can't end well.

"It's been a pleasure, Ma'am, gentlemen," Asa says, giving one of his devastating megawatt smiles that burn down houses and hearts, and then... he staggers back, his golden hair flying.

"Asa!" I make a grab for him, but Ryu is faster, grabbing him around the waist, steadying him.

"What the fuck, man?" Ryu demands, glaring at the angel. "Told you, you should be in bed, resting."

"It's the dome," Asa breathes. "The dome is about to come down. We have to go."

"Now? The dome is about to come down *now*?"

"It's starting," he says, looking up, as if he can see through the ceiling to the invisible barrier that has kept us isolated from the rest of the world these past few days.

It feels as if months have passed.

And I feel it, a lift in the pressure, making my ears pop.

Oh, shit.

"What is going on?" Aunt Mia has paled. "Did I hear that right, the dome is coming down?"

"Sounds like it," I say, distracted, as the guys glance around, frowns on their handsome faces.

"We're on our way to you," Uncle Emrys says as I lose grip on my magic and the image fizzles. "Be careful and wait for us."

"We can't wait." Asa pushes off Ryu, getting back on his feet. "We need to get going."

"Wait, Asa... How did you know? I thought.... I thought your angelic powers would be gone now that Heaven cut ties with you. If you never rose to Heaven... if you never became an angel, and this was your mission, to rise..."

"We'll figure it out later," Asa says. "What matters now is escaping."

He's right.

"Are you ready?" Tir says, taking my hand. "I'll open the portal into Faerie. It may not be the safest place but I know a spot where the Wild Hunt sometimes goes. Maybe we can hide there for a while."

Ready? No, I'm not ready but I nod anyway. "I thought we had more time."

"Raziel managed to speed up the process," Asa grinds out. "A new spell, perhaps."

"He probably forced all the archangels to pour their power into rending the dome," Rook mutters. "No big surprise. I just thought not everyone would agree with him."

"The other archangels aren't around," Asa says.

"No?"

"It is said they live in the higher spheres these days. We don't even know if they take any notice of what is going on in the other planes of existence. Only Eremite has remained, managing Heaven."

"Awesome," Tir grumbles. "Whoever this Eremite is."

"Might be for the best," Ryu says. "Imagine having more power behind Heaven. It's bad enough with Raziel as it is."

And it makes things even more confusing. How would Asa know all that if he hasn't even risen yet? The others didn't hear what Raziel said about his past, about who he is, and he hasn't brought it up. Do the others know that he used to be a mortal? That he may have never been an angel and was only temporarily imbued with angelic powers for this mission?

At least, that's how I understand it.

"We should stop talking and be prepared to go," Tir says.

My breathing echoes strangely in my ears. The others gather around us, all touching Tir and me, preparing for the jump.

"How will you know when it's time?" I whisper. "Asa, do you feel it?"

"Now," Asa says. "Be ready."

Tir murmurs something. For the portal, he needs demonblood and as I watch, he brings his wrist to his mouth and bites down. Those sharp Fae teeth tear through his flesh, and I smell coppery blood, like pennies.

He lifts his arm up, the blood snaking down to his elbow. Speaks the incantation.

The portal appears, showing nothing at first. But then the air ripples, a pinprick of light that expands larger and larger until it's big enough for us to go through. A forest is visible through it, a castle, and a cloudy sky.

Faerie.

A place where no technology can work, where iron is forbidden, where elemental magic is everything.

A hiding place; a respite.

"Let's go," Tir says, tugging on me, stepping closer to the

portal, and everyone follows us. "I should go in first, check that it's all right—"

The portal snaps shut and bursts into glittering fragments like glass.

Throwing Tir to the ground, throwing all of us down. I roll with him, hitting the floor in painful bursts, coming to a stop with his arms tight around me.

Ow.

Shit.

"What the Hell happened?" I wheeze.

A deafening crash jolts us as five angels land, wings flaring open.

"Going somewhere?" one of them asks, smiling with teeth sharper than Tir's. His eyes are a solid blue, like lapis lazuli stones set in his face. "You're caught. It's over."

32

FRANKIE

*T*ir and Rook and Ryu and Kass close ranks around me. Asa tries to step in front of me, but I duck under his arm and plant my feet—facing the angel squad.

It's a standoff, I think.

I feel crazy.

This is crazy.

"Francesca," the angel with the solid blue eyes says, like one would say *"Well, shit."*

"That's me. Took you a while to come get me, though. Why?"

"We don't discuss the will of Heaven," he intones. "Only execute."

"People, or orders?"

He doesn't blink. That's a little unnerving. "Both."

Right... I lock gazes with him, refusing to look away. I'm tiny compared to him and I pretend not to notice. "Execute away."

Tir makes a sound, slowly getting to his feet. "Frankie..."

"Do you know who I am?" the angel asks.

"At a guess? Raziel."

"Archangel Raziel."

I narrow my eyes at the pompous ass. "Are you here to kill me?"

"Heaven could use someone like you."

"For the greater good, I suppose."

"Exactly."

I almost laugh. "Right."

"But it's unlikely," he says in that same impassive voice. "Which is why the Four Houses sent the order to terminate you. It's why Asariel received the same order, which he refused. And why we're here now."

My boys gather around me as the other four angels lift their hands and white, shining spears appear in them.

I'm getting annoyed, the emotion competing with my fear. "What are you doing?"

"All of you will die. But the Four Houses will see to the other emissaries. We're here for you and Asariel, who proved to be a traitor and will die for his sin."

I cock my head to the side. "Oh. Die again, you mean?"

The angel's face contorts. Looks like they have feelings, too. Interesting. Rage, at least. "He will be burned to ash, so you can't bring him back."

"Inventive," I say, though my blood grows cold.

"How dare you," Raziel hisses. "Hiding your abilities from Heaven. Killing, destroying, and resurrecting. Have you no shame? No fear of yourself, of what you might bring about?"

"See my jar of fucks," I mutter. "It's empty and spent."

Asa produces a choked sound. I don't know if he's upset or laughing—but why would he laugh, right? Nothing funny here.

Only crazy.

I think I've gone around the bend. It's too late to save my sanity.

Just a few angels and an archangel come to fetch me to Heaven, having a little chat beforehand so that I feel the fear and remember my place before I'm whisked Heavenward.

Nothing to see here. Just a little dust down, just a little telling off. A small exchange, charged with anger.

"And you." The archangel turns to my guys. "Hiding her. Hiding the two resurrected amongst you. Disobeying orders. As if you were given a choice."

"We all have a choice," Kass says. "Always."

"Because you failed," Raziel rumbles, "and didn't get what you wanted? Is that why you gave up? What if you could win your prize? What if your true heart's desire were available to you?"

"What are you talking about?" Tir laughs. "Nonsense."

But they all grow quiet, staring at the angels. What can Heaven do? Can it bring back those gone forever? Can it turn back time? Who knows?

The archangel points a finger at me. "Is she worth your loss? Your failure and pain?"

Yep. Crazy. And growing more afraid by the second.

What if Heaven pits the boys against me again? Would they be convinced? Would they give me up?

And wouldn't it be best for them? How can I hold them back? Insist on their punishment?

"She goes with us," the archangel goes on. "It's too late."

Par for the course, really. I'm a weapon and I've been bought. This is what happens when you finally locate the weapon you wanted to get for your home. Something decorative to place over the fireplace. Something to boast about to your friends. You go and get it.

I mean, I may be a little angry myself. I never set out to hurt anyone. Only killed people sent to kill me. Speaking of which...

"Who sent the assassins to kill me in the first place?" Since the fight is over, I might as well satisfy my curiosity. "When I was still a teenager, when I manifested my power for the first time—but also here at the College? All those assassins, all those students paid to eliminate me... Who was behind that? You owe me at least that. I want to know."

"Asariel." The archangel scowls. "Did you tell her she has the right to pester us with questions?"

"I don't have to tell her anything," Asa says. "She has her own tongue and her own mind."

I smile at Asa. He nods at me, his face hard. He knows what comes next.

Or thinks he does.

We all think we do.

And I think, no matter what they do with me, maybe there is a way to save them, not to take them down with me.

The angels' spears glow brighter and brighter with Glory. Time is running out.

"Wait," I say. I should have known not to let this conversation drag. These are angels, unhinged pawns of Heaven with no real moral compass or empathy to distract them. "Look—"

"Frankie, stay back!" Kass grabs me, hauling me away. His eyes are growing crimson, his fangs lengthening. He lifts his lash from the floor, where his pants were left in a pile. "We got this."

Oh no... They are going to fight for me.

Rook is a blur of black mist, long black hair and eyes that flash, swinging his staff, while Ryu is already half-fox, all claws and hissing. Asa is glowing white, his sword materializing out of thin air—yep, still an angel, it seems.

And Tir roars, looking half-beastly with his black-on-black eyes, the horns, and the claws. He doesn't even look for his staff. He jumps at the angels, opening a mouth full of razor teeth. They shout something and swing their swords at him.

Magic flashes. Crashes. It splits the air with supersonic booms as it clashes with the angelic Glory the angels are wielding. Their swords are blinding streaks of power.

But what if they're hurt—and for what? Fear grips me. "Wait, Tir. Wait, all of you! Stop. *Stop!*"

I don't think they will listen to me, either side. My boys have gone into full protective/aggressive mode, their darker sides coming out to play, and the angels are so focused, well-oiled machines of war, their swords moving in synchrony. A choir of death.

So I enter the fray, searching for the magic inside of me. It comes rushing, I shove at the angels. They screech as they fall back, energy spiking around them.

"Stop!" I yell. "Stop now!"

Rook lifts his staff and steps back. "Frankie wants to talk." He thwacks at Tir who's still going after the angels. "Stop. Looks like we have to use our words."

The angels turn to Raziel, spears in their hands, silent but obviously awaiting instructions. They act like lifelike robots. So different from Asa.

"Take her," Raziel says.

"Wait." I lift a hand. "Just a moment. You saw that we're not exactly helpless."

He produces a weird sound that might have been laughter, though he's not smiling, so... maybe not? "If I needed more angels to subdue you, I'd have called for more. The outcome of this scuffle was inevitable."

Rook growls like a wolf.

"I don't believe you," I say. "I think that you had other reasons to only bring four angels with you. Could it be that Heaven doesn't want my death?" He says nothing, so I go on. "You wanted to test us. Or maybe you wanted to see if I'd try to scream and kill everyone. Maybe something else is keeping the angelic battalions away. After all, if you're so afraid of me you want me dead, wouldn't you have given me a better show of power?"

No reply.

"Now listen." I lift my chin. "I want to propose a deal. A new contract."

"Frankie," Tir says, his gaze on me now. "What are you doing?"

"I have an idea," I whisper, but I can't tell them. Won't. Because they may refuse.

"A deal?" Raziel is staring down at me. "What sort of a deal?"

The fact that he seems willing to discuss this tells me I'm not completely wrong. That there's a chance he might agree.

"Frankie," Ryu says. "Don't."

"Making deals with the angels is even worse than making deals with the Fae," Tir says, "and I should know. What could you want to negotiate with them about?"

I give him a faint smile. God, I love these guys. Even if they are tempted to turn away from me again, I'll still love them. The heart, once set on its course, isn't easily swayed.

The things you learn right before the end.

"Take me," I say, "I won't fight back. I will come willingly."

"Frankie, no! What are you doing?" Kass hisses, but one of the angels lifts a hand and Kass is thrown back to the floor. I glance back to make sure he's okay. "Don't listen to her."

"What's the point of all of you going down with me?" I tell him. "It won't change anything."

"Frankie…"

I ignore him. Ignore them all, though my chest hurts. "I will come on one condition: don't punish them. All five of them leave here and will not be punished for this, not now, not later. You take them to a safe place, give them a new identity, let them live their lives in peace and happiness."

"Frankie, goddammit, don't do that!" Tir roars. "We don't want that."

But I want them to live. "You are amazing guys. The world needs more of you, not less. I will be content at least knowing you are all right." I turn back to the angels. "Do we have a deal?"

Raziel seems to be considering it. "You will come calmly, not trying to kill anyone with your scream."

"That's right."

"Not now, and not later, when you are in Heaven."

"I won't."

"Fine," he says and I have a moment of shock that he would agree so easily, "so we—"

Another crash, a boom of thunder, and a beating of great black wings herald the arrival of another presence.

Booted feet slam on the ground and the angel in front of us folds his arms over his chest. Pale hair, those angelic solid blue eyes, a square jaw. Black leathers.

"No deal," he says with a voice like thunder.

Shadows wind around him like snakes.

A tremor goes through me. Raziel and his buddies step back, bowing their heads, and this is bad.

"And who are you?" I ask even as I know, I *know* who he must be.

"I am Azrael. Your father."

———

I almost laugh. This is like a line from a movie. "I see not all archangels chose to live in another sphere. Some chose to fuck a witch and create a weapon for Heaven to use."

"Have some respect," Raziel says, lifting his gaze. "Azrael is one of the ancients."

I glare at my father. "Well, nice to meet you. It looks like I'm going with Raziel with whom I have made a deal. Have a nice day."

"No, you don't have any deal. And you're not going

anywhere, daughter," he says," until I've decided what to do with you."

"Really? Nice of you to show up after all this time and try to control me."

"You don't seem to understand," he says, "how serious this is."

"Oh, I get it, don't worry. I've had plenty of opportunities to find out how much every single side wants my death."

"You won't die," he says slowly. "You will ascend. Lose all emotions. Learn about Heaven's will. And all that power is yours to use in service of Heaven to which you will then belong. Angels have no free will, they have a divine purpose."

"Really." I curl my hands into fists. "And if I don't want to ascend?"

"Then Heaven will destroy you."

"Read my lips. I. Don't. Care."

"You are making this hard." As if he didn't expect me to disagree with him, put up any resistance, but instead go with him like an obedient little puppy.

Surprise?

"Help me get out of this," I tell him. "You're my father. I don't want to ascend. I want to live here as a mortal. Help me!"

He scrutinizes my face for a long moment. He watches me through lidless eyes, that solid color that looks so animal-like. Demons have the same eyes, I think. How weird.

Then he says, "You're staying here."

And with a woosh, he flies up—through the ceiling and the roof? What the Hell?—and is gone.

"Hey, come back here!" I call out after a stunned moment. "Hey!"

But he's vanished, leaving me alone. Well, alone with my boys and five pissed-off angels.

Then something shifts again in the air—no, deeper, inside me, inside and outside of everything.

A shift in magic.

I see everyone shudder, looking around and up.

"What the Hell just happened?" Rook mutters. "Was that...?"

"Fuck, "Asa grunts.

And then I feel it, too, concrete for the first time, a feeling of containment, of dampening, a metaphysical slam on doors and windows, on the very air surrounding us and the College.

Azrael closed the dome over us once more.

The angels seem as surprised as we are.

Well, right now the only thing that matters is that we're trapped inside again.

Together with Raziel and his angels.

Speaking of whom...

I turn back to the angels and... *Oh shit.* They're turning into monsters, rising taller and wider, their faces twisting into those of animals, their spears blazing.

"On them," Raziel says, his lip curling, the anger back in his flat blue gaze.

"Run!" Ryu yells, grabbing me and setting off toward the door. "Come on!"

"And then what? What's the use?" I let him sweep me along, through corridors and halls. "There's no escaping from the dome or the angels."

He gives me a grim smile. "We live to fight another day."

GLOSSARY

General notes

Please note that this is a made-up world that only looks like ours, therefore the language isn't always the same. Except for Italian. Italian is universal.

Combined words particular to this world

Scale-ball = a game with an enchanted ball
Bat boy = a vampire boy
Demonblood = the demonic element in the blood that lends particular magical abilities to those who have it, that is the magical creatures descended from demons such as demons, vampires, fae and werewolves (in the context of this world)
Faeling = young fae

Words having to do with the Fae

Fairfolk = all fae (fae, fairies, elves, goblins, trolls, gnomes etc.)

Seelie = good, benevolent (refering to the faerie Seelie court, of court of Light Fae)

Unseelie = bad, malevolent (refering to the faerie Unseelie court, of court of Dark Fae)

Pukha (or pukka) = a goblin-like creature

Fae-speak – used by Tir

Danu resh = gods of the deep

Quentesh = Done

Abesh = fuck/fucking/fucked (a swearword)

Abesh (k'emel) = two-dick fuck (Fae-speak can be very eloquent)

Arawn = God (actually the Celtic god of the dead, war, revenge and terror)

Elenyi = girl

Enkeleth = Highness

Kerel = lawless bastard

Kraish = damn (and not *lily-white* as Sindri claims at some point)

Kraish bedash = damn this shit (unicorn shit in particular)

French in the text

Fleur de sel = flower of salt (a type of sea salt that forms in a delicate crust on the surface of evaporating seawater)

Italian - used by Kass

Minchia = shit

Vecchie pettegole = Old gossiping ladies

Che cazzo vuoi? = What the hell do you want?

Cretino/cretini = idiot
Stronzo/stronzi = asshole
Che volete de mi? = what do you want from me?
ragazza bella = beautiful girl
(Ma che) cazzo = well, fuck
Piacere = a pleasure (to meet you)
Porca miseria = dammit
Giocattolino = little toy
Giocca = toy
Merda = shit
Ragazza = girl
Amico = friend

Japanese - used by Ryu

Baka/ bakayaro = stupid
Kitsune = Japanese fox shifter
Sayonara = goodbye
Nani = what?
Kuso = shit

Angel-speak – used by Asa

Alal = destroyer
Fravash = protector
Umbar umsa = esteemed brother
Urun-en = your servant
Malakh = Messenger (ángel)

ACKNOWLEDGMENTS

To Haeley Rochette: lady, you rock and without you this series wouldn't be the same
To Lainey Da Silva: my friend, I couldn't do it without you
To all bloggers, instagrammers, tiktokers and to all amazing readers: thank you from the bottom of my heart for making this dream real

ABOUT MONA BLACK

Mona is a changeling living in the human world. She writes fantasy romance and reverse harem romance, and is an avid reader of fantasy and paranormal books. Check out her paranormal reverse harem series Pandemonium Academy Royals and Brutal Never Boys, and her fantasy romance series Cursed Fae Kings.

ALSO BY MONA BLACK

A completed Paranormal Reverse Harem series! Welcome to Pandemonium Academy!

"Of Boys and Beasts"

One's a werewolf with an ax to grind

Two's a vampire with a heart of coal

Three's a demon with a taste for pain

Four's a fae with a past of woe

Five's a girl who will take them down all

In revenge for the pain they've sown

So what if they're gorgeous? They must atone...

My name is Mia Solace. You know, the girl who will take them down all? That's me.

When my cousin is returned to us by Pandemonium Academy in a glass coffin, in an enchanted sleep she isn't expected to wake up from, I grab her diary and head to the academy myself.

Because her diary, you see, tells of four cruel boys who bullied her and broke her heart until she sought oblivion through a spell.

Four magical boys, because that's the world we live in now, heirs of powerful families attending this elite academy where the privileged scions of the human and magical races are brought together in the noble pursuit of education.

As for me, I cheat to get on the student roster, and once I'm in, well... it's war, baby. I'll get those four sons of guns, steal their secrets, make them hurt. I'll transform into an avenging angel for my cousin, for all the girls they've wronged, and I bet there are plenty of those.

While growing up, my cousin was my only friend. Now I'll be her champion.

Only these boys aren't exactly as I pictured them. Devastatingly handsome, deliciously brooding, strangely haunted, they're getting under my skin and through my defenses.

Kissing them surely wasn't part of my plan...

Getting into bed with them even less.

———

Book 1 in the Cursed Fae Kings series (standalone fae romance novels series):

The Merman King's Bride

A cursed King of Faerie

A princess betrothed to a man she doesn't love

A kiss that will change everything

The last thing Princess Selina expects to find in the lake in the woods is a handsome merman. His name is Adar and he saves her, teases her, kisses her, and tells her she could break his curse.

Because, as it turns out, he's a Fae King, cursed to remain in merman form until he finds a princess to kiss him.

But one kiss is not enough and Selina has other problems.

Such getting engaged to a prince she isn't sure she even likes, let alone loves. Marrying him and having his children is not on her list of favorite things.

And now she's falling for the merman.

He's everything she could wish for in a man. Handsome, protective, kind. Except that he is Fae. And has a fishtail.

Still, she can't stop thinking about him. Keeps going back to him. Craves his kisses.

Would gladly have his babies.

Is this a spell, or is it love? Can she break the curse and save Adar? Will there be a happy ending to their story?

All a girl can do is try. After all, true love is worth fighting for and Selina knows she has found it.

This book is standalone novella-length NA romance fantasy novel, featuring mature situations with some dark themes and adult language. It is a retelling of the Frog Prince, with all the emotions, romance, spice and heat.

———

Do you like contemporary RH omegaverse? Check out my new series The Candyverse. Start with book 1: Bee and the Honey Crew (The Candyverse #1)

Bee Robinson's dream is to be an omega. What she is, though, is a weird beta on the run from her ex and her small town.

Weird as in *unusual*, as in being a lot like an omega, rather than her official designation. It's what got her into trouble with her ex and her family.

But now she's about to get her life straightened out. A new town, a new job, new friends, and a chance to accept who and what she is.

Learn from your mistakes, isn't that what they say?

What doesn't kill you makes you stronger.

Only her new friends also seem to think she may be an omega, and so do the members of the St. Laurent pack who instantly start courting her.

A pack of four gorgeous males, each with their own insecurities and doubts, a pack needing her to cement the bonds that make them a family, needing her to join them as their mate.

A family...

Does it matter if you're a beta or an omega when all you need is to accept yourself as you are and see where it takes you?

Her new friends and the pack seem to think so, and in the end Bee may have to let nature take its course, come what may.

At the end of the rainbow, there will be a happy ending.

———

Or maybe you like dystopian paranormal RH omegaverse? I have you covered, too. Try my series Golden Cage Omegas – and start with book 1: Caged

Finding out I am an omega in a world ruled by betas was only the beginning of my troubles...

Alphas and omegas are considered non-humans. We're thought of as animals, some of whose traits we share. Furry ears and tails, anyone? Oh, and also mating cycles. Finding out I am an omega in a world ruled by betas was only the beginning of my troubles...

That's right.

Not something I thought I had to worry about. See, I thought I was a beta. I thought I was human.

And then, my world is upended once again when my parents are killed by a pack of rogues. Escaping, I head to the city, and there I am captured and sent to the Golden Cage.

A Cage where omegas are kept, to be sold to an alpha pack. To the highest bidder.

I came to the city to find a gang of boys I met many years ago, to beg them for help, but instead I am being sold to an unknown pack, the choice not up to me.

———

Do you like dark paranormal romance? Do you like fairytale retellings?

Try my completed Brutal Never Boys trilogy!

King of Nothing (Brutal Never Boys 1)

No man has ever managed to satisfy me—until Peter Pan carries me away to Neverland and now all bets are off…

I never thought that there is another reality beyond this one. My life is normal—work, routine, a few disappointing flings—when a man grabs me from the street and carries me off the Neverland.

A madman.

Granted, he probably saved my life, and the island he has brought me to is beautiful, the sights including three more hunks like him.

He says his name is Peter Pan and this is Neverland, he says they have been waiting for me and I may be the one…

Yeah, he sounds like a madman, all right.

A pity. He's so pretty. And so are his friends.

Peter and the Lost Boys, living on an island where the mermaids sing in the sea and creatures named Reds roam the land.

It sounds like a fairytale.

But if Peter is mad, the rest aren't much better. Dark forces seem to be at work here, and I'm caught in a web of fear and doubt.

The Lost Boys turn out to be violent, vicious men and I am their plaything.

Caught in a web of desire and pleasure.

Am I really the one they have been expecting?

Can I save them?

And do I even want to?

———

New series to check out if you like omegaverse, RH and epic fantasy! The series is called Hunted Fae – check out book 1: Unlikely Omega

I am just an acolyte in the Temple, sworn to purity of mind and body.

An average young woman with doubts and hopes and dreams.

I'm certainly *not* a prophesied Fae omega who will help bring back the lost Fae race.

Not me.

And I'm definitely not the woman who will gather a clan of alphas and maybe betas and deltas around her and start popping out their babies.

No way.

I'm human, as human as they come. Just a girl, with all the imperfections and traumas to show for it.

Abandoned at the Temple by my mother.

Not sure I have a single real friend in the world.

Lost.

But when I awaken—as Fae-blood and yeah, as omega to boot—one thing is for sure: the Temple doesn't want me. The Empire abhors me.

Bringing back the Fae doesn't seem to be an option the Anchar Empire is willing to consider.

Every Fae-blooded man or woman is to be eliminated to avoid any chance of the Lost Race returning.

And I'm apparently the Empire's worst fear.

www.ingramcontent.com/pod-product-compliance
Ingram Content Group UK Ltd.
Pitfield, Milton Keynes, MK11 3LW, UK
UKHW021107170325
456354UK00008B/508

9 798230 082668